REMEMBRANCE OF
THINGS PAST

Max closed his eyes, and the memories welled up like music. Amanda, running toward him, opening her mouth. "Help me."

Max's face paled. Or had he imagined it? Two sets of memories. The Amanda he had found on the floor of the music room, and the Amanda who had come running into his arms: the silent Amanda and the one who had spoken.

He looked at the clock. Only seconds had elapsed, but his world had changed immeasurably. Two memories, two sets of sensations. His head spun, and his heart began to flutter. He felt hot and cold.

20/20 VISION

Pamela West

A Del Rey Book
BALLANTINE BOOKS • NEW YORK

This story is fiction. Any resemblance to real persons or events—
past, present, or future—is coincidental.

ccl
3108
1399

A Del Rey Book
Published by Ballantine Books

Copyright © 1990 by Pamela West

All rights reserved under International and Pan-American Copyright Conventions. Published in the United States of America by
Ballantine Books, a division of Random House, Inc., New York,
and simultaneously in Canada by Random House of Canada
Limited, Toronto.

Grateful acknowledgment is made to the following for permission to reprint pre-
viously published material: Harcourt Brace Jovanovich, Inc.: Excerpt from "Burnt
Norton" in FOUR QUARTETS by T.S. Eliot. Copyright 1943 by T.S. Eliot.
Copyright renewed 1971 by Esme Valerie Eliot. Rights in the U.S. administered by
Harcourt Brace Jovanovich, Inc. Rights in all other territories administered by
Faber and Faber Ltd. Reprinted by permission of Harcourt Brace Jovanovich, Inc.
and Faber and Faber Ltd.; Excerpt from MODERN MAN IN SEARCH OF A
SOUL by Carl Jung. Reprinted by permission of Harcourt Brace Jovanovich, Inc.;
Excerpt from "The Love Song of J. Alfred Prufrock" in COLLECTED POEMS
1901–1962 by T.S. Eliot. Copyright 1936 by Harcourt Brace Jovanovich, Inc.
Copyright © 1963, 1964 by T.S. Eliot. Rights in the U.S. administered by Har-
court Brace Jovanovich, Inc. Rights in all other territories administered by Faber
and Faber Ltd. Reprinted by permission of Harcourt Brace Jovanovich, Inc. and
Faber and Faber Ltd.
Macmillan Publishing Company: Excerpt from "Lines Written in Dejection" from
THE POEMS OF W.B. YEATS: A NEW EDITION edited by Richard J. Finneran.
Copyright 1919 by Macmillan Publishing Company. Copyright renewed 1947 by
Bertha Georgie Yeats. Reprinted by permission of Macmillan Publishing Com-
pany.

Library of Congress Catalog Card Number: 90-93132

ISBN 0-345-36736-7

Manufactured in the United States of America

First Edition: August 1990

Cover Art by Hector Garito

For my grandmother Naomi

Time present and time past
Are both perhaps present in time future,
And time future contained in time past.
If all time is eternally present
All time is unredeemable.
What might have been is an abstraction
Remaining a perpetual possibility
Only in a world of speculation.
What might have been and what has been
Point to one end, which is always present.
Footfalls echo in the memory
Down the passage which we did not take
Towards the door we never opened
Into the rose garden.

Four Quartets. Burnt Norton, 1935
T.S. ELIOT

The meeting of two personalities is like the contact of two chemical substances: if there is any reaction, both are transformed.

Modern Man in Search of a Soul, 1933
CARL JUNG

1995

Saturday, April 15, 3:44 A.M.

Amanda tried to scream, but no words came out. She couldn't breathe. She had been at a party, with a man, dancing. And then the music had turned wrong. A limpid little strand, so very simple. She didn't know why it changed things.

It was dark suddenly. She had been decoyed. Water everywhere, rolling over her like drumbeats, and beyond the pulsing beat she could hear the sluggish dragging gait, repulsive. The man was following her, slowly, dragging one leg. She tried to run, but her arms and legs were jelly.

The music came from below, a dark bow resonating from a deep well, unsyncopated, relentless, and perfect. The jaws of death swimming toward her, taking away her air, burning her lungs.

Scream.

If you can. Even a whimper will suffice.

No, stay still, a voice cautioned. Let it pass. But the music commanded obedience: *Follow*. A slow, marching bass fugue pulled her like a tide. Hide, she told her heart, but her heart was out of her chest, pounding to the drum's beat. The dark frothy waters rolled over her, moistening her, anointing her, and she felt a hot breath at her neck, savage and pitiless. Then the gnashing jaws were upon her, opening wide.

Scream.

She managed a tiny squeak. She woke.

She was covered in perspiration, but she wasn't drowning. Her mind was there, within her body. She was in her room. It was dark, and there seemed to be a lot of noisy music. She moved her leaden limbs, her skin atremble with the strain of being flesh. No, not music, only noise: loud creaks and low whines, steady rhythmic knocks, the single loud blare of a trumpet. And then there was silence. She could hear her heart beating loudly.

"Jenny?" she said, gulping in air. But her voice, small as it was, didn't penetrate the deep REM sleep of her roommate. Amanda rumpled her pillow in a ball and curled herself around it. *I wish I were home*, she thought, knowing she was too old for such fear. *Go to sleep*, her mom would tell her, only her mom wasn't there to tell her. *Stay awake*, her brain told her. She felt the veil of sleep lowering, calling her back. The undertow of music tugged at her mind, teasing her: *Sleep, precious*. No, she told herself, jamming her nails into her lower lip, straining to keep her mind awake.

The hour bells sounded, muffled and far away. Four o'clock, the hour of the wolf, the hour when souls depart the earth. She shivered as she sat up and looked out the window, at the Dipper, high above with the polestar Polaris. Then at Cassiopeia and Cepheus low on the horizon. She found the star in Cepheus that would some day mark the pole. She did algebraic problems in her head, then recited a poem, anything to keep the music at bay.

Go to sleep, a deep voice whispered out of the well as she lay her head back against the pillow. *We will play the rest for you. Don't you want to hear? Go to sleep, Mandy*. No, that couldn't be. Mandy, her dad's old pet name for her. But her dad was dead, long dead. It was a trick.

The bells tolled the next hour, "Blackwell's Tune." Almost time now, she told herself. Then you can let go. It's all fading now. It's only last Monday's sixties music class, Professor Bannon's collection of period newspaper clippings.

You had the dream the first time that night, remember? That horrible account of Kitty Genovese. Poor Kitty, screaming out for help as she was stabbed, taking a long and noisy time to die while city people hid their heads beneath their pillows.

It's time now, a voice said as dawn broke, and this time it was her mother's morning voice. *Rise and shine, time's awasting.* It was all right now, she told herself, floating off with the dawn. She could see her mother sitting there on her covered porch with her piebald cat, drinking her solitary cup of morning coffee.

Sleep now child. Her eyes fluttered closed, and her hands fell from her ears to lie like wounded doves upon the pillow.

She didn't hear the morning bells when they rang; she slept through her roommate's rising and departure. "Blackwell's Tune" played four more times before she stirred and opened her eyes.

3:44 P.M.

His face in the mirror was black as pitch, oily. He smiled and his perfect teeth gleamed, a Cheshire smile. The mirror behind him caught it all, flashing the receding scenes.

Backward: the smile, the faience, the slice of still green life below. He was lord and master of it all. Above him hung the past, high and light. Below, the future, somber and dark. It was all there: the shuddering elms, the squirrels frolicking, the sleeping beauty—soon to be victim—even the name of the killer. And it was time now. Time to ring out the old and ring in the new. Time for the tolling of the iron bells.

4:00 P.M.

The man with the fox-colored eyes stood stock still as the bells finished tolling. Four o'clock, time for tea. He looked down at his hands and saw the drop of red on the scabbard.

Sweet Mother of Christ, what have I done? He collapsed in his chair and waited for the thunderbolt, the girl's voice echoing in his brain, frantic. It would come now, the high-pitched screaming of the girls in the computer cluster. "O, sweet Mary," he said, closing his eyes—now he understood the master's words: "Now the Devil dances with me, too. Madness takes hold. Destroy me that I may forget that I exist."

Silence. No angry bolt from heaven. It would come more slowly. He opened his eyes a slit. Across from him in the hall was a lavender flier decorated with notes of music. Next to it a bird-watcher's club bulletin printed in canary. He could hear two sounds, a loud whirring and a rhythmic thumping. He located the first sound: the large-faced impulse clock across the hall. The clock creaked as the minute hand jerked past the twelve; the second seemed to drag out endlessly; then the thumping speeded up. Muffled by something. Amanda pounding on a door? Telling it all? How long could she run? Long enough to name him? Sweet Mary, if she could run, she could talk. They would come soon, the women; they would cluster round with their cackles and sharp, painted nails and tear his flesh.

Silence still? He drew in a large breath of air and held it. Had he imagined it all? Was she standing there waiting behind him, that crooked grin on her face, bow poised? "Again," he had said, "mit höchster Gewalt." And she had played, oh how she had played, the music and the feeling swelling effortlessly out of her, coming exactly as the master had wanted. Sweet, malefic Alma, a perfect vessel. He had turned, and his eyes had met hers, and her smile and his had been one. The miracle had begun to unfold.

He wheeled around. No, there was no goddess smiling and drawing the bow of the cello. Only his bow on the chair—and the music sparkling like diamonds in the expectant air. What he had thought dross she had woven into gold. He turned toward the waiting notes. He was quite mad, he knew. She wasn't Alma, not underneath. Her face had gone quite soft when he hit her.

His eyes glinted as he narrowed them. Quite mad. The music was everything, wasn't it? Maestro, your work. They were waiting for him, waiting to be plucked and played. He reached out his hand, and his fingers made a little pincer and tried to pluck a note. It slipped through his fingers. Another. No, the notes evaded him and danced among the air motes. Not time yet. He realized he was waiting for something. What? A sound, the tap of the conductor's baton—something. He turned back toward the door—the hall was deserted, the veined marble floor shiny and clean. But below? In the subterranean world, what waited?

Presently, the minute hand creaked as it rounded the six and swept upward. He focused on the yellow and lavender sheets: thirty chickadees, fourteen sparrows, forty swallows. April's early bird count. Mahler Prize: $500,000. A chance for fame. Just turn slowly and approach the keyboard, roll your fingers, and play.

If only the pounding would stop. Each beat seemed louder. The music was all there, every strand of it. And Mahler was alive in heaven. He would want to hear it played. He looked at the MIDI instrument, staring at the button that would activate the E-mu digitizer. The sequencer lay ready to record the snapshot of sound. No. Left brain jumped in and grabbed him back. Beware. God punishes those who cannot listen.

"Word of honor," she said. It wasn't his fault. She had laughed when she first saw the pictures, laughed and ran her hand through her gun-barrel-blue hair, and flushed red. It was warm in the room; he always kept it warm.

"Go on, you can touch them, dear. Art is meant to be experienced. These are seventeenth-century aquatints."

"I don't know, really." She pushed them back at him, giggling. "Really, sir."

She was tense as a bow, her knees pressed together, her breasts between her arms. She needed drawing out.

"Sir? Can't you do better than that?" He watched her squirm in the hard chair; her panties under the leather would be sticking to her buttocks.

"I can't, really."

He moved toward her, his eye on her damp cleavage, smelling her woman's musky wet-hay scent. Year after year of sweet, tormenting Amandas—always young, always ripe.

His hands had risen of their own volition toward her swelling breasts. Sweet Mother of God, let me touch you, your skin is so soft. His hands were blameless; couldn't they touch that perfect body? His hands were perfect, no part of his vile body. He looked down at them. They were smooth and blemishless. His fingers weren't long, but his palms made up for it. Strong hands.

She had hit his hands away and jumped up with fire in her eyes.

"Don't be afraid, sweet thing. I just wanted to touch— you're like a cello string yourself, so much tension quivering in those wires, so alive . . ." He had experience with coeds. There was a time to retreat and woo with words. Or music. But he couldn't stop his hands.

"Please. Stay away from me!"

"I won't even make you give up your music this time. And I'll bring you gifts. Scent—you like that, don't you? It's fate, don't deny it. You and me—built on the foundation of old ruins." He grabbed her around the waist. "Don't you know who you are?"

She pushed him away, hard. "And you're crazy! Or strung out on something. I should report you. Trying to seduce me with your sordid little pictures."

He laughed and folded his hands. "Sweet child," he said, "I didn't mean to discomfort you. I thought you had enough breeding to recognize art when you see it. Those sordid little pictures are rare and priceless." He sniffed, wheeling back from her.

She wasn't frowning when he turned. It was working. She

was feeling guilty. She would come and lean over his chair.

He came toward her. "I'm sorry," he said. He reached out his hand. She didn't take it. He didn't know what came over him then. His strong hand behind him tightened on his bow. He reached up with his other hand and touched her buttocks. She gasped and pushed him away, against the wall.

"Damn it, you creep! I'm reporting you to Dr. Garver!"

He had risen then and raised the bow, to threaten her, and saw that she was ready to scream. He *had* to quiet her.

Only it wasn't a bow. He adjusted the glasses on his nose and passed his tongue across dry lips. He hadn't meant to hurt her, hadn't even thought of striking her until he had done it. His whole life had flashed before him then. Arrest, disgrace, ruin. It was all her fault. Didn't she see? He'd have done anything for her.

He bowed his head, his words a soft whisper: "Farewell, my lyre."

⌐ 2040

Saturday, April 14, 11:44 P.M.

It was a night like any other night in Shawneeville, dark and warm with just a hint of a breeze. The young woman came out on the porch after her shower, her close-cropped yellow hair still damp, spots of moisture darkening her linen underwear. She moved to the railing of the porch, setting her white china mug next to the citronella candle, and looked up at the spot of hazy light. Behind that fuzzy veil lay the waxy-faced moon. She had seen the full face once or twice a year when she was younger, but her memory was still vivid: in her mind's eye, the man in the moon was always smiling.

Somewhere off in the distance a dog howled. Sweet night music fiddled up from the cool darkness below: bullfrogs and cicadas. The house was at the end of the block on the edge of the canyon, an old turn-of-the-century solar single, a good fifty yards from the thirties Plexiglas double dozens that capped the block. "Happy Hunting Pueblos," they called themselves, sort of art deco Navajo with soft sienna-and-turquoise trim, and totem pole fixtures. No two units were the same, two rows of twenty-four, each with a double garage and an oxygen unit. Old folks went to bed early. No lights on in the treated glass windows. No night noises.

She reached down and took a sip of hot brew. From the distant campus library tower, the bells began the carillon-neur's tune. She waited for the sweet high E and winced when it came. Was something wrong with the bells? Or was it just the acoustics in the canyon?

The breeze scudded a bank of purple clouds across the dusky sky, and somewhere far off down the canyon road a cow lowed. The woman stretched in the warm night and planted her bare feet square on the soft, moon-washed pine planks. She closed out the night and started her t'ai chi: body forces centering, fingers like lilies floating on the still waters, now lowering, hands coming around to hold the magic sphere. No.

She moved to start again but stopped. A chill went down her spine, and the hairs on her neck prickled. Too much caffeine, she thought. I've got to cut down. But no, it was more than that. She opened her eyes wide and strained against the night. The canyon music had stopped. Dead silence. Even the cicadas had stopped humming.

As she watched, the sky began to shake. Her hair stood on end, charged. And then it happened: the haze lifted and a pocket of black night turned itself out. The moon's gold face shone down. She drew in her breath. Her shadow shimmered long and angular across the milky pine planks.

The solar flares were acting up, swathing the planet in a luminous veil of gold zodiacal light, enough energy erupting up there in a nanosecond to light every light bulb in the world forever.

All at once, the Happy Hunting Pueblos erupted in noise. Forty-eight desert-rose and cactus-green garage doors yawned open in unison, the sound splitting the night. Then, on cue, before the echo had even died, they all cranked shut. The moon molded like cheese, grew green as jade, then rotted black. The night sealed itself back up.

Now the Pueblos were waking up. The day people were turning on lights, opening their pastel front doors, and coming out in their night clothes to exchange excited queries. But they were too late. The show was over; the zodiacal lights were already dimming.

She picked up her mug and slipped back into the shadows. Let them read about it tomorrow. Time to go to work and earn her nightly bread.

She dressed without thought, buttoning the blue coat and putting on her shoes between bites of crisp toast. E E L, STATE POLICE, ARCHIVES, her ID tag read; she fastened the chain around her neck and dropped the tag inside the dark blue coat lapels. She put a few hard-boiled eggs and biscuits in a brown paper bag and put the bag in her ample pocket. By the time she came back outside, all the commotion had died down. Only two lights remained on in the Pueblos; as she stood on the porch attaching her bicycle clips, one of them winked out.

It wasn't till she was coasting down the canyon road that she thought of work, of the file she had left in her processor bank. "Baaz," she said out loud, as she pedaled past the hedgerow; she should have put a protect tab on it. In the field beyond the hedgerow, a black and white milk cow lifted its head and lowed back. Not smart, Eel, she chided herself. And yesterday of all days. She pedaled faster, toward the little town of Shawneeville.

⌐ 2020

Tuesday, April 14, 4:00 P.M.

Badge 77, Detective Sergeant Maxwell Caine, leaned back in his ancient swivel chair and put his feet on the edge of the scarred gunmetal desk. In his hand was a coin; he turned it idly between thumb and forefingers. The coin was worn nearly faceless, but the silver still weighed richly in his hand. A Kennedy cupronickel-clad half dollar, forty percent silver. The famous "vanishing coin," rarer these days than a blue moon. Minted by the millions, intended as the last prestige circulating coin of the realm, it had disappeared into collections as fast as it could be issued, even after the date was frozen in 1965. He had been carrying this particular one in his pocket for a quarter century, holding it, twisting it, flipping it, worrying with it until the face and seal had become faint shadowy reliefs discernible only under strong light. It was going to be hard to let it go.

Cadaveric spasm: the death grip. He had been in plain clothes for two years that spring of '95. Before that, three years in blue; a degree in criminal justice had speeded his promotions, but in those three years he had seen the victims of booze and icy mountain roads—he could spot the death spasm as good as the next fellow. He should have pegged it. It was just that most all the cases he had seen had been gripping steering wheels.

"I've got smelling salts," a shrill voice had said above him.

11

"Call an ambulance!" he yelled, beginning mouth to mouth. Then there were more voices jabbering around him, talk about her studded leathers and hooligan hair and how it had to be a narco fit. Assumptions. There had been so many druggers those days; it had been natural for onlookers to assume.

"I felt a pulse," Max said as the first attendant knelt beside him.

The young man reached to find it.

"I think it's crack or ice," the younger man said as the medic came up with the lifepack, and it seemed as they worked that the color was returning to Amanda's face. Her skin was ruddy, flushed with life. It was natural for everyone to think that it was the life-force that kept the coin in her hand. Even the attendant who pried open Amanda's fingers and held up the coin for Max had not known.

Max slipped the coin in his pocket and stood up, clearing the way to the door. Someone found the girl's purse and set it beside her on the pallet. When they carried her off he went to the men's room and splashed cold water over his face. Then he took the coin out and inspected it. A fine piece.

Max knew about coins. Anyone who grew up in Shawneeville couldn't help but know a little about coins. Coins and music, the trademarks of the burg. It was the Welsh-Indian mountain blood, the love of music and precious metal. Numismatic knowledge came with the territory. A full tenth of the National Numismatic Society's membership lived in Shawneeville. There was not much chance of finding a rare coin locally, but outside the sleepy college town, numismatic knowledge could be quite profitable. Max had once, the summer he turned twelve and stayed with his grandparents in Kansas, garnered a thousand dollars by visiting various banks and buying penny rolls and nickel rolls, weeding out the wheat pennies and buffalo nickels, and selling them on his return to the Numismatical Society shop. Within Shawneeville, the wheats and buffalos never made it to the bank. Anything of value circulated by outsiders was quickly pocketed by locals.

Max flipped the coin. Every contact leaves a trace. Wasn't that what they taught in forensics? Heads. The "1965" had blurred out long ago. Kennedy's profile was a thin trace, slender as a sliver of new moon. Three score minus seven years. He flipped it again. Tails. The Great Seal was but a faint imprint. A piece of silver. A few more tosses and it would not even serve as diviner—it would be talisman only.

Twenty-five years. He grimaced at the jumble of boxes surrounding him, what his wife Connie had bitterly called his "magnificent obsession." He had married late, just before the turn of the century, along with the other mass marriers, part of the great tide of couples who, like lemmings, had pledged themselves to twoness as the century turned. The last demidecade—not much to brag about—five years of myopic greed as the baby boomers reached their majority, a great spiritual vacuum waiting to be filled.

A dog-eared bound report lay on his desk, its spine creased open at a double picture page. On the left was a repro of the pinup photo. One of the twelve prettiest girls on campus, or so said the caption. Amanda with her perfect hourglass figure, frozen in a fading rectangle. She was wearing a black and white, vertical striped, off-the-shoulder jersey, a red neck scarf, and leather pants. She was standing next to the panther shrine, one arm draped along its back. Dark skin and almond eyes, rosy cheeks and jet black hair cut spiky short, suggesting a trace of Oriental or Indian. In the background the leaves were orange. The picture always reminded him of one of those Halloween cats, hair on end. Only she didn't look scared; she looked as if she were about to laugh. Maybe it was just because she was Miss October. And the orange leaves and great sassy jack-o'-lantern smile. "How I envy maple leafage, which turns beautiful and then falls . . ."

Some seventeenth-century Japanese poet, Kagami Something, Max recalled. He hadn't graduated college for nothing.

Opposite her on the page was a composite sketch of a man's face: sharp chin, wide forehead, a sailor's cap, glasses. Not much of a suspect. No name, few particulars. His only witness had first thought him short, then changed her mind and couldn't say; she had not seen the color of his hair or eyes. Still, they had gotten this image under hypnosis: a mean-looking lowbrow face, the hint of a mustache.

Max crossed his legs over the man's face and thought of the girl. Case #665-1995: Amanda Zephyr, a devilish case. His slate was clean, save for her. And there was so much of her. Six 1,500-page documents submitted by thirty-six investigators; sixteen boxes of assorted photos, lab reports, sketches, and index cards; a giant carton of videocassettes and Xapshot floppy disks; a key to a physical evidence locker somewhere in the basement. Case #665, a story of blind alleys and dead ends, his Nemesis.

All of which had to be filed before he could check out. He reached around and turned up the screen, plucked an antistatic wipe from the console, and used it to clean the gold bull's eye browbar of his Ray-Ban Shooters; they gleamed in the mirror opposite, twenty-three-karat gold. One of his few vanities. They only blocked out 98 percent of the hellish UVs, but he loved them. What did he have aside from these and his vintage BMW that he really cherished? One salty geriatric African Grey parrot who bit the hand of every female he had ever brought home? A few souvenirs among the crufties in his desk drawer, some old photographs: life on Woodland Drive, Max with his parents; Max in his little room next to a wall of cats that were wearing red sneakers and singing about eating mousies . . . little pieces of a past long gone. Nothing new, nothing perfect, nothing that could not be packed into Lady's backseat and trunk and taken with him. Or given away. There was not even enough for a garage sale. He had done all that. He had closed up the big house the previous summer, cleaned out the attic, and sold or thrown away the boxes his mom had kept all those years: GI Joes and Incredible Hulks and plastic Cooties. He had not brought much baggage when he moved to the condo.

He looked out at the jumble of boxes. So much and yet so little. A mystery from the very beginning. Knife-impaled hearts weep blood under average conditions. Unless a particularly careful planner, the average killer leaves clues, traces of himself or herself. And yet they had found nothing. No blood, no motive, no weapon, no prints, no pattern of premeditation. No one had even called it murder until the infirmary doctor had called. Max stroked his graying mustache. As usual, it needed trimming. He had read once years earlier that stroking a mustache was a sign of vanity and since then did it only when he was alone.

He had been clean-shaven at twenty-five. A nice-looking young man, people used to say.

Just the facts, he reminded himself. He had just gone off duty and was passing Mahler Hall when he felt thirsty and went in for a drink of water. Walking by the music room, he had seen Amanda. It had all happened so fast. Amanda, wobbling on her feet, her mouth opening and closing like a fist. She looked familiar. Was this the cellist? She saw him and started toward him. She raised her hand to him and then . . . everything seemed to blur. Memory was encrusted in the piles of reports he had written, in the frozen words of the interviews he had given to the media.

Amanda, falling, grabbing out for the music stand. Amanda looking at him with her eyes wide and her mouth making a big O as he caught her. Her face was flushed, her flesh warm; he had tried to prop her up, but she had collapsed. He had knelt beside her and felt her neck next to the double lightning bolt ear cuffs, felt the hot nape of her neck.

The ambulance was there in five minutes. The coin was placed in his hand. They used a siren when they sped off.

Miss Tilly came up behind him and offered him a plastic cup of coffee. "I'm Miss Tilly," she said. "If you need anything, just holler. I hope Miss Zephyr's okay." He palmed the coin in his hand and took the coffee with a smile. Miss Tilly reminded him of his favorite aunt, soft and fleshy, smelling of gardenia, but agile as a sparrow, always fussing over someone.

It was Miss Tilly who called him to the phone. "It's Dr. Scutari, from the infirmary," she whispered. He remembered his conversation exactly. He had replayed the transcript many times.

"Detective Max Caine here."

"Detective, this ain't no social call. I thought I'd better call so you can secure that goddamn hall."

"What?"

"Hold on to your hat. That girl you sent over?"

"Yes."

"She didn't just faint. Foul play, I'm afraid."

"What?"

"She's dead."

"Dead?" He lowered his voice. "What do you mean, dead?"

"As in doornail, Caine. DOA. I've called the coroner. And I've checked her purse. Name's Amanda Zephyr, lives in Bruckner Hall. You'd better notify the department head and call State. I've bagged the clothes—you'll want to get a CSI unit over to look for latent prints and trace material."

"I am CSI. Christ. But I felt a pulse." Max looked over at the pale-faced Miss Tilly standing in the doorway. "Narcotics?" he asked, keeping his voice low.

"No, this one's for the books. She was stabbed, Caine. Knife cut down through the leather, through the wishbone of her bra, into her heart. Double-edged blade, thin, maybe four inches. Not something you'd cut cheese in the dorm with."

"But—" Max lowered his voice. "Stabbed? There wasn't any blood."

"Bled into her chest cavity. Tamponade. Had to be a pretty strong and tall person to have done it—left the imprint of the hilt on her breast. You can eliminate the little old ladies."

Max remembered how he had hung up the phone and looked up at Miss Tilly, at the women and students milling behind her in the hall. "I need to speak to the department head," he said.

Miss Tilly stepped forward. "Dr. Garver is in Arizona—a convention. What's wrong?"

"I'm afraid Miss Zephyr is dead," he said, taking charge at that point, scanning their faces with professional suspicion. "I want everyone to stay in the building till we can collect statements. Miss, uh, Tilly, can you get Maintenance to barricade the entrance?"

She nodded, flushed with excitement. A wisp of damp hair clung to her cheek, reinforcing his previous reaction. She did look like his aunt, like Aunt Emma, doing housework, intent on her task. He turned and picked up the phone and called the station.

So much to do. Seal off the building, fill in the arriving detectives, bring in the metal detector and search for a weapon, take Xapshots of the room, talk to anyone who might have seen anything, notify the next of kin. He had just shown the forensic crew where to mark the chalk outline on the music room floor and was helping to set up the video surveillance camcorder when Miss Tilly appeared in the doorway of her office and beckoned him across.

"It's probably not important," he remembered her saying. A strange look came over her face. She was, Max thought, smiling for the camera. She no longer reminded him of his aunt.

"Yes?"

"But I did see a man hurrying down the main steps at four. He was carrying sheet music."

"Important? God, woman! Of course it's important. Hey, Fred, you getting this on the tape? Hank, you'd better get over here, too. Pull half your men off the internal check and send them out to the air terminal and station.''

''I remember exactly,'' Miss Tilly said. ''The bells were just striking four. I was standing at the window and saw him on the outside stairs, going down. He seemed to be limping slightly.''

''Would you recognize him if you saw him again?''

''I can't say. I only saw him for a moment. He had this funny hat on, more like a cap really.''

''Damn,'' Max said. ''And I was coming up the Mall at four, with a good view of the hall. And then I stopped to watch this stupid squirrel.''

''Squirrel, Caine?'' Fred said.

''It was an albino. Damn! I must have just missed him.''

''For want of a glance, a promotion is lost,'' Fred joked. ''Ah, Caine. Well, better call in the 'artiste' and get him to work with Miss Tilly. Better yet, I'm going over to headquarters—I'll take her to the man himself.''

''Would you?''

''Oh, I couldn't possibly go just yet,'' Miss Tilly put in. ''You send your artist over here. If we're barricading the building, I'll be busy taking round tea and coffee.''

So the artist had come, and Miss Tilly, between service runs and calls, had set down her description.

By daybreak there had been thirty-six men on the case and a $100,000 community reward. A reward never collected. The killer had too much of a head start. Amanda had never had a chance. Tamponade, the autopsy confirmed. The knife had cut downward through the aorta into the right ventricle, severing the pulmonary artery. The shock had compressed the heart and stopped its pumping. Blood had poured into the pericardial sac, the internal hemorrhaging flooding her face with color. A freak blow, the killing stroke. The faint pulsation he had felt had only been her heart quivering in a cushion of blood. She had died in a state of anoxia, gasping for breath. There was nothing anyone could have done. The pathologist told him that had she been stabbed in the operating room with five heart surgeons standing by and an unlimited blood supply, they could not have saved her.

Max flipped the coin and recrossed his legs. There was no statute of limitations on murder. As long as there was a chance of conviction, the file would remain open until it was archived in 2040. A quarter of a century had brought them no closer than they had been that first day. Amanda had become "that girl who was killed in Mahler Hall," a campus myth, something to scare freshmen coeds with. Not one out of a thousand people still remembered who had been the first to find her.

He flipped the coin. When he retired there would be no one left who had worked on the case, no one who remembered the hundred times his team had thought they had found the lead that would take them into the light, only to find themselves at the end of another blind alley. A hundred coincidences that had slowly burnt away intent, a fruitless human jigsaw, exhaustive, exhausting, and in the end, futile.

The time had come to file the final blue paper. He pulled his console closer and activated Manual mode. He was old-fashioned, he told everyone. He liked beginning his work with the same ritual. Hands on, the old way. He hit ENTER a few times, and then logged in: MAC. The plasma screen brightened. He typed in his password, PEGASUS, and then took a shiny optical lasercard from the cardfile and popped it in the laser scanner. Case Summary #665-1995. He typed in the date: 4-14-20. The ides of April, not a lucky time. In those hours, Lincoln was shot and died; the maiden *Titanic* struck ice and sunk; the great earthquake and aftershock of '99 rocked LA. April 14–15. Death and taxes. He sighed; he would have to do his own taxes very soon.

He looked at the large, ancient clock in the hallway of the third floor of police headquarters. Six o'clock. Once or twice a year they came and fixed it, but it never worked for long. It had stood at six o'clock for weeks now. He wondered if it was A.M. or P.M. The digital on his desk read 4:02:13 P. Just past the time Amanda had died. Tea time. He knew her whereabouts almost to the minute that day. She had slept late and skipped breakfast, but she had made her ten o'clock music class; she had worked the lunch shift at Boscoe's Diner, bought a textbook at the HUB store, and sunned herself on the library steps. They had found her cello in her locker. Nothing out of the ordinary. He looked at her photo. A delicate face, but not fragile, not at all. The image of a hooligan, the very antithesis in real life. She had passed the blood test clean. No narcotics, not even a trace of alcohol. No seminal fluids on the vaginal smear. Red Cross certified AIDS-free. No enemies. He had personally cleaned out her dorm room: a book of Russian poetry under her bed, a big white towel bathrobe on the bedpost, an unfinished letter to her brother on the desk. He had talked to her roommate and spoken at length with her parents. Amanda's idea of fun was to kick a soccer ball fifty times or sit on the steps of her dorm and play her cello for the squirrels and chipmunks. He had read her diary. She didn't have a lover; she didn't even have a date for that Saturday night. She was saving herself for the right man.

Maybe she had just been at the wrong place at the wrong time. Unlucky. Like himself. If the coffee had not been so hot at the diner that day, he might have reached Mahler Hall earlier and collided with the mystery music man. If he had not stopped to watch the albino squirrel romping with the black squirrel . . .

No one knew what kept her that day from her music, and there was no use thinking of what might have been. He rapped the coin on the desk, then laid it on the blotter and looked at the amber screen.

His hands on the keyboard twitched, and he stored the introduction. Then he hit VOICE.

"A cop gets to thinking crazy when he can't find a motive

or a weapon or a suspect. The killer could be anyone in Shawneeville—a student, a teacher, the guy sitting next to you in the diner. Maybe Amanda didn't even know him. Amanda Zephyr was the last name in the college directory. Maybe he just picked her out of the book. A random motive. Except for one thing: Amanda herself. She wasn't random, wasn't any ordinary girl. Amanda was gifted and beautiful. Surely she attracted her own fate.''

Max killed the switch and sat thinking. Amanda was like Snow White in her glass coffin, frozen in time, forever young. And now she had slept a quarter century . . .

⌐ 2040

Saturday, April 14, Midnight

The campus bells were chiming as the young woman flipped down the kickstand, leaned her bike against the vegetations house, and approached the low, domed booth. The air smelled of tomatoes, acidic and crisp. OMNIPOL CENTRAL the gold gas plaque read. She lifted her ID to the scanner and made eye contact. "E. E. Lacoste, let me in."

The sensors rumbled. "Pass," the electronic bass voice sounded. The smooth round metal doorway glistened and rippled, then formed petals and opened; she stepped through the doorway and walked quickly down the sloping ramp to the first moving ramp. On the second moving ramp she came up behind a few pairs of stragglers, then stopped walking and let the rampway carry her at a distance.

NEWS ROOM, the arrow said, fifty yards before they reached the tunnel turn. *JAVA*DONUTS*PAPERS*COKE*CONDOMS* GUM* the rainbow neon flashed every five yards. The two couples ahead of her moved to the turning lane's slower track. She stayed on and rode swiftly past the open door of the gathering room. People talking, drinking thimblefuls of hot brew, making faces, catching up on gossip. People in pairs and trios and whole clumps, sometimes the same clumps, sometimes different. She reached in her pocket, took out her earbug, and slipped it in. Her morning mantra, juice for the soul.

The track ahead was deserted now. She checked to her rear

and then stepped up her pace, covering the next ramp in crisp
seconds flat. FILES, the approaching arrow pointed. She
judged her speed and alighted on the slower track, the ground
coming up short beneath her. Baaz, she thought as her knees
crunched, I misjudged it. She steadied herself against the
rubber rail and limbered out her knees; then she bounced on
down the track toward her section.

As she turned right at corner thirty-three, she smacked into
a stranger coming off the ramp the wrong way. The air came
out of her. Her earbug popped out and went sailing down the
corridor. "Ouch!" she cried.

The man had half fallen himself. "I'm sorry," he said,
picking himself up and uncrumpling his freckled face.

He had a Texas accent, the sound of wide open plains. He
smiled at her. "Are you going to report me for shortcutting?"

"I ought to," she said, retrieving her earpiece. "Except
for one thing."

"I have an honest face?"

"No, I was speeding."

He breathed an exaggerated sigh of relief. "Thank God for
honest criminals. You okay?"

She surveyed herself. "No damage done."

He followed her gaze. "No," he said. "You new here?"

She laughed and shook her head. "Heavens no, I'm just
late today."

"Never see you in Klatch." He stuck out a big hairy hand.
"Clay Adams. Canonical Files."

"E. E. Lacoste, Archives," she said, dipping her head
formally in the first degree. A polycop and she had con-
fessed. Not smart, Eel.

She moved to the side to let him pass, and he moved, at the
same moment, to the same side. There passed between them
that panic of amusement strangers felt when they met and
could not pass. Deadly embrace, the phenomenon was called;
she had studied it once, analyzing its proteins in the brain.

"Shall we dance?" he said, holding up his arms.

A man with a tiny cleft in his chin and blue eyes and soft hair and freckles stood there waiting for her answer and it was all a joke—life, too. Canonical Files: the pol was probably as rigid as the pearly gates.

"Are you crazy?" she asked. It broke the spell, and she found herself gliding past. "I've got work to do," she said. Wasn't that what one told a polycop?

"Java sometime then," he said, not making it a question, but he was already talking to a fleeting glimpse of her back as she turned the corner to ARCHIVES.

She had to laugh. "New here," he had said. Ten years that month. A decade archiving the State's collection of unsolved turn-of-the-century crimes, ten years of scribing short concise crime summaries in her perfect 150 wpm calligraphic shorthand: twenty cases a night, every night. "How do you do it?" people would ask when they found out that she was "that" E E L, and she would smile a wan smile and tell the truth. "It suits me fine," she would say. There was a satisfaction akin to shoemaking or cutting hair in her work. Her marks would stand as history.

Besides, it left her energies untapped for the later nightly fare. She would do her twenty cases by 4 A.M. and beat the power crunch, would be deep into Wormwood, many levels down, before the rest of the game hackers began to log on.

The first thing she did when she entered her cubicle was to get out her Virus Buster and sweep her files for Friday the 13th worms. No DenZuk III killers; no Jerusalem bugs. No "Yankee Doodle" or "Daisy." She let out a sigh of relief and poured coffee from her hotpack into her zarf cup and changed her earbug. In her right brain, Tangerine Dream's "Rubycon" began, cradle music. She closed her eyes and remembered the previous morning's encounter with the red-eyed dragon. She had used the basket of swallows to lure him near and then frightened him with the centipede. She had been close enough to grasp the spinning pearl, but at the last minute she had slipped and had to retreat. So close.

A soft *feep* made her open her eyes.

"Foo?" she murmured, switching focus.

The yellow turbo light was blinking. She rubbed her chin hard as she stared at it. She clucked. Who knew what solar flares could do to a file. Let's see, what was this case anyhow? She remembered the number, 665. She remembered loading it up last night, but then she'd started thinking about the pearl. She'd put the file on backburner while she played Wormwood.

The turbo light stopped flashing and she called up the work screen. The AA program came up: Archival Analysis. She entered the code and the case file number: 665-1995. The Crayette began to make appropriate noises. Good, the gallium arsenide chips were still doing their teraFLOPs. She picked up her stylus and set its point on the clean slate, already composing her opening. She liked her history neat.

Feep, feep. She spun her stool around. BAD FILE CODE, the screen read. Damnation, it had barely begun. What in Crayation? She retyped the number: 665-1995 and pressed DEF. In the half light of the cathode, the letters radiated cool orange. File #665-1995 defined itself:

HOMICIDE, stabbing. Zephyr, Amanda, white female, 19. Mahler Hall music room, April 15, 1995, Shawneeville. Maxwell Caine, Investigating officer, badge #77.

The computer-coded evidence files had all been transferred to digital. Now her Crayette would file them as she wrote her summary. She pressed ARCHIVE. The turbo light blinked as the Crayette gulped down the data.

An odd case, she thought, composing the capsule summary in her head: A young coed stabbed in the music room on campus, found by the local CSI officer who just happened to be passing by. Weapon: Never Found. Motive: Unknown.

One possible suspect, seen limping from the scene, never located. Clues: three bags full but all of them leading down blind alleys.

A loud *feep* from the Crayette made her look up. What now? The error light was blinking wildly. ERROR #66 ELLIP-TICAL CONFUSION. CANNOT PROCEED.

Hogwash. She reset the system and tried again. ERROR #66 ELLIPTICAL CONFUSION. CANNOT PROCEED.

She tried to file it, error and all. The Crayette bleeped back: LOCKJAMMED. Baaz, now she couldn't even move backward. And her Crayette didn't have AIM—it couldn't fix itself the way her old mainframe could. Error #66—she didn't remember ever seeing that. She rocked back on her knee chair and rolled the kinks from her shoulders, feeling the screws loosen in the stool's frame. It was an old stool, but she loved it; she kept a solar screwdriver in her top drawer so she wouldn't have to send it to Maintenance. She wiggled her fingers and lay them on the keyboard. Try again. She twiddled and tweaked, but the cursor would not move. The Cray-ette continued to feep and blink like a baby bird without its breakfast. She rapped the machine on its curved mirrored exterior. "Hey, Kludge, what gives?"

She shrugged and pressed the HELP button and waited for the robotic technician, scrawling doodles with her mouse on her auxiliary note screen. A border of roses around the file number, garlands. A knife, with a drip of carmine blood; a badge, number 77.

She was scrolling gothic flourishes around the badge to the electronic Teutonic sounds of her earbug when the robotic technician wheeled itself into the cubicle. She put down her mouse and tipped the pad to erase the doodling.

"Having trouble, E E L?" the robot croaked.

Eel smiled. "'Oh, it's you, Seventeen. My loops won't loop. My file's catatonic.''

The robot had been programmed for light self-mocking patter. "Well, we'll just have to have a look at the cretinous thing," it said, rolling forward. The robot extended its sensor finger and inserted it in the access socket. "Tsk, tsk," it said. "You left her on auto last night, didn't you, E E L?"

She gulped. "Yes."

"Without a protector." It wasn't a question. "Lucky for you the worms didn't get to it."

Robot Seventeen uncoupled and recessed its sensor. "I'll check the cards. We've had a rash of glitzes tonight. Old Sol doing her thing." It raised the screwdriver finger of its multi-jointed digit. It approached the curved mirrored Crayette from the side, stealthily and softly, as a vet might approach a wounded animal. "How you doing, gal? Somebody bump your gizzards?"

"I don't think it's in the cards, Seventeen."

"Won't hurt to check it out." It reached out slowly and touched the Crayette's dark mirrored side. "This won't hurt much," it said, yanking the plug as a person might have yanked a bandage from a child's knee.

"Now we'll just have a look inside," it said, wheeling around the curved table and swiftly unscrewing the back. It checked the cards one by one. The O card was loose; it pressed it firmly in place, then pushed the cover back over and screwed in the plates. "Okay, try it now. From the beginning."

Eel powered up and entered her code: EEL. Initial screen loading fine. Lights whirred within the mirrored surface; then the screen glowed amber. Her file came up and started to archive. Then it jammed. ERROR #66: ELLIPTICAL CONFUSION. CANNOT PROCEED.

The robot pulled a blue manual from its solar plexus cavity and pressed a code. "Here we are, under extraneous errors. 'Error number Sixty-six: elliptical confusion. Cannot proceed.' Read as: 'Do not pass. Go directly to Canonical Files.'"

"Uh oh. The manual's current?"

"Affirmative."

"A deliberate lockjam?"

"Affirmative."

"Uh oh," Eel said again. "Nothing else? No code?"

"Negative."

When Seventeen had wheeled out, Eel sat staring at the screen. Finally, she got up and went next door, looking for the twenty-first-century archivist.

Zelda was in her cubicle, her eyes glued to her amber screen.

"Having a rough night, dearie?" the old crone asked when she saw Eel in the doorway.

"I've got to go to Canonical Files. Some kind of error."

"Good luck."

"Er. You don't think it could have anything to do with the game?" Zelda played the game, too, albeit at a novice level. Eel played deep, but she was always careful to play several levels beneath their deepest probe; still if the wrong person looked in the right place . . . Canonical Files were the purse strings of Omnipol, the Big Guns, the Keepers of the Code. They had access to channels most people never dreamed existed. She had no desire to get on one of their probe lists.

"I can't see how it could have anything to do with that, dearie. More likely you're in line for credit for some statistical improbability. The Millionth Case since Crayation."

"Or maybe someone turned me in for speeding." Eel laughed, remembering the polycop in the hallway.

"Probably they want to commend you for your consistent persistent work, make a model out of you. You've exceeded yourself. They're going to promote you."

"Zelda . . ." Eel's voice was sincerely worried. "They can't. Besides, I never exceed myself. I'm very careful not to draw attention to myself." Very careful—she did just well enough on her summaries to get a plus rating, but was never so efficient as to risk promotion. She was never rated malcontent, so they let her be. But if they promoted her to a real job—it could ruin everything.

"Mediocrity is rewarded every day. They very well can." Eel sighed.

"Don't give yourself wrinkles worrying," Zelda said. "Maybe it's just some kind of quality control. Just take them your summary."

"I haven't got it."

"You read it once, didn't you?"

"Yeah."

"I've seen you whiz through a case. You only need one mind photo. I think you'd better take them a draft. Just write from memory."

Back in her cubicle, Eel activated the stylus and tablet and wrote the case number. In her head she composed the skeleton of the case, constructing it as one might a poem. Voila: there lay history in less than a hundred words. She took a deep breath. The fellow in the hall had not seemed too ominous. Cocky and arrogant, yes, but not sanctimonious. Baaz, it really wasn't worth a nano's thought. Even if they had caught her excess usage, they would never suspect how deep she was going. She always entered their system silently, without noise. A few credits docked for jamming a file, a fine for trespassing on political property. She had more credits in the bank than she would ever need in three lifetimes. Humans made errors. Really, she was working herself into a tizzy for nothing. Maybe that cocky Mr. Adams had just used his power to tinker with her program and get her to come up there for who knows what Texan polycop perversion. Well, she wasn't about to hurry. It took her three drafts before she got it right.

2020

The bells chimed the quarter hour. It would be getting dark soon. Max didn't know how to end the report. What could one say about a life cut short? Such a waste. He exited the program and stared at the blinking screen, the Muzak in the corridor pouring over his mind like embalming fluid. It was Ravinsky for the masses, not exactly his favorite. One fifteen-minute segment ended, and a new sugary-sour soundscape began. He should start his taxes. Simple short-form stuff—it would take him ten minutes. Or he could log in a few of the physical evidence codes. No need to think. Time to get his house in order. He wanted no evidence of sloth or avarice left when he passed out of this world. He pressed FILES and stared at the entry IRS SHORT, but he didn't retrieve it, just stared out the window at the fading dun light. He had enough time if he hurried. He picked up the phone and checked his balance. Then he got up and shoved his way past the jumble of un-opened boxes, pausing to take his hat off the peg at the door.

"Got a couple errands to run, Agnes." His secretary of eleven years was cutting coupons from the *Shawneeville Shopper*.

"Want me to lock up, boss?"

"Don't bother. I'll be back."

He walked home and got scissors from the kitchen and went out back and cut a bunch of bicolored purple irises. Iris, the winged messenger of the gods. Then lilacs from his back

30

hedge, Persian lilacs, heady, sweet flowers, dampening the newspaper he used for wrapping.

He opened the garage, fired up Lady, and backed out. A short drive to the Numismatical Shop, where he picked out a shiny Kennedy half dollar from the velvet tray; the keeper put it in a soft mole-gray pouch while he transferred the funds by voice print. It set him back a half a week's wages.

On the way to the mountain, he turned on the radio and listened to a first-round qualifying match for the '22 World Cup. USA versus Uruguay, and the US was up two-nil. He exited the highway at Juneville and took the back road past the magnolia- and mimosa-lined canal up to the old cemetery, passing under the GREENWOOD sign on the white-painted iron gate.

Amanda's thin marble headstone glistened in the dull heat.

AMANDA ZEPHYR
Born November 28, 1975
Departed April 15, 1995
TAKEN TOO SOON

Max laid the flowers on the stone; the lilac buds had closed; the amethyst iris scrolls hung limp.

"Good-bye, Amanda," he said. The words echoed in the sultry glen. He looked past the grave, out toward the hazy valley and distant bucolic Shawneeville.

Shawneeville, an optimistic little town. Murder didn't happen there. Its inhabitants were knowledgeable and friendly, good with their hands and minds and voices and admirably suited to their faces. People took their time to grow vegetables and watch after their neighbors, to stop on the corner for quiet chats. Everyone hummed and whistled as they went about their work. It was a little Camelot, a small oasis in time, protected from life's storm.

"Except for you, Amanda. Whatever happened to you?"

He swept the old dead flowers from the marble and laid the

new ones gently down. A breeze stirred the trees, picking up the scent of purple petals. The cedars in the grove sighed, and his whole body seemed to sigh with them. He let out a deep breath.

"I won't be coming back, Amanda. I wanted you to know that." The wind picked up a notch, starting the maples chattering. His hand in his pocket clutched the talisman coin and let it go; with his fingers he located the small soft pouch and flipped the velcro seal. Two coins in his pocket now, one new, one old. Clink of silver: Eeny, meeny, miney, mo. Old or new? He found the new coin with his fingers and rimmed its ridges with his fingernail. No harm in token gestures.

"Maybe this one will bring you better luck," he said, laying the bright coin on the worn marble. He turned and walked softly away, imagining that he heard music, the sad strings of a cello. The sound of loss, someone once called it.

He had listened to her playing since September '94, never knowing her face. September's awkward sounds had smoothed into October and November. By Christmas he had begun to look forward to hearing the cellist. He had missed the music over the holidays, counting the days till the next term, hoping the cellist returned. And not a day had gone by since that he didn't perk up his ears to listen when he walked beneath the music room window of Mahler Hall.

When he got back Agnes was still there, fanning herself with her bouquet of coupons. He went into his office and raised the UV shade. Was it his imagination, or could he see the glint of metal high on the mountain?

The day was going fast. He didn't turn on the fluorescents, just sat and watched the lighted, weatherized, glass-and-steel office cubicles in the building across the way. People were milling about behind the lighted windows, getting ready to begin their other lives. He looked down: the lights on his switchboard twinkled red and white as the staff made going-home plans, the lights blinking out one by one. He heard relaxed voices in the hallway, saying good nights, the Muzak soundscape fading.

Then silence. The sun would not set till 6:38, but it was dark already, the last light swallowed by the deep haze. He pulled the old coin from his pocket and looked at it. Liberty, In God We Trust. The words were illegible, just small chicken scratches in the silver. He took the chain-of-custody record from the file:

M. Caine to Evidence Locker
Evidence locker to SIB Crime Lab
SIB Crime Lab to Property
Property to M. Caine.
M. Caine to . . .

He could return it to property, or route it for destruction. The only thing he couldn't do was to keep it. He closed the coin in his hand, trusting that God would understand if he kept the evidence just a short while longer. Let it serve one more night as talisman.

The Angelus began, the call to prayers, but Max didn't notice. He slipped a vintage U2 disc into the player and sealed out the world.

The day went out like a candle. Nightmode.

2040

Sunday, April 15, 2 A.M.

"Better get it done with, dearie," Zelda said, popping her head through Eel's doorframe.

Eel looked up. "I know. I just—"

"Procrastination is the thief of time." She gave Eel a wink. "Good luck, child."

CANONICAL FILES, CENTRAL DISTRICT POLICE HEADQUARTERS, read the platinum letters on the ebony seal that hung above the massive polished and carved mahogany door: a gnarled old man holding a scale, a warrior with a shield, an ancient blue coat with a cap and badge and billy. The wood was gleaming with oil; the knob was heavy brass, scrolled and scalloped.

Eel grasped the doorknob and pulled. The lobby was old-world elegant, with thick, dense Oriental rugs and a massive carved desk. Behind it sat a tiny boy with large, round, green glasses.

"May I help you?"

"Number Seventeen instructed me here. Error sixty-six."

"Hmm," the boy said, eyeing her. She eyed him back. No child prodigy was going to get her goat.

"Hmm?" she said.

"Hmm. Interesting, error sixty-six. Very interesting. May I have the code, miss?"

Eel laughed at the boy who looked so much like an old tiny man, imagining this is much how she must have appeared

34

when she first started working in Gore Lab. People were forever not taking her seriously. She gave this microtot about four years. He was already showing signs of technostress. She gave him the code and watched him call the case up on his screen. "Why interesting?"

The boy straightened himself up. "You may be eligible for a prize, perhaps even a promotion."

Eel made a face. "For an error?"

"A misnomer, I assure you. You may have tripped over a perfect case. Our curators are always looking for new cases for the Hall of Justice. Perfect crimes are very popular."

"Perfect crimes. I thought criminals were the bad guys."

"Of course they are. But when there is no longer any chance of prosecution, when all who were alive are dead and there is no one left to sue—then, we must let go. The thing is, a perfect crime is very rare, a kind of fluke, an error of nature. Perfection occupies a special dimension. It's our duty to preserve such things. Of course, first it must pass some 'checkpoints.' We don't make awards and promotions lightly."

Eel saw a glimmer of hope. "You mean I don't necessarily just qualify?"

"Exactly. The computer has identified certain key elements about this case, but it hasn't the ability to judge. The recognition of art is a uniquely human quality."

"Who's going to judge it? A panel?"

The boy shook his head. "We do it differently. Let me explain. To be a perfect crime, certain elements must all be there, certain clues visible in plain sight. The criminal must be masterly; he must not only get away with it, but he must do so with public abetment. All the discrepancies must be ironed out, but the ending, nevertheless, must be ambiguous. There are strict canons that must be met, rules that must be satisfied before the case even comes to our notice. This case, number six six five, has those elements. It's got a nine-point-nine rating. But to be a perfect ten, it must go beyond. The work must act as an infinity of mirrors, interpretable to different people in different ways and on many levels. The problem is in judging. What is art? What is perfect?"

"I see your problem. Emphasis and proportion are elusive, at best."

He smiled, looked closer at her name tag, then nodded and went on as before. "If it is art the Central District will appropriate a large honorarium for the complete archiving of this work. The case will be preserved for public viewing. A lengthy summary will be commissioned, and photographic exhibits recreated."

"So who's the judge?"

"Oh, we don't use a judge. What we have is an adversarial decision."

"What?"

"A prosecutor of last resort. After all, as you say, we're the good guys after the bad guys. Our top dog gets a go at the case—with unlimited credits. If he can go back through channels and change the proportions, he has a good chance of disqualifying it. If he can get a confession or a retroactive prosecution, *he* gets a prize."

Eel let out her breath. "Is he any good?"

"He's the best," the boy said. "And he'll be able to use SMT."

There was hope yet. It was only forty-five years. If the principals were still alive, he could do it easily.

"Have you checked the principals?" she inquired.

"Afraid he's going to have to use Deep Subharmonic Memory Transfer. It's still experimental, but we've had some recent successes."

"DSMT." She whistled. "That takes a whole lot of credits."

"Oh, you're aware of that? Yes, but you see—" The kid smiled happily. "—he's got unlimited credits." He looked at Eel's report and then studied her face carefully.

"So you are *that* Eel, aren't you? I thought you were."

"I'm credited for the first SMT experiments. Unlimited travel, eh?" Maybe she could help.

"Okay," she said. "So where's this prosecutor of last resort?"

"Second door to the right. He's green, but he's good. He's cracked his last four cases straight. And he's notched up two retroactive prosecutions. Two more and he'll hold the record for rookies."

It was a plain door, white ash, with a plain brass lever. She knocked, and a strong voice told her to come in.

"Change your mind about java?" It was Adams, blue eyes and cleft chin, smiling at her.

Eel flushed. "No. You see—" She lifted her file. "I've got an error sixty-six."

If he had been happy to see her, now he was positively beaming. "Hot damn!" he exclaimed. "I love Sixty-sixes. I see you brought the report. May I?"

He read her history slowly, nodding. When he finished he didn't look up, just sat, his face unreadable. "Unsolvable. That's what you conclude?" he said finally, tapping the tablet in his hand.

"That's the only objective conclusion."

"But what do you *think*?"

"I'm not paid to form opinions."

"But you must have suspicions. Like what was the cop doing there?"

"I have noted that coincidence and its degree of randomness."

"Quite a coincidence, I'd say. A little too perfect. Come on, don't you think he did it?"

It brought her up short. "It's not my role to judge, only to archive." She kept her face a blank.

"Well, let's take off the lock and see this perfect crime your Crayette has identified. But I'll tell you, your baby's no match for my mainframe's Police Blotter program."

"I'm familiar with the base program. Out of Avalon Hill, isn't it?"

"Well, yes," he said sheepishly.

She shrugged. "Nothing to be ashamed of game programs. Your rookie in the thirteenth precinct has a good mind."

He smiled. "Yeah, you're right. My right-hand man. Anyhow, we've closed a half dozen of these, no problem. Tell you what, if I crack it, I'll buy breakfast."

"I bag my breakfast."

"Well, first I've got to crack it. Hey, are you in a rush or anything? You want to watch?"

"Sure." Maybe she could even help him out. No need to insult the man, especially now that he'd gotten a sort of hang-dog look. He turned away from her and got a code book, and then inserted the file and typed his entry. Error sixty-six vanished and the file appeared. "A nine-point-nine, eh? Okay, now we run it by the rookie who eats perfect crimes for breakfast."

He initiated the program, and it began running, sorting out the parameters, toting and weighing the files, analyzing and printing the conclusions and directions: CONSULT SVHS TAPE #1-A. FRAME 336–337, QUADRANT 18. EVIDENCE. HIGH DEGREE INCRIMINATION. NOTE: DISCREPANCY MESSAGE; TEST TAPE 18, FRAME 339–350.

"What's a discrepancy message?"

"Never got one before. Something the Boolean search has picked up at this crossroad. Some sort of minor error. Anyhow, we don't worry about trivia. Tape One-A, that's the nitty gritty. You want to come down and help me lug the equipment?" He didn't wait for an answer.

Eel followed him with a light step. Really backwoods, this fellow. All the small anachronisms delivered without embarrassment. Those firm beliefs in black and white, right or wrong. He didn't know, did he? He had lived all his life on one world. When one had experienced alternate realities, one didn't get so rooted. Boggled the mind, really—someone

whose feet were planted firmly in one terra, who didn't know
that reality was just a plastic projection of the mind.

"Why not?" she said, following. He stopped and looked
back at her, and then one corner of his mouth twitched up.
"With a little luck," he said, "we'll crack this thing before
the crows start cawing."

He led the way down the elevator to the sub-subbasement.
The air was denser down there. Everything seemed to congeal, even time, and it no longer seemed to matter that she
would be an hour late getting on the system. Last morning's
quest for the pearl seemed as distant as a dream.

They took the glow track to OBSOL and requisitioned the
tapes. A young girl in a white smock handed them a shoebox.
"You'll need some equipment, too. I'll warn you, handle it
with care. Remarkably immature circuitry."

Adams signed out a video player and monitor, circa 1988.

"I'll wheel it for you," Eel said.

Adams carried the box and helped Eel push the cart back to
his office. "Maybe we have a foot fetishist," Adams joked as
he set the shoebox on his desk. He opened it. A plastic tape
case lay inside; he opened the clasp and lifted the lid.

"Good, at least they're marked," Adams said. "Let's see.
We need VHS number One-A. Number Eighteen's here, too,
in case we need it." He picked it up, and as he did, a small
velvet pouch sealed with velcro came unfastened from the
velcro tape mount.

Eel lifted it up. "We picked up a hitchhiker."

"What is it?"

She opened the pouch and spilled its contents into her
hand. It was a wafer-thin silver coin, worn almost smooth. A
chill ran down her spine. She knew this coin; she'd touched
it before. She handed the coin to Adams, who studied it. "A
Kennedy, I'd say." He looked at his physical evidence list.
"Transferred to property from Maxwell Caine, April fifteenth, twenty twenty."

"Where's the profile in courage?"

He held up the coin and turned it over. "Anyone's guess. I'd have to check the catalog, see which scratches are which." He handed the silver coin back to her. "Well, let's take a look at the evidence," he said, plugging the player into the adapter. He took out a pack of Halycon and offered her a stick of pink and black gum.

"No, thanks," she said. She had kicked narco gum the previous year. "Need some help with that?"

"Nothing to it," he said, popping two sticks in his mouth, but he had a little trouble getting the tape to go. At one point he removed the back and did some fiddling. Finally he got it going: a jerky grainy image began to play on the wall screen; it made her eyes water. A man appeared. He was medium height, with short-cropped reddish-gold hair. He was wearing amber aviator glasses and had on a soft camel-colored sweater and a checked shirt.

"That's the tec," Adams said, consulting his printout.

"He doesn't look like a murderer."

"What does a murderer look like?"

"I don't know," she said. "He just doesn't look the type."

"You just don't want it to be the cop. Come on, that era was riddled with cop violence and greed. You want to deny history? The program tagged this crime because it resembles art. The late-twentieth-century-novel twist, using the badge of trust for evil ends." Adams reached for the master switch and dimmed the lights. "Okay, let's play it forward a bit."

The camera panned the room and then focused on the chalk outline of the victim. Then the detective reoccupied the foreground; in the background a door across the hall opened and a woman came forward from her office into the hall. The woman crossed the hall and filled the frame. "I don't know if it's important, but—"

Adams froze the frame and cut the audio. Frame 336–337. 4:30:00. On the quivering screen 1/24th of a second was frozen: the woman talking to Caine, her office beyond.

"Quadrant eighteen," Adams said, checking the data. He

zoomed in past the desk, circa 1995, past elephant mugs, elephant paperweights—and she just a little bird of a thing. Quadrant eighteen held two faces: Maxwell Caine and Miss Tilly. He focused.

"Look at them," Adams said. "The way he's looking at her. He knows this woman. Can't you see it? And that look she's giving him. It could fry the tar off a chicken roof."

"And he claims he never met her. I'll admit, it looks suspicious. Maybe it was love at first sight."

"Clear as the nose on my face. He did it, and Miss Elephant-lover is covering up. Don't count on getting this case to the hall of fame. I think I can crack this one."

"So much for art. I hear you have quite a row of notches on your gun."

He laughed. "A few. I believe in putting criminals behind bars, not eulogizing them."

"You really think he did it?"

"Don't you? He was in charge of the investigation. He promptly went charging off in the wrong direction. 'Barricade the bus station, surround the airport.' He led them a merry chase and she helped him. The question is, is SMT prosecution possible?"

Eel didn't tell him the kid at the desk had already checked. Let him find out for himself.

"My bad luck," he said, reading the screen. "Both dead, died within two weeks of each other—twenty years ago. Hmm? Some sort of pact—to the death? Oh, well, I'll just have to go deep, try to get a proactive confession. We've got rudimentary wormholes back that far. I'll just need a top-notch demidecade channeler."

"And credits are no object. Must be nice."

"I suppose you'd prefer art?"

"No, I wasn't thinking that." Eel was looking at the woman's face. And beyond, studying the fuzzed grainy items on her desk. Elephants galore: elephant erasers, a small elephant vase with silk flowers, a packet of elephant Gummi Bears. On the shelf above, a whole row of late-twentieth-century bodice rippers. She felt strangely deflated.

"There's art involved in this as well, you know," Adams said. "A man's soul is involved here."

"And you're going to rescue it."

"Save it. I use DSMT and hit the tec in twenty twenty, see if I can improve his vision."

"Repent while ye may. You sure about this?"

"Rookie Bob never gets the wrong man."

"You believe that?"

"I've full trust in the program."

"Well, let's pull the public files. See what we're dealing with before we zap him."

He looked up. "You're an awful good sport about this. I mean, it's your reward and all."

"I'm a cop, just like you. If he did it, he's got to pay."

Maxwell Caine's public biofile was on the screen by the time Eel got back from the necessary room. Adams had his feet on his desk and was scanning several screens at a time: wall-size copies of 1995 blue final reports. She looked around his office: very canonical—neutral tones, a few sepia photographs of extinct wildlife.

"Here's your tec." Adams dimmed the two side screens and magnified the center: a mugshot black and white of Caine when he entered the service, dated April 15, 1990. A color deathmask photo before his cremation on April 30, 2020.

"Twenty twenty, we'll have to use a very narrow channel," Adams said, pacing back and forth in front of his faux window. "We've only got rudimentary wormholes available. But I've an ace up my sleeve." He stopped and lit the left screen. "Visual acuity, so-so. Audio talents: high. Reflexes: above normal. Martial arts: brown belt. SAT scores six hundred eighty math, five hundred sixty verbal. Majored in criminal justice, minored in music. IQ: one forty-nine. Just a shade better than your typical average cop."

"Social adjustment?"

"Never rated below seven."

"Wonder why he juiced it?"

"Says here depression." Adams removed his gum and put it in the turquoise boomerang gumtray. "He called for a priest just before he checked out, then changed his mind. I bet he was all set to confess. One megadose of guilt should do the trick." Adams dimmed the screen and held out his hairy hand. "Got your walking shoes on, little lady?"

She got up and brushed back her hair. She didn't know why she kept following him. She hated going anywhere without a precise agenda. And no one called her "little lady" and got away with it. He just sort of seemed to bungle through life, colliding with random particles. She couldn't have him botching it now. Sure, keep the joker company, why not? Besides, it had been a long time since she had seen Moby.

"EEL, MY LONG LOST FRIEND!"

She had to stifle a giggle. Still, Moby did seem to be genuinely moved. Adams was standing, jaw slack, struck speechless as the usually stentorian jumbo blue-gray monolith continued to chat in a frolicsome voice.

Eel smoothed her hand to touch the icy blue mirrored face.

"It has been a long time," she said, not really lying. She might enter Moby's system each night, but they never acknowledged each other. This was the first time in many years that she had been there face to face. Not that Moby mattered with faces; it was mind that mattered to Moby. Still she felt her mouth ripple in a smile.

"I never get greeted like that," Adams said. "Who are you anyway?"

Eel smiled. "Moby's an old friend."

"I see that. Well tell him we want to do a gens cross search. Here's Caine's voice code. We want to access the RNA/DNA file for peripheral referent intelligence. We know Caine reviewed these tapes sometime April fifteenth, twenty

twenty. We wormhole back to the section of time *before* he looks at this tape and prime him. Hit him at night and vibrate his membranes. A typhonic timpathy of guilt.''

''An ambush.''

''Yes, precisely.''

A blink later, Moby was running the cross check and a Boolean search of contacts for the night of April 14, 2020—Maxwell Caine—Shawneeville.

''SHALL I PRINT THE LIST?'' Moby asked in his normally deep voice.

''Yes, please,'' Eel answered.

''Beginner's luck,'' Adams said, studying the printout. ''We've got a section of memory with approximately eight possibles and at least half are local. Only two males—they do make better senders. C ratings, though.''

''And we'll need both ends open.''

''You're right. A female then. Hmm, Emily Struthers—a Piscean Mage, Shawneeville College Maintenance Staff. Reliable rating. She worked on the Chippewa Springs Klas/Koop AIDS vaccine project last year. Got an *A* rating. She's requesting local jobs now. Last job: a lab fraud case. As a janitor she has keys to the right places. She's considered a local eccentric so people don't ask questions. Always wears blue.''

''I think I know her,'' Eel said.

''How's that?''

''At least to say hello. I'm a Shawnee Valley girl. Never knew her name, though. She was always just the Blue Lady.''

''Why the blue do you think?''

''Just her patina. How about her harmonics rating?''

''Pheromones off the wall, but she's a little insular. Not used to dealing with people. You want a white rat trained though, she's a wizard.''

''We don't need much, do we?''

''Keep it simple, that's our motto. If we try to change

things too much we won't change anything. Go for the subtle solution every time. A megadose of guilt. When he looks at the tape, he's already thinking confession. He sees that someone's on to him.''

"How does he see that?"

"Ah, that's my ace up the sleeve. I'm going to use cold fusion on the tape, warp it on the incriminating frame.''

"Warp it permanently?"

"How else? Who knows, we might just wrap this up back in nineteen ninety-five when he first shows the tape to his police team. Can you see him, at the weekly briefing, standing behind the projector, getting flustered when the tape jams on his guilty mug?"

"Hmm, I wonder. Well, we'll just have to aim and hope.'' Eel lifted her hand and used her index finger as a gun barrel. "Right between the eyes.'' She blew off the imaginary smoke.

"Okay, Annie Oakley, what sort of harmonics shall we give him?"

"Harmonics? I don't compose anymore. Ask Moby—he'll find you a snapshot of sound.''

Eel watched Adams as he set eagerly about his task. He loaded the variable sets and keyed in the power variables, then typed XQT. Billions and billions of electrons lined up in exact formation and went flashing back over the wrinkles of time, warping the tape for a nano in timespace and splicing off a section of electrical memory. The ceiling lights dimmed as the power surged through the system. He smiled at her. "Okay, there's the basics. Now I just have to figure out where to put the bells and whistles.''

She wasn't so sure. The terra firma in the last demidecade had not been so firma. Some of those wormholes were riddled with fault lines.

Adams switched on his intercom. "Mazie, set me up with AIS, will you? I'll need a few seconds. And see if Agent eight-six-one-nine-seven-four-three is available for work to-night.''

''Yes, boss.''

During the next few minutes, before the buzzer on Adams's desk sounded, Eel looked closer at the room. Perhaps it wasn't so canonical after all. Degrees papered the wall, along with plaques and certificates, a few sports trophies, and a Water-bury Crystal soccer trophy. He would have scars under his Levi's.

When the buzz came, Adams pressed a green button, and the ash door opened. An old woman dressed in a blue dress and stockings and blue hat stood in the doorway; she was leaning on a cane decorated with blue stripes.

''Emily Struthers?'' Adams said, standing up.

''Sometimes,'' she answered, smiling a crooked smile.

Eel smiled at Emily. Emily nodded. Ritual gestures among local freaks, the way they had greeted each other for years on mean streets. Eel backed up a little. She didn't read minds anymore, but she still had trouble when she was in the room with a channeler; their wavelengths were too accessible, op-erated on the audio and visual cortex like a live hologram. But then, that's why Adams had picked Struthers rather than one of the others on the list, for her leaky filter. Normals screened out the fourth dimension, kept their egos encapsu-lated by skin. Necromancers had no cultural filter.

A mage, Adams had said. Adams used all the terms, but he didn't quite realize just what Struthers was. Mage Struthers played the Game. This woman had been down the wormhole and back and was willing to bilocate again. A winged angel of mercy. And justice. She sat there like a small swallow, waiting to become mage, waiting to do battle with the dragon.

Justice—at least Adams seemed to have that first on his mind. She wondered. He wasn't the kind of man one curbed. Trying to knock some sense into him would be, she thought, like riding a wild horse—not that she had hands-on experi-

ence, only Cray sense, book sense—but she was pretty sure
one had to be careful with the mouth, not try to curb a wild
horse. A soft bit, and he might come around.

Old fortune-tellers read tea leaves to find the secrets of the
world, Eel thought, picking up Struthers's thoughts in spite
of herself. You need a fortune-teller to see through time.
People don't understand. Time is like a giant pousse-café,
flaming with St. Elmo's fire. You stare down through the
flames and layers to the bottom of the glass, down through
the ages. The past doesn't go away unless we sweep it. Synchronized past is present—it is only that we go through life
taking the side view of the glass. We see the layers, each with
their specific gravity. Struthers was about to look down past
the flames.

"Have you got anything that belonged to the subject?" the
woman asked as Eel attached the electrodes to Struthers's
temples.

"How about the coin?" Adams placed it in the woman's
gnarled hand.

She closed a blue-nailed fist over it, decoding its repository
of psychometric data. Then she closed her eyes and entered a
deep somnolent trance. Adams winced when the woman went
out of body.

As the timer reached 3:00:00, Adams activated the electrodes, and Moby accessed her memory for that night, iso-
lating the moment in timespace when her energy field crossed
Caine's.

"What do you see?" Adams prodded.

Struthers's voice was deep and flat. She spoke slowly,
without affect. "The man is coming toward me, just stepping
off the curb."

Adams made a minor adjustment in the temporal coordinates and replotted the velocities. "Okay, right there—hit
him with the harmonics, play him a little night music."

2020

Tuesday, April 14, 11:50 P.M.

It was almost midnight, but Max couldn't sleep. Finally he got up and dressed, put on his hat, and started back to the office. Something was nudging at the back of his mind. Something wasn't right. He checked his pocket for his keys. Something nagging, something he couldn't pull out. It was a night like any other night, as banal as its murky salmon sky and fetid dry wind. He should be sleeping. He took his usual path, down the drive under the old oaks past the eighty-year-old frame-and-stone one-family homes, right at the corner. On auto.

It wasn't till he looked up at the youngsters sitting on the backporch swing of a larger century-old farmhouse, now gone to boarders, that he realized he had turned into the alley instead of the next street. He was seeing the backs of the houses instead of the fronts. And he would come out in a different patch. His old route. Steps fell easily and softly. He could hear the bats high above, happy. Some people claimed not to hear them, but Max had always had a high range. He actually cringed when people blew dog whistles.

"Twinkle, twinkle, little bat, how I wonder what you're at, up above the world you fly, like a tea tray in the sky." His mother's daffy song, one she had learned from his dad when they were both young. One of many. He was the only person he knew who didn't duck when bats swooped down; he kept looking for the teacups. Of course since global warming had brought the vampire bats north of the palm latitudes, he might have to duck. He didn't fancy any teacups filled with blood.

At the corner Max stopped. The moving sidewalk rolled past. His stomach rumbled. He didn't want to work, he wanted to eat. He rode the slow lane to the top of the hill, stepped off, and cut through campus, backtracking his old beat. Open slits of starless sky shone pink above the buildings. Campus was quiet. He passed two rabbits beneath a ginkgo tree by the mansard-roofed Victorian that housed Humanities. The rabbits froze as he passed, sat like statues until his footsteps hit concrete, then went back to nibbling the soft vegetation. He came around the side of the music building; across the piazza he could see the lighted clock in the turreted library tower. Almost midnight. He came out the side of the building onto the top tier of the piazza, crossed the piazza quickly, and took the shallow flight down to the first promenade; only then did he look back. Old Mahler Hall rose behind him, a physical presence, female, glowing. He knew her by heart; she had even invaded his dreams. She was high turn-of-the-last-century Italianate, all false front and features, lit à la 1999 in night queen colors.

She was lit tonight at the edge of the blue-violet spectrum of April, soft Italian deco pastels trimmed with fluorescent yellow. By day she was primly lovely, but by night, beneath these Piscean-Aquarian violet lights, she was the evening primrose, calling bees and butterflies with ultraspectrum. Her arched window eyes were on him, iridescent insect eyes. He leaned his head and listened for music. No music, not even the master's.

He turned and walked on down the Mall, thinking of his future. This time next week he would be a civilian with an engraved onyx Shawnee Panther statue and a Shawneeville Police ebony rocker. The badge would go into the case, and he would indulge the final wanderlust. Better that than an unplanned trip. His mother had died an iatrogenic death, her house in disorder. Better to know.

He descended the short staircase onto the Mall's second tier and walked beneath the clone elms. Far ahead he could see the lights of the main street, yellow and red. He paused and took a deep breath of air. Just there at the turn of the century he had stood and watched them cut the last fungus-infected natural elm. It had left a great gaping hole in the sky above the row of straw-bedded and stringed cloned saplings, like a space left when a tooth is pulled, a sudden new space, nude and raw. Like the way he felt listening to Mahler and Wagner. In the years since, the clones had grown to be as tall as three men, arching gracefully on either side of the walk-way, reaching up and up; in another fifty years they would link branches and weave a canopy.

"I grow old, I grow old, I shall wear the bottom of my trousers rolled." His eyes had started going the previous year—macular degeneration, his doctor said, normal for a man his age. That explained the white lights that had started speckling jagged holes in his vision. At least he had not started shrinking; he could still wear the dress whites he had been forced to buy when he joined the force thirty years before. It was just that the children around him had grown like crude preozonic corn, high as an elephant's eye. Children's faces in giant elongated bodies filled the world. When had they started letting children take care of the world?

No one was out tonight. He passed the science building and looked up at the dark floors. Where were all the night-worms tonight? A power drainage, maybe. The wind picked up as he walked down the last promenade to the campus gate, and with it came the scent of full-blooming jasmine and wild roses. It hit him hard, like a woman coming across his senses, that feeling a man might get touching a woman he had dreamed about too long. Stop, Max. Don't. Repent of your sins and ask them for an extension. Keep working. You only have to swallow that yard of pride you've built up over the years. Stop waiting for them to ask you.

A woman passed him on the walk, swirled in her alpaca

cape, head down, thinking. Stop waiting for some woman to rescue you and find one. Live, why don't you?

For what? To grow older without blood or affiliation? No, too late, he thought, but he couldn't stop himself from inhaling the short-lived heady sweetness. June flowers, abloom at April midnight. In the preozonic days winter had stayed later. There had been no wild flowers when Amanda died. In her diary he found a small violet pressed between the pages. He had bought hothouse violets for her casket.

Fifty years, a half-life. A fragment of Yeats imagery came to him: "And now that I have come to fifty years, I must endure the timid sun." The prophet poet, master of dejection. The timid sun, the smoky starless skies. Too little ozone above. Turning and turning in the gyre. Slow toxic strangulation. The cruel month of April, born before its time. He was glad he had not had children.

And now that I have come to fifty years . . . He had lived his half-life; he knew what path beckoned him, knew which road he was going to take. Down the Mall, under the adolescent elms, through the looking glass into the arms of sleep. Mother Goose and lullabies: "How many miles to Babylon? Three score miles and ten. Can I get there by candlelight? Yes, and back again." A dry wind whipped his silvering hair, bringing with it more scent. He sighed. He would have liked to see the canopy.

Max stepped off the concrete path and took the path of pine needles into the thicket. A small stand of breakfront pines and oaks shielded the shrine. The ground was soft and pliant beneath Max's leather shoes. The cat sat at the top of the knoll, crouched low, gleaming in the murky air. It was a marvelous panther, cast larger than life, slunk low to the ground like a linebacker on the goal line, easy for children to climb on, strong enough to hold a kissing couple, too big to be carried off, the perfect college shrine. Of course, in the tradition of such shrines, it was annually attacked by rival tribes and decorated with their colors, festooned also with other public offerings: beer bottles, flowers, women's under-wear.

He took a step up the path and then stopped. He held his breath, listening. Just the breeze in the foliage. He went up to the cat that had been part of his beat once long before, check-ing that it had not been desecrated or decorated, smoothing his finger over the acid-damaged flank, running his hand down the sleek body. Drops of perspiration beaded on the polymer body; he wiped the beads away. The cat seemed to be purring beneath his fingers as he surveyed it with his fingers and eyes. Shrine intact.

He came back down the path and stepped from pines to pavement. As he took the turn toward Main Street the carillon bells began their midnight song. Dark and deep. An oppres-sive tolling that seemed to drag on forever. Guilt. Shame. Remorse. But whose? He had always felt there was some part of him that lived in some room of his house that he had not yet discovered. Some other more carefree self. Didn't he dream recurringly of a room, a high turret room, white, where that man lived? Didn't he from time to time hear echoes of his easy laughter?

When he reached the curb, he stopped and stared across the street at the diner. He was hungry, wasn't he?

The twenty-four-hour diner's Plexiglas doors swung open at that instant, and Max saw the Blue Lady come out and cross the side strip. Emily Struthers, that was her real name—he had read her file. A local moonstruck loonie but harmless. She had a job chopping carrots or sweeping floors in some dorm, and apparently she functioned adequately there. Pre-sumably she was able to buy groceries and pay her bills and keep a roof over her head. She lived on the other side of the canyon; he had never seen the house, but she seemed to take care of herself. She was always clean. It was just that she always dressed in blue: dark blue shoes, azure blue dress, teal purse, blue-green stockings. Even her hair was a shade of acid-rain turquoise.

She was his age, maybe a few years older. She had accosted him once years earlier during the Musical Festival and started a Hemingway sort of dialogue, something about coming with her to the zoo. Her eyes had been pale blue and watery, serene and shimmery. She had been very soft-spoken, sincere, without a trace of eccentricity—except for the fact that there was no zoo in Shawneeville. Farms and pens and stables but no zoo. Never had been. Ah, well, it took all kinds. They tolerated their eccentrics in Shawneeville. In a mashed-potato town of homogenized steer-fed children, a little local color never hurt.

There was still no zoo, Max thought as he stepped off the curb. The ground came up to meet his feet, and he almost stumbled, knew in that sudden instant of catching up to the world that the Blue Lady would speak to him tonight. Déjà vu. He found himself meeting sea-nymph eyes. He could see her pupils expand and contract. She smiled a strange, sweet, Cheshire Cat smile. "The wages of sin is death," she said sweetly. She seemed to be looking out from sleep and dream, and her voice seemed to float above him.

"Ivory . . . elephants . . ." he caught. "It's very important . . . music is . . . message . . ."

Her face clouded and the hood lifted from her eyes. She seemed startled to see him; she jumped in her skin.

"What's very imp—" He stopped. She had already stepped on the conveyer tube and was riding silently off, chin held high, skin glowing a translucent alabaster.

Elephants? Max thought. Ivory? Ivory Tower Diner with elephants at the stools? He smiled. Pink elephants? He shook his head as he pushed open the swinging door of the diner and surveyed the S-curved Formica counter. It was almost as old as the college, this place, always populated by a few unsavory locals. When Max had joined the force it was "Ye Olde Ivory Tower Diner," its sign a flowery calligraphy. During the Revival Period the sign had been replaced with a neon replica of the original: The Ivory Tower. Inside it looked pretty much the same as it always had: a cracked linoleum floor, red vinyl and chrome stools patched with industrial tape. The station numbers at the end of the counter no longer lit up, but Max couldn't remember that they ever had. The booths in the back were seedy and comfortable, genuine relics. The diner was a far cry from Boscoe's, the town's trendy table.

Max took his usual stool at the counter, wrapped his legs around the chrome stand, and stared across at his unshaven chin in the backwall mirror. The waitresses were fast, at least on the graveyard shift, and one could always find a newspaper on the undercounter rack, or an easy conversation, if one had the mind to. The fan still whirred overhead, and the china cups were still thick and solid and pitted soft around the rims. And then there were the grilled hot cross buns. Why change when one can have the old world every day? If only they still had coffee, it would be heaven.

There were a couple of students at the middle curve drinking chicory and soya. On the last curve, back to the door, sat a kid with lots of frizzy white-gold hair. Pretty hair, though it looked as if it needed a good brushing, huge dark gray eyes, and an unwashed face. She couldn't be more than seven or eight, Max thought, that is, if she's a girl. Thin freckled legs poked out of purple and green checked pants; the shirt was black-and-white stripes, horizontal, worn tight across a prepubescent frame. The remains of a soyacake waffle were pushed off to one side. The kid was spinning the stool and kicking the counter with one purple high-topped sneaker while playing with a thin piece of computer feed strip.

Who was she with? he wondered, looking toward the necessary rooms. When no one came out after five minutes, Max frowned across the Formica island at the waitress. Carlotta and Lester were on tonight. Carlotta looked up, and he quirked an eyebrow at her, nodding toward the kid. "It's okay," she said when she came over. "You want the usual, Max?"

He nodded. "Out late for a kid, isn't she?"

"Eel? You don't know Eel? Of course you know her. You guys made *World Magazine*'s cover last year arresting her and that monkey for erasing the IRS files."

"That's the April Fool kid?"

"In the flesh."

Max eyed her surreptitiously while Carlotta served a man at the next island. The girl would be just turning seven. He hadn't been on the case, had seen no more than a glance at the courthouse steps. The system had gone to great lengths to protect her minor status. A picture had been printed, but it had been taken in a standard uniform, and her hair had been arranged in the appropriate student style. The urchin before him looked nothing like that picture.

Max stared at the wafer of a child spinning aimlessly back and forth on her stool. A podtube child, selectively created, undesirable genetic qualities removed with laser intervention, smarter by half than anyone else in the room. Must be a lonely life. She looked like a kid, except for that crazy hairdo and those weird clothes. He stared at her, but she was lost in her own inner space. They had dropped the charges against her. Her lawyer had convinced them that she was just copying campus behavior, having a final fling before she turned six. A little April Fool's joke, that was all. A harmless little worm that got out of hand.

Carlotta came back with his water. Max was still looking at the kid. "I wonder what she does for fun now that she's almost seven?"

"She's a loner. Nightmode—she usually comes in later, more like around dawn." She took a cup from under the counter and poured fresh soyachick java into his cup. "Watch your thoughts," she said.

"One of those, eh? Thanks."

Max waited, hungry, and looked over at the scrawny little kid. It was all hocus-pocus, wasn't it? She had learned certain neuromotor signs that indicated in what direction people were focusing, whether they were thinking or remembering. It wasn't as if she could really read minds, he told himself, not the words anyhow.

There was a *Midnight Gazette* on the stool next to him; he picked it up and turned to sports, checked the World Cup qualifying results, read Brenner's column. He had read an article the previous month on the microtot program—a complete educational immersion for a group of supernova pod-raised kids. Kids who started talking at six months and developed higher math at two. The college brought them in and spoon-fed their education. The stars of tomorrow, they were supposed to be. Max wondered. He thought of Harlow's monkeys clinging to terry-cloth mothers, only half as neurotic as the baby monkeys with the steel mothers. In her own spoon-fed brilliant way, this kid was probably as crazy as the Blue Lady.

He glanced up and found her looking directly at him. She scrunched her face at him and looked away. From the kitchen Max smelled butter roasting, and his mouth began to salivate. An Ivory Tower hot cross bun, one of the few unchanged things in the world.

The bun was just like it always was, hot enough to burn the roof of his mouth, soft and twisty and cinnamony with plump raisins that never came burnt. He chewed contentedly.

A couple came in the swinging doors and sat at the first curve of counter, heads bent, holding hands, laughing. Max watched the girl's radiant face until she noticed, and then he looked away. And he had somehow reached this time and place alone, he reflected. Lost dreams. Heartstrings unplucked.

A sour note played on the gut string. He hated feeling sorry for himself. Face it, he had married his dream willingly. He had married in passion, in love with the rustle of Connie Calloway's Parisian silk, swept off his feet by her flashy beauty and winner's smile. Miss Shawneeville 1995. And then the passion had faded, leaving only frosty monosyllables and frozen gourmet diet dinners. Connie Calloway, a Mercedes body with a Yugo mind. They had not even fought; in the end, it had all seemed as inconsequential as a summer shower. Connie Calloway had come home one day and packed up her makeup and designer clothes; she had left him the house and cat and dog and parrot. They had not kept in touch.

He took another bite of hot cross bun, finishing as he always did by licking his buttery fingers. He smiled and wiped his mustache on the napkin. If he juiced it he would miss the buns. It was a joke, wasn't it? Life came down to that, a taste for something. He hoped there were hot cross buns where he was going.

The couple across the way were on one stool now, unable to keep their hands off each other. Max saw the kid Eel purse her lips. That's real life, kid. She caught him looking and made a sour face. He shrugged. This fledgling had probably solved several secrets of the universe, but she still had a few things to learn about life. He closed his eyes. A quarter of a century. Twenty-five years. Amanda would be forty-five now. And he was fifty. Fifty, Max thought. That's so old. Strange how he imagined Amanda's voice. Sometimes passages from her diary would come to him while he tried to sleep. "Men, what foreign creatures they are. He looks at me and imagines me as he will. He will not let me invent myself."

Max closed his eyes and stroked one side of his mustache. "Men, what foreign creatures they are." A musical voice, the sort of voice men fell in love with. He realized with a start what had been nagging him. That picture of Amanda in his office. He had seen the picture that afternoon, perhaps for the thousandth time, and suddenly—he couldn't remember her face. Couldn't remember how she smiled, only that she was smiling. Across from him the microtot cleared her throat and stared at him. She seemed to be getting ready to go. Max turned back to his newspaper. Odd. Or not so odd. It was just further mental deterioration. He could see the picture in his mind's eye, but the face wouldn't focus.

He looked up when the kid spun off her stool and started out the swinging door. Max looked at the clock. Time for him to go, too. He paid his check and came out on the sidewalk. He still wasn't sleepy.

He stood on the corner with his hands in his pockets. It was getting muggier out, and there was an acid hint of rain. Better get inside. Yes, it was definitely going to rain; already the buildings across the street were shining an eerie green. His office was just a short walk away—he could go back and tackle those boxes. Or he could risk getting caught in the rain and go home, watch a movie. His hand fastened over his silver coin and drew it out. He flipped it. Heads I go to the office, tails I go home. He missed the toss, and the coin rolled to the sidewalk.

"Truth is underfoot," a small voice said, stopping the coin with a purple sneaker.

"Heads or tails?" he asked.

She lifted her foot. "Tails," she answered.

He took the coin, wondering if the kid had just guessed, or if her young eyes were really so much sharper. "Thanks, kid." He was going to offer her a Lifesaver but decided against it. He walked home slowly, feeling guilty about not going to the office. Something was troubling him, a heavy feeling of doubt and remorse.

He let himself into his condo, turned on the tube, and pressed MENU. A shoot-'em-up western on 56; an ancient black-and-white Hitchcock on 78, Slavic classics on 99. He keyed in 78. Alfred himself was ascending a train, cello case in hand. Max had seen it twice and had always wondered what was in that case. A cello? A body? A machine gun? He tried 99: The one o'clock movie was just beginning, an old Czech classic from his teen days. *The Unbearable Lightness of Being*. A girl with long dark hair was swimming underwater; a man stood poolside, fully dressed, watching her.

Max settled on his futon and watched the film on the bedroom wall screen. The man was in love with two women, one sophisticated, one totally naive. One of the women wore a hat when they made love. He married the other woman. Max fell asleep sometime before the ending.

His dreams were tormented by the girl swimming underwater, but in his dream the girl was a mermaid with Amanda's face and hair. She swam toward him, mouth making bubbles, her wet hair bruising his wet cheek. Music pounded at them, tumbling them against the sandy bottom of the deep.

As morning brushed away the memory of his dreams, the face dissolved. Yesterday blended into today. If anyone had asked him as he arose whether he had dreamed, he would have denied it sincerely. His conscious mind still worried at its losses. He couldn't wait to get to the office and see Amanda's face.

2040

Sunday, April 15, 3:00 A.M.

Emily Struthers blinked and stared at Eel. For a moment her eyes flickered recognition and then they shifted to Adams.

"Take it slowly," he said, patting her blue hair. "Just let it come slowly."

"I made contact. I spoke to him. 'The wages of sin' spiel. I delivered the message and the harmonics. I don't think he was really listening. I think my pitch was too low for him." She opened her hand and held the coin up for Eel to take.

Adams was studying the U-curve. "Terminal salience in effect," he said. "Good vibrations beginning and end but the middle got garbled." He picked up the file. "I was hoping the file would be marked closed." He flipped open the file and scanned its contents. "Eureka! One change. He's noticed the warp."

"When was that?"

"The afternoon of the fifteenth. He's penciled in a note to have the tape checked out by Technical. Could be a sly ploy. Get it declared damaged evidence and get it disposed of."

"Except for one thing. It's here, innit?"

"And he's made a call to Miss Tilly. The plot thickens."

Adams shrugged. "I'm not giving up, though. We've dislodged two items. We just have to keep working. Struthers, you up to another hit?"

"Not tonight. One a night is all I do. Otherwise it eats up

my REM sleep. Besides, I'm not sure I'm in his range. My vibrational level just isn't reaching him.''

"Well, another operator then. I want to get this sewn up.''

"Use her,'' the old woman said, pointing a bony finger at Eel as she headed for the door.

"Her?''

"She was there, ask her. That kid I was sitting next to before I came out of the diner. You were playing with a little paper toy and making a mess with your food. He'd respond to you.''

"You?'' Adams said, when Struthers had gone. "That's right, you said you were a local.''

"Afraid so. Probably somewhere on the list.''

"Lacoste.'' He ran his finger down the list. "Yes, but they say here you may be—'' He hesitated. "Unreliable. Do you remember speaking to him?''

"Vaguely.'' The spring of 2020. Her blue period. Her house parents had been in Crete on sabbatical. They had left Moby in charge and let her run up a tab at the Ivory Tower. She had been into cetacean songs that spring, that and the game.

"What did you say to him?''

"It was a long time ago. I spoke a few words to him on the street, I remember that. Then I went home and played a Game.''

"What game? Not IRS Wars, was it?''

"Certainly not. The outside system locks I helped them design were in full working order. I never went off campus after that. You're welcome to access the structure. Moby will have the whole thing on tape. He kept elaborate records of every second I was in the lab.''

"I wasn't prying. It's just that if you were on the system in twenty twenty, we can get you back quite neatly. Just tunnel in and hit behind the target, tunnel out. What exactly did you say to him?''

"Very little, as I recall. He dropped a coin. I picked it up.''

"Did you make physical contact?"

"Only with this." She held up the worn coin.

"It's worth a try. Go back and see if you can extend the crisscross. I know it's not fair, it being your prize at stake and all."

Eel had forgotten her original intent. She had gotten involved. She could kill two birds with the same stone: get the cop and guarantee her safe, anonymous job. Strike the cop a glancing blow as she crossed his path, throw him a curved ball, and then get back to Wormwood. Nothing that would actually tear the fabric. If he did it, he deserved it. If he was innocent—well, that was a different story.

"What do you want me to do?"

Adams smiled. "Just extend the contact long enough to get the subharmonic suggestion working."

"Hmm," Eel said, probing her memory. "I might try something else."

"What?"

"I lied to him the first time, about the coin."

"You lied? Why? How?"

"Well, he didn't exactly drop it; it was a coin toss. I suppose I just wanted to please him. I picked the answer out of his head. He wanted to go home and watch the movie."

"Instead of what?"

"Instead of going to his office. If I'd told him the truth, he might have gone back that night."

"And seen the tape while he was still resonating with guilt. I like it. Subharmonics always work best at night. So, tell him the truth."

"Trying to make an honest cop out of me?" She smiled and raised her right hand. "The whole truth and nothing but the truth," she lied, knowing she would have no such control over her actions. She would do what she would do—there was no changing channels.

She looked up. Adams seemed to be struggling with the new temporal coordinates.

"Don't forget to adjust for the added displacement."

"First thing I did. It's just that I'm not used to dealing with tots. The wormholes are kind of spongy."

"Need any help?"

He couldn't help rubbing his knuckles on his chest. "Ph.D. Stanford, class of thirty-three, Intelligence Transfer."

"I'm class of twenty twenty, Shawneeville. NFD."

"How's that?"

She laughed. He *was* the new boy in town. "No further degree. It's a local expression. Just wondered."

She leaned over his shoulder, monitoring his progress. Yes, that might work. Hadn't she made up the rules for subharmonic memory transfer? Here's the game: Go down and battle the forces of good and evil. It was a neat cuspy world, where if one weren't too careless, one could go on forever, gaining skill and power. If one went down far enough, one would come to a place where time itself stopped. And there, through a hard-to-find keyhole in that concrete slab of time, one could peek through and see the light coming in backward, blinding.

Go back and stand at the keyhole, shout at the poor man to confess his sins. We know, man. The game is up. Shower him with subharmonics, accost him with his past, give him a chance to save his soul.

The painter moves his brush and the paint shifts upon the canvas, she thought. Art or not?

"Done yet?" She asked, leaning over his broad shoulder.

"Almost. Ready to play?"

"Been ready for minutes. Come on, let's get this piece of worthless art exposed."

"You're a game woman."

Eel looked at him. Was that a corny compliment or a bad pun? She decided not to care. The past lay ahead of her. She had only to wormhole down through the depths of the subterranean world and go spinning back across time to the spinning stool in the restaurant. Just a little push, enough to careen her back through time with a slightly different trajectory, at a slightly different angle. Easy as slicing pie.

Adams was working out the last program details, setting up the show. "I'll go on open channel right about here. You can broadcast the optical acoustics."

Eel took her place in the pod. "Well, what are you waiting for? Wish me happy hunting."

"Happy hunting. Let's get that goat."

She settled back in the pod, then turned around and looked directly at Adams. She winked.

2020

Wednesday, April 15, 12:01 A.M.

There was a burst of static in her left ear; when it cleared a new ancient oldie was playing: ". . . I've just got to get a message to you—hold on—hold on . . ." The last note dragged on and on. Noetic thought. Hypnogogic vision. A cool, deep pool of nonbeing: a myriad of smells bombarding senses, essences of old dead memories.

Falling. Dizzy as any mortal.

It had happened to her before, this falling, but only in dreams. Dreamfalls she had called them, filtering them out with her analytical left brain. The ground comes up to meet your feet, and you say you have stumbled. But it was night now. She was awake. On a spinning spool. She caught herself, and felt the world congeal beneath her fingers.

She took a deep breath to calm herself. Yes, she thought, savor the moment without sensors: watch the electric current running, let be. She spun the small paper Möbius strip slowly around and around. Each point on the Möbius was infinitely farthest from the point directly past the thin membrane of paper—and infinitely closest.

She noticed the man when he came in. He sat across from her as she somehow knew he would; she watched him in the mirrorglass. A man who looked as if he had fallen on bad times. Sad speckled eyes, unkempt. Reddish gold hair just going to gray. Familiar somehow. Erratic wavelengths. Peripheral thoughts.

She listened when the waitress spoke to him. She watched as he raised a newspaper, reading it back to front. She looked at her own reflection and got a fright: how big her eyes looked in the mirror. She closed her eyes and sifted through the conversations in the diner, came back to the mindspace across the counter. He wasn't reading; he was thinking. Strong pheromones. A quick burst of visual projection; a woman's body, arched and supple, spiked hair, the face blurred, the whole scene seen through a juniper-green haze.

She picked up the cool, glass, hexagonal shaker and poured a few NaCl crystals in one palm; she dropped them one by one through the small rotating hole of the Möbius strip. She searched her memory file of faces. She had never seen the man before, but he was curiously familiar. She thought there was something she wanted to do for him.

She swept the salt off the counter onto the floor. He was thinking again, a clear picture ungarbled by concepts. The girl with the black hair was lying under a stone; she was dead. There was a coin on the stone. The date was 1965. And then she saw another slab and another coin, and the man's thoughts were covered with a thick, black cloth. His brainwaves were tormented. Worry and anguish, depression. A veil, not tightly woven but present nevertheless, not close to his face but around and over him like a loose net.

A man planning to take the final trip? She ought to warn him. Mister, don't do it. If you juice it with a girl on your mind, you'll never rest in peace.

Not her business though, was it? Time to go home and play the new game. She finished her soyacake breakfast, spun off her stool, and paid her bill. She went outside and stood in the balmy night and, for the second time that night, caught a mindwave: the silver coin. An eagle. The door of the diner swung open, and the man came out. He looked up and saw her standing there in the shadow of the bank pillar. He reached in his pocket, pulled out the silver coin, and tossed it in the air.

Precognitively, she knew: He would miss the catch.

"Truth is underfoot," she said, coming up behind him and stopping the rolling coin with the cushioned sole of her purple high tops, but not before she had made out the thin crescent on the top of the rattling coin. The profile.

She knew what he would say next.

"Heads or tails?"

She didn't hesitate for a second, just scooped up the silver. It was like him and almost as strangely familiar. "T—" She stopped herself. "Heads," she said, laying the coin in his palm. He looked at it carefully, touching the faded profile with his finger.

"Bat guano," he muttered.

She smiled. It was a mean trick, but she wanted to know something. She leaned on the lamppost to watch. Would he keep his bargain with himself?

She jumped when he spoke to her. "Hey, kid—" He had exchanged the coin for a crystal-green roll of Lifesavers and was peeling the silver foil. Wintergreen, her favorite. "Want one?"

Never take candy from strangers. Never take candy from strangers. Moby would be ashamed if she did. She shook her head. "I don't eat things that glow in the dark."

He laughed. "Just checking. You know you should never take candy from strangers. Good girl. What do you mean, glow in the dark?"

"Your candy."

"That's a good one. You're a funny kid. You sure you're okay walking home alone? It being so dark and all."

"Quite."

"Don't you have a curfew?"

"Not since I graduated high school."

He laughed. "Where is home, anyway? I could call ahead and tell them you're coming."

"Twenty Fibonacci."

"On campus?"

"Yes."

"Funny I never heard of it. Where is it?"

She thrust her hands in her pockets. "I'm not at liberty to divulge that."

"Good. Excellent self-defense skills. You carrying a flashlight?"

"No."

"Maybe some candy just to light your way?"

She giggled and took her hands out of her pockets, but she didn't reach out. Not noticing that the paper Möbius toy had fallen to the ground, she shook her head and started up the street. It came to her suddenly what she wanted to say.

"Hey, mister," she said, turning back and speaking over her shoulder. "You know, if you juice it with a girl on your mind, she'll haunt you forever."

"Yeah, yeah, and the sky is blue."

"It used to be. Some old tales happen to be true."

"Is it so obvious what I'm about to do?"

"You're a broken switch. You broke down a long time ago, only no one told you. How'd you make it this far?"

"They promised me an onyx panther and a college rocker."

She laughed. "Maybe there's hope for you."

"You're not one of those antieuthanasianists, are you?"

"Hardly. I just like to fix broken things."

"Some things can't be fixed." He turned and started to walk off, then stopped. "Kid—" He shook his head. "—never mind."

She shrugged and took a step, then yelled back over her shoulder. "Call me if you're ever in the dark." She wasn't sure if he heard her or not.

12:35 P.M.

Max let himself into his office and promptly barked his shin on a cardboard carton. "Ouch," he said, pulling back and snapping on the overhead. "Who moved the damn box?"

He took his stool, pulled up his trouser leg, and massaged his leg, looking down at the picture of Amanda. When his eyes were full, he swiveled around to the portafridge and took out a pony of extra pale Rolling Rock 33, seven little ounces of pure spring Latrobe brew, same as it ever was. He popped the cap into the gunmetal ash can and pushed a U2 DAT cassette in the player. He put his feet on the desk, across the face of his star suspect.

A rumor had begun the year after the crime that the mystery man was the fugitive Charles Manson. Hadn't he broken a leg when he escaped from San Quentin in '94? Didn't he hide his scar with a slouch cap? The FBI had come in on that lead, and Max had been promoted as a result of it, commended for his helpfulness. In 1999, the winter of the double blue moons, he had led a Manson spelunking posse, leading twelve G-men up ancient boulder-strewn river paths, deeper and deeper into the land of bats and limestone. Stalactites and stalagmites, trickles of moisture on walls, inner shapes still forming, leading them farther and farther from the sun until his own heart had started to beat doubletime. They had gone five miles down the main tunnel and turned back. He got a perverse kind of pleasure in seeing their relief when he led them back into light.

And now caves were prize commodities, naturally air-conditioned refuges from the annual dust and heat storms. Max knocked his knuckles against the imitation knotty pine desk. Shawneeville excluded, thank God. A more tranquil oasis didn't exist. The town was a meteorologist's dream, a geophysical fluke. The weather remained temperate, even in summer. Plenty of clean water, and the acoustics were perfect. Everyone was good or lovably eccentric. There wasn't really any crime, just the happy-go-lucky delinquencies that come when thousands of youths are taken away from home for the first time and plunged into a passionate, rowdy bath of music and freedom, when they are exposed for the first time to 30,000 other symphonic ears in a mass orgy of music.

Watermelons stolen in August, black cats kidnapped in October, experimental spruce cut down in December. Youth really was innocent. Oh, accidents happened, people got killed. And people juiced themselves, more and more. But criminals?

He laughed. Murder didn't happen here. Murder was brutal and sordid and bloody. Its motives were shallow. This murder was a stage death, recited ad nauseam. The life drained from Amanda's body as the color rose in her cheeks.

He sighed and shifted his feet on the evidence, then sat staring at Amanda's face. Memory was playing tricks on him. Hadn't the red scarf been tied to the right? He moved his foot and stared morosely at the scuff mark he had left on the man's high forehead. The mark of Cain. So be it.

The music came to an end and the cassette was ejected. Max picked up an evidence tape and put it in the video slot. When he retired, the case would be deep-sixed. Technically Donovon would take over, but Max knew that Donovon was a form man; he would check the inventory sheet and wouldn't bother to crosscheck. Max reached in his pocket and took out the coin and the kid's paper toy. He turned the paper idly, his fingers moving over the strip of even holes. Paint a road on the twisted treadmill and one could travel forever, only gradually becoming aware of a repeating landscape. Loop the loop, in and out of time.

His old fluorescent started blinking. He saw himself reflected in strobing light in the glass of the print behind him. A Hudson River School print in Indian reds: *All That Is Glorious Around Us*. He appeared to be a man with a tic, a bizarro. He leaned back and looked at himself in the wall mirror. Tired eyes. A mirror contains all it sees, and it contains nothing, he thought. One unreal world is as unreal as the next. And the real world, perhaps, was buried just within the depths of time. He tossed the paper toy on the desk and looked up at the clock. It was almost one. He waited for the bells. They came, deep and somber, a dark acoustical clock.

Time. He wondered what it would have been like to live in a time when man believed he was the central beast. Slower and more graceful, less concrete and linear. Hours were not in widespread use till the Industrial Age, unless one lived close enough to a church to hear the bells. Nanoseconds had not been used popularly till the twenty-first century. And all that time, all that history, was just a whisper in the life of the universe. Only man's grandiosity proclaimed otherwise.

How tormented man was. Only man thought of death. Only man paid taxes. That thought brought a smile to his lips. He should start his income tax, that's what he should do. Then he swiveled and took out another pony and guzzled it down. The bells sounded the quarter hour. He picked up the toy and twisted it around again. Perhaps humans were special midworld creatures, trapped at the fulcrum in three-dimensional stillness. Weren't there 10^{16} neural connections in the brain, 10^{16} stars in the galaxy? Man was a microcosm of the planet, composed of the same percentages of water and earth. Perhaps we really do occupy center stage in the architecture of the universe; perhaps our role is to perform some cosmic juggling act.

Max laughed and tossed his pony in the can. What pretention, he thought, remembering his high-school biology. A tenth of a watt, that was how much the brain energy produced. Not enough to light a strand of Christmas lights. No, in the book of planetary history, humans were but the last word in the last sentence on the last page. And they lived happily ever . . . after.

Another beer? After. After what? He reached over and pressed PLAY, and the cover lifted on his video work screen. His twenty-five-year-old celluloid self appeared before him.

"Testing, one, two, three. Testing, one, two, three."

His half-life self moved closer to the camera and smiled. "Picking me up out there?"

"Yes," Max said to the screen. "Why don't I trust this man?" he asked out loud. His younger self stepped off camera for a few moments and then returned. Max found that he was shivering as he watched: a pan shot of the music room, milling men in hats, a shot of the chalk outline on the floor. Then the young Max was back, the camera moving jerkily.

The shivering stopped. The ghosts that had been haunting him all day seemed to draw back. It had not been his fault. A half-life away Max watched his naive body move with supple grace. And through the arched window of the music room he got a shot of deep blue sky and one perfect white fluffy cumulus cloud. He sat transfixed, bathed in an aimless tenderness. The sound track had picked up a bird song. A wave of nostalgia flooded through him. You can clone elms and blueberries and turkeys, but you can't make the birds sing again. You can't grow me a real coffee bean. You can't give me back my blue sky and white snow and cold starry nights. Can you?

The woman's voice spoke off camera, and the camera swung away from the clouds to the door of the music room. Miss Tilly, coming to describe the suspect. Emotion showing on both their faces. Miss Tilly's little bird voice: "It's probably not important, but—"

And then the tape stuck and blinked brightly.

"Damn," he said, hitting the stop button. He backed up the tape and replayed it, up to the same blinking full stop at the door with Miss Tilly. "It's probably not important, but—"

Such an odd expression on her face, as if she knew that she was frozen in that stance and only her eyes could touch out. Such a look in those eyes. What was it? Now he couldn't even remember what she had been telling him. He seemed to drown in her eyes.

He shut the machine and made a note to call Repair. He reached in his coat pocket and took out the roll of Lifesavers. What had the kid said? Things that glow in the dark? He leaned across and shut the lights, then rolled his chair closer to the mirror. He popped the Lifesaver in his mouth and crunched it. Blue-green glowing lights seemed to decay in his mouth. He tried another, with the same effect.

In case you're ever in the dark, he thought, wheeling around and picking up the kid's paper toy. Twenty Fibonnaci. He checked the directory. No Fibonnaci Hall, no Fibonnaci Lab, no Fibonnaci nothing. Twenty Fibonnaci. Hmm. Fibonnaci of twenty. He remembered something from a genetics class; they had been studying brother-sister incest, working out some symbolic formulae for the Egyptian eighteenth Dynasty line. That name.

FIBONACCI OF TWENTY

Very funny. Easy for a microtot.

He looked up at the blinking screen. Fibonacci of twenty. He took a pencil and pad and wrote out an equation, then balled the paper and tossed it in the can.

Leonardo of Pisa, the Moorish joker. His quaint symbolic series merely a jeu d'esprit, of no practical use for over six hundred years, of use now only in the Mendelian science of inbreeding. If he could just . . . Half a pad of paper later, he got the same answer twice in a row. He drew two lines below the number, then he picked up the phone. He'd call her and then head home; he punched the code: 6765.

"Fibonacci of twenty," the kid's voice machine answered. "I'm gronked out right now. Leave a message if you want."

Max spoke when the tone sounded. "This is Mr. Caine. You gave me your number. I wanted to know——" It seemed silly now. "I just wanted to know, why did the Lifesaver glow in the dark? And one more thing, can you fix a jammed demidecade super-VHS tape? Phone me at home: six-five-four-three."

He ejected the tape and took an evidence bag from the shelf and put the tape inside, wrapped a rubber band around the package, and put it in his jacket pocket. The bells chimed the quarter as he left the office. Maybe he would catch the last of the one o'clock movie when he got home.

└ 2040

Eel blinked when Adams snapped his fingers; she opened her eyes. Somewhere far away bells were ringing. Adams was standing above her, smiling, the curls of his hair pitching over, expectation on his face. Strange, she had been here before . . .

"I—" She tried out the word. It seemed to fit fine. The walls around her met at the proper corners. "That was strange," she said. "He called me, didn't he? He left his number."

Adams was playing the transcript. "Yes. You extended the contact considerably. Your subharmonic projection was excellent. I was sure he was set to confess when he called you back. He's a tough bastard."

She closed her eyes. The subject's ego defenses had been about what she had expected, ill-sublimated and infantile but still fairly open. "Something's not right," she said.

"He called you!" he exclaimed. "He figured out your number. Why didn't you call him back?"

Eel was silent a moment. She remembered getting the call. 6-5-4-3. It was the number that had stopped her. How odd, and what a coincidence.

"I don't know," she lied. "I guess I was just too busy. Deep into my game. Besides, he asked *why* the candy glowed. I would have just given him a flippant answer."

"What's wrong with *why*?"

74

"Why does a stone roll downhill? I just hate anthropomorphizing. Perhaps if he had asked *how*. And altruistic I've never been."

"You're helping me."

"Yeah, I know." She didn't correct his good opinion of her. "You know, I've been thinking . . . maybe we're wrong about him." She sat up and peeled off the silver electrodes. "Maybe there's been some mistake. Struthers contacted Caine at exactly the right angle, but he didn't fall into the pocket. I made contact, hit him with the full range of harmonics, and he still hasn't budged. Maybe your rookie made a mistake. I hear there were a rash of glitzes tonight."

"Just routine proton bursts, nothing concentrated. No major geomagnetic storms."

Eel smiled. She was remembering the symphony of the garage doors, and the smiling face of the moon before it was eaten by the night. Obviously he had not been outside.

"What about the discrepancy your program picked up?" she asked.

"I told you, it's of no significance. May as well check it out, though." He found the interview tape and played it to the indicated frame: a white ivory elephant letter opener on a tray; his pal Ryan conducting the interview.

"I told you," he said, "it's just errata."

"But that's Miss Tilly holding the tray."

"Yeah. So?"

"I don't know. Maybe it means something."

"Not according to Rookie Bob."

"Random errors are not unheard of. Maybe the solar flares thrust some small pivotal premise out of place. I just can't see Caine as a killer."

"Anything to back that up?"

"Nothing concrete. It's just a feeling." She stopped and examined her memory, but found nothing that touched her private history. Then why did it feel like she was Eve in the garden and had just tasted of the forbidden fruit and lied to

Adam? She had not changed at all; everything was okay. She looked at the blowup of Caine and Tilly on the wall. The background was a blur, but the looks on their faces were unmistakable. Still, there was this feeling.

"What if there's something we're not seeing? What if she's not looking at Caine but at someone behind him? I mean, Caine called *me* back on the street. He knew I picked brains. If he had anything to hide—I don't know. I just get the feeling we're doing something wrong. I just don't get the feeling he's a bent cop. I read and get true-blue copper."

"Why don't you take the candy from him then?"

"Early conditioning—or maybe I just thought he was baiting me."

"Why didn't you call him back?"

"I told you. I was playing a game. I was too busy."

"Well, go back and call him, then. Extend the contact a little longer."

"Now what do I say?"

"I'm sure it will come to you. You've not afraid of losing a little sleep, are you?"

"I wonder if those amber glasses are prescription?" She turned to the mainframe. "Moby?"

Moby's sonorous voice sounded. *"STIGMATIC. CORRECTED TWENTY TWENTY."* In recent years Moby's accent had become pronouncedly Minnesotan; he sounded like an overstuffed Hubert Humphrey doll.

"Thanks, Moby, that's all I needed to know. Okay, Mr. Clay Adams, I'll try once more."

"Once more is all we get. Last chance."

Eel settled back in the soft leather of the pod.

"Great Seymour, you're a wonder," Adams said. "Be careful though. If he's killed once, he can kill again."

"Cross my heart and hope to die." She was teasing him again. "Yes," she finally said, when he wouldn't stop looking at her like that. "I'll be careful."

"And keep an eye out for that ivory opener. One never knows."

"Yes, sir." Eel closed her eyes when the playback began. Her halfling self tunneled downward in the dark, toward the pinprick of light. Help him, help the man with the sad, fractured eyes. Help him see in the dark. Give him back his twenty twenty vision.

Noetic thought. Fractured vision. A loud and steady ringing in her ear. Eel, phone home. Phone home. 6-5-4-3.

⌐ 2020

Wednesday, April 15, 1:59 A.M.

The light on Max's message unit was blinking red when he came through the kitchen door. He tossed the brown evidence bag on the enamel table and lit the message screen of his Navigator. The kid's freckled face appeared on holograph.

"Six-five-four-three: The question is not why but how. Methyl salicylate crystals. As for the bollixed tape, if it's made of bits, I can fix it. Gore Lab basement, Mary Shelley Building. Nightmode." The message cube darkened.

Max hit replay and watched the kid again. She was in a lab of some sort. Machines everywhere. He reset the machine, went into his bedroom, and took off his hat and glasses, then inspected his mouth in the dark mirror. No sparks, nothing blue or green. Methyl salicylate crystals had all dissolved within. He emptied his pockets, putting the kid's toy on the bureau: Fibonacci of twenty, Nightmode. He smiled. Some people just won't be reduced to numbers, he reflected. He wondered if she got many calls. He put his change in a pile, then turned on the tube and checked the menu. The wall blinked rose and pale blue. There was an old eighties film on 99, Czech: *The Unbearable Lightness of Being*. He had seen it, hadn't he? Haunting cello. A fifties John Wayne western on 56, which he didn't even consider. A Hitchcock thriller, but he had seen that, as well. Besides it was in black and white, and he couldn't bear that tonight. Oscar Favorites on 100 had a 1999. Best Picture,

Best Score. Viennese music, Ravinsky. Not his bag. Three stars though. But it had just started. No, he didn't want to be up all night. Max kicked off his shoes, leaned back on his futon, and punched in channel 99. He was a product of the eighties: he couldn't defy it.

The movie music started him thinking of the music room in Mahler, the old grand with the ivory keys. He had spent a lot of time there in the days following the ides of April. Days trying to piece it all together. Often he had found himself at the piano, trying to pick out the strand of musical notes he had found in Amanda's pocket. Such a simple little piece, but he couldn't quite get it. Now he couldn't even remember the notes. A perfect "Chopsticks" was all that was left of four years of preadolescent piano classes. That and one or two classics, a passable "My country 'tis of thee," which he had learned in the second grade, and a horrendous rendition of "O say can you see." Piano was not his forte. He didn't have the fingers for it. He could fiddle, that was about all.

At least he could carry a tune. But then who couldn't in Shawneeville? America's most musical town. Shawneeville had carried that banner more than once, especially since the Revival. Home of the Sing-in, herald of the demise of *Weltanschauung*. It had started there, at Badger Stadium at a July 4th soccer game in the year 2000. The first mass singing.

The singer rose to deliver the national anthem. The crowd rose to mutely salute the flag. She told reporters later that she didn't know what came over her. She had misheard, perhaps, or just forgotten. By the time she realized her mistake it was too late. She was singing "America."

A loud murmur went through the crowd. Then a small voice joined in. A child sang out the words. A wave swept the stadium then, and other voices joined in, a great swell of 85,000 voices. Of one heart, they sang the simple tune, and as they sang, tears began to stream from their eyes. Two centuries of pent-up song burst out en masse as the audience wept and sang "America." When they finished there wasn't a dry eye. Not there, and not in the eyes of those watching television screens across America. The country had a new anthem.

And such a moving ovation of music to follow: mass musical festivals, global songs. Unbearable happiness had accompanied the turn of the century. It was a time of new composers and new music, not all of it sweet, much of it searching and sad. Great mass symphonies that left all present with tear-streaked faces, a celebration of sound to announce the century's turning. For a decade Max had been swept up in the movement, as they all had. Like lemmings, they had embraced the mass revivals, the mass marriages, the masses to the new century. The world sang, at football stadiums and at county fairs, at pageants and parades. Into the waiting eager ears new composers brought forth new universes of music: Stringfellow, Ravinsky, the new world revivalists.

On the screen, a man and a woman were eating. Max's stomach started rumbling, so he went into the kitchen alcove for a drink of milk. The little brown bag on the table seemed to glow in the dark. He assumed it was the waterproofing waxy surface catching the hall light. He opened the refrigerator, took out the milk, and drained the carton.

He went back in the bedroom and put on his glasses. The girl in the bowler hat was naked, beckoning. He watched her in the mirror, and realized only gradually that he could leave his mirror self watching her while he looked back out the door and down the hall to the alcove. The bag was still on the counter, glowing even brighter than before.

The bag looked suddenly alive.

Max shut the screen and quickly crossed the hall, plucking the shiny bag from the counter. The glowing stopped, but all the way to campus, Max had a funny feeling.

He had put one tape in the bag. He should feel some

heaviness in his arms. Instead, he felt as if the bag were tugging him along, urging him into the night.

The two creamy yellow lights atop the tower of the Mary Shelley Artificial Intelligence Building brightened to white as Max approached, but they faded quickly, almost to amber, as a power surge robbed the circuits of juice. Originally people had gone Nightmode to get cycles. Now the big power drains all came at night as midnight hackers ran their programs. Max entered the building and located the directory: Gore Lab, Subbasement 3.

He took the escalator down. A green door. Shiny gold letters: GORE LAB. ENTER.

As he opened the door he heard music, scales rising and falling. It was dark within, but he could make out some sort of outer office. A crack of light just ahead: the sonorous music was coming from there. He felt along the wall for the panel and flipped on the lights; he was walking past a white marble fireplace with holographic logs. The music deepened as he approached the inner door. He cocked his head. Voices? It made him smile whatever it was, an opera or a ballad in a foreign tongue . . . no—bassoons?

"Eel? Yo, kid! Anyone home? What is that unearthly sound anyway?" He pushed open the door and looked for a light switch. He couldn't find it, but there was a dim blue light aglow just beyond the closest partition. He put his hands over his ears and waded through the vibrations of the speakers. A horrible sulfurous smell enveloped him, and he raised his hands to cover his nose and mouth; it quickly wafted past. Ten feet in front of him he saw the kid; she was sitting on a leather cushion in a large crystal pod, hunched over a wraparound holographic stereographic wall screen, operating her mouse commander with skinny little nail-bitten fingers. The blue light of the screen made her skin glow; he watched as a scaly, wormlike monster slithered toward her.

As Max took a step forward he heard a loud screech and a small furry ball came crashing down on his shoulders, skittered down his body, and attached itself to his leg. He froze. This one was real. The furry ball climbed to his knee. He looked down into the inquisitive face of a small, sharp-toothed monkey.

"Does this thing bite?"

The girl didn't answer. He chanced a step. The monkey clung with one shaggy arm, the other arm shielding its eyes from the photon ray of bright lilac light the kid was blasting at the red-eyed, scaly creature.

"Got him! Yes!" The creature dissolved in a cloud of yellow smoke that smelled like rotting eggs.

The monkey climbed a bit higher on his leg.

"Hey!" Max yelled.

The kid started and twirled around.

"Sorry, I didn't mean to frighten you," Max said quickly. "Can you get this thing off me?"

"I wasn't frightened. Come here, Lucy." She pursed her lips and gave a little whistle. The monkey jumped into her arms.

On the holographic screen, a two-legged, one-eyed giant approached. "Hey," Max said again. "You've got company."

Eel whirled, mouse in hand, and sent out a spell that turned the beast to cold stone.

"What was that?"

"Just a stone-giant."

"Big brute."

"Fortunately, he's dumb. But he'd just as soon eat me for breakfast as smell me."

"Nice holography," Max yelled over the music. "How do you do that?"

"How? Oh, that's simple. Vision is a result of a pattern of light hitting your retina, not what is actually out there. The

scene reflects a pattern of light in your brain. You think it's
out there, but it's really in here." She tapped just above her
eye. "So, I just re-create the same pattern of light and project
it, clone a wavefront of reality, a virtual image. This setup is
just the next step up. A live holly."

"Live?"

"Advanced optical programming: a program that learns
from its experience with its player, creates infinitely more
challenging and terrifying mythical monsters. Of course, I've
got help." She glanced sideways at the monolithic computer
that sat just beyond the wrapped holly screen.

Max whistled. "I'll say. You got permission to use that
thing, kid?"

"I've got permission as long as I don't violate any present
systems outside the campus. I've taken an oath to that. But
there are no restrictions on my usage hours. Besides, Moby
and I are in the midst of an important optical laser experiment. The State wouldn't dare interfere."

"Moby? A colleague?"

The kid laughed. "Sort of," she said, glancing behind her
again. Max realized that she was talking about the mainframe. It was a large icy blue set of cylinders, arranged in a
cruciform, a mainframe XY-Y Cray 4000.

"Nothing but the best for you microtots, eh? That is a Cray
four thousand, isn't it?"

"Yes."

Max raised his eyebrows. "No wonder your game's so
real. Go on, don't let me stop you. I'm fascinated."

On the floor of the subterranean cave lay gold and jewels,
all the riches of the world. It was right there for the plucking.
Only the kid was ignoring it, going down a set of worn stairs.

"What's down there, kid?"

"I don't know. Depends on what it thinks I'm after."

"It?"

"Its neural network."

"You're saying it thinks for itself?"

"That's what artificial intelligence is all about. It may not actually think, but it thinks it thinks. It believes it exists to thwart me, to beat me. A perfect game partner. It couldn't cope in the real world, of course. It's not really there at all. None of those creatures are real. I know that 'cause I made it all up. Just 'maginary creatures. It's just a game to pass the time."

Max shuddered. What would she be doing when she was eight? His eyes were finally getting used to the gloom. The lab was a crammed jumble of wires and racks and blinking lights and shiny surfaces without any apparent organization or order. There was a pair of megaspeakers balanced precariously atop a yellow file cabinet, their meshed covers vibrating violently. A man's kindly face smiled benevolently on the disorder from the wall.

"Who's that?" he asked, nodding at the picture.

"Seymour," the kid said.

"Seymour Who?"

"No, Seymour Cray. The computer wizard. He's kind of a holly himself. A virtual image."

"I don't understand. I thought he was dead." Max took a closer look at the close-mouthed wizard in the blue button-down shirt. He had beady eyes but there was a twinkle in them.

"Cray disappeared from public sight in the nineteen eighties under a cover of eccentricity. Cray Enterprises, though, continued to turn out more and more advanced computers."

"No one saw him after that?"

"Around the turn of the century, there were some reported sightings. They say he looked younger than he had twenty years before."

"So, what do you think?"

"I think he found the secret."

"What secret?"

She smiled. "Back in the seventies Cray built a deep cedar-lined tunnel in his Minneapolis backyard. I think he cheats time. He's got a secret world we can't share.''

''You really think so?''

''That's why he can't show his face. He's nearly a hundred years old but he's got the face and body of a sixty-year-old. He's found the fountain of youth in a cedar-lined time tunnel in his own backyard.''

''You believe that? You believe that time travel is possible?''

''Why not?''

''The well-known law against causality violation.''

''How long ago did you go to school? Relativity was disproved years ago. In UF theory—''

''What's that, flying saucer stuff?''

Eel laughed. ''Unified Field Theory. U-F-T. As I was saying, we may have random causality violation, as long as the violation is only a glancing blow. Quantum theory not only provides for causality violation, it practically demands it.''

''Yeah, I read that somewhere. It's like an onion, isn't it? You're supposed to be able to peel off different layers. Only you can't prove it in this world, so what difference does it make?''

''It doesn't, that's just it. It's like the old UFT joke, what if the sky turned pink overnight? It doesn't make any difference as long as it turns pink for everyone.''

''I'd take pink over dun yellow any day.''

Eel clucked.

''So how did he do it, this Cray fellow?'' Max asked.

''I wish I knew. I've a hunch he found a simple answer. You see, the world *is* synchronous. Events are intertwined and contiguous, not causal. Reality isn't bound by space/time parameters. Micro time travel happens all the time; it's just a matter of sustaining it.''

''What do you mean—micro time travel happens all the time.''

"You know déjà vu?"

"Yeah."

"Déjà vu's just a memory mirror trick. It's your future *psi* self remembering, robbing the past. A brief flash of neurons as your future self links itself to the memory and borrows a bit of timespace. When you reach that section in linear time, the ground is still spongy. Timespace has been violated and the person trips into a déjà vu state. Hocus pocus and you're no longer condemned to Euclidian three-dimensional space. Think about it."

Max shrugged.

"In theory—" Eel stopped and sniffed the air. "Just a moment, while I deal with—" She turned to her screen and fried another odorous monster. As Eel moved her mouse north and another vista appeared before her, Max studied Seymour Cray's face. A kindly face; neatly folded hands. The only human portrait in the room. Seymour kind of reminded Max of a figure from his childhood, Mr. Rogers, with that Harris tweed jacket and wide black tie, that apple smile. He looked like a man buying time. At whose expense? Had he taken anyone with him or was he perhaps the loneliest man in America?

He looked at the kid, playing her game on company time. A birthright. Genius brought with it its own punishments. Moby was her only real friend. The lab was her home, and the game was her real world, infinitely variable but ultimately controllable. No wonder she preferred it—a castle where she could garner strength and wisdom and never lose control.

"What do you call this game, anyhow?"

She answered without looking up. "Wormwood."

"I used to be pretty good at these games," Max said. "Played some megagames when I was growing up—Hack and Zork, a little AD and D. I battled Baal and his evil undead, swam the pool of radiance in the fabled ruins of Phlan on the shore of the Moonsea. A few bodacious space fantasies: Sentinel Wars and the like.'' He didn't mention the other games he had played when he got bollixed by his studies: Leather Goddesses of Phobos, played in lewd mode. What he wouldn't have given for sensory graphics like Eel's. Though he could have done without the olfactory effects.

"What's wrong?" he asked. The kid was making a face.

"Sentinel Wars. How could you stand it?"

"Great musical score."

"On a high tweeter? That game sucks pond scum."

"Such a mouth. You probably didn't like Captain Blood either."

"Nice EGA graphics. Zero content."

"Well, thanks a lot," he said. "Er, think you could turn that music down? Whatever it is."

"Oh, that? Angels," she said.

"Yeah? Well, they sure can't sing."

Eel laughed. "Great winged angels, actually. A cetacean courtship song. They're tinkering there with the score. Cetaceans are inveterate composers, you know."

Max had not known. Cetaceans? He had never been much for geography.

"Whale songs," Eel said.

"Oh," he said. "Well, I never was much for biology either."

"What you're hearing is a ten-million-year-old primordial melody, recorded off Patagonia by a quartet pod of humpback bulls, *Mysticeti*. Of course, you can't hear it all. Humans don't hear the whole range of sounds."

"Ten million years? Don't tell me you have a cedar tunnel, too?"

She laughed. "I just meant that it's the same basic song poem; of course, the variations are infinite. This one is mid-twentieth-century. A man named Roger Payne recorded it before the seas were clogged. It's primordial, played on a universal scale."

"Payne, eh? That figures. How long is it?"

"This tonal poem runs about an hour. If you listen carefully you can pick out individual voices. Males only, of course."

"Why's that?"

Eel shrugged. "Female whales don't sing tonal poems."

"You understand that stuff? I mean, are there words and all?"

"Words? Not exactly. Feelings, expressions."

"A tonal poem. Yeah. It's—" He stopped. "It's—" The music was getting to him. "Could you turn that off?"

Eel punched a button, and a DAT cassette ejected. The room filled up with machine sounds, the steady roar of fans. Max let out his breath. Dreadful stuff, oppressive as Bach.

"Would you prefer some Paul Winter? Some loons or wolves, or something in a higher range. Porpoises, perhaps?"

Max declined.

"A beer? While you're waiting?" she offered politely. "I'll be through here in just a nano."

"Beer?"

"In the cooler next to the vending machine. Help yourself."

"And whose beer is this I'm drinking?"

"My houseparents, Dr. and Dr. Stukowski, but they're on sabbatical this spring. Help yourself."

Max went over to the vending machines and found the cooler. No Rolling Rock, nothing but Leinenkugel. What the hell was Leinenkugel? "German?"

"No, Chippewa Springs. Good for the brain. Seymour Cray's home brew."

Worth a try. He uncapped the bottle and raised it. "Here's to you, Seymour." He took a sip. Not half bad. Max walked back with the bottle to the console.

The kid was doing battle with a very large, very ugly, black, smelly spider.

"Wormwood, you said."

"Wormwood," she said, her voice solemn.

"Never heard of it."

"Sort of my own invention. I'm still inventing it. The basics are in C."

"Sort of advanced D and D?"

"Sort of." In front of her, a small red dragon appeared and Max felt the air around him grow hot and singed. "This fellow nearly wiped me out once when I started out. I tried to kill it with a fireball." She laughed and blasted the creature with an ice spell. "Have to fight fire with ice." The dragon snorted, and smoke puffed from his nostrils. Then he turned and slithered down a distant staircase.

"Just a nano, I'll save this," the kid said, hunching over the screen. The little monkey was perched on her shoulder, chattering at the screen.

Max nodded. Just a nano to a D & D player was like a couple of beers to an alcoholic. Max pivoted on his heel and finished surveying the room. There were photographs of computers on the walls. In the corner he saw a child's cot with a threadbare patchwork quilt; it was blocked on two sides by salmon pink metal cabinets. So the kid slept here.

Next to the child's cot was a small crib. The monkey's bed, he guessed. He turned back to the strange pair. The kid was standing up, good as her word, looking curiously at his brown paper bag.

"Okay, three guesses, Miss X-ray vision. And it's not my midnight snack."

"Your broken tape?"

Max shrugged. "Think you can fix it for me?"

"Like I said, if it's made of bits, I can fix it." She took it out. "It's awful old. You some sort of antiquarian?"

"Ha, that's a good one. Didn't I give myself away by now?"

"You don't look like a cop."

Max laughed. "That's what they all say. And by the way,

about the Lifesavers? How's that work? Methyl—what?''

"Salicylate—it's a chemical reaction. The cracking sugar crystals stimulate the methyl salicylate to emit light. A micro-optical trick, sort of like a hologram in your mouth.''

He unrolled the silver and offered the pack for the second time that night. The kid hesitated and then helped herself to a candy, took a bite out of it, and grinned a green-specked smile. Still crunching, she fed the tape into an old multi-adapter and played it forward to the final catatonic scene.

"Who's that you're talking to there?"

"My star witness, Miss Tilly.''

"Tell me, have you always parted your hair on the right?''

Max reached up and touched his crown. "Yes, always. Since I was six anyway,'' he said, remembering how his mother had combed his hair once, on end, like the crest of a cedar waxwing.

"Just as I thought. But look at the screen.''

"You're right. It's parted wrong.''

"No, the tape's been wound wrong. Looks like a job of careless threading—nothing serious. Just a nano and I'll have it twisted right.''

She fixed the tape and replayed it, up to the same blinking dead end. This time, the part was on the right.

"It's still broken, kid. And what's making it pulsate like that? Boy, that bothers my eyes.''

Eel was staring at the blinking light, mesmerized. The blinking light was now illuminating the quadrant opposite the two faces. An elephant pot holding an elephant book-mark and an elephant letter opener, a pencil with an ele-phant eraser.

"Strange, very strange,'' Eel said. "It's still stuck.'' She rewound it and sat thinking. Presently she got up and ejected the tape. "Back in a nano,'' she said, going into a small cubicle behind the Cray.

When she came back, her eyes were wide and glowing. "Any idea how the tape got this way?''

"I just figured it had gotten old. Those old VHS tapes brittle with age. It's not melted, is it?"

"No. It's been stored where?"

"In the basement at Central."

"The submountain station?"

"Yes. The files were in a lead vault, climate controlled. They were there a long time. That is, until this week. I've had it in my office a week."

"Very, very strange," Eel said. "If I'm right, this tape, this section, has been subjected at some point to an extremely strong gravitational pull."

"You mean it's been erased? Like with a giant magnet?"

"No, something stronger. Like a micro black hole."

"Whoa! Whose black hole?"

"There's the mystery. You know how the stiletto heel of a hundred-pound woman can make a puncture in a rubber mat, yet the soles of a three-hundred-pound male won't make a dent. Well, I think this had been *made*. Someone's been playing God—tinkering with your biography."

"You mean God is a hundred-pound woman with stiletto heels?"

Eel laughed. "Maybe just one stiletto heel. I don't know how it happened, but your tape's warped, permanently. You can back it up and play it forward but it will stop again just here."

"Can you unwarp it?"

"Theoretically, yes."

"But in actuality?"

"I'd need about a teaspoon of neutrino material, more than all the cold fusion machines in the world produce in a decade."

Max whistled gravely.

"I think that bit of tape beyond the warp is caught up in it," she went on. "It's still happening in there, and it can't get out. Some sort of tremendous gravity is keeping the light from getting out. What else was on the tape?"

"After that? Just routine surveillance. We kept the room under monitor for six weeks. I used to come in every day and change the tapes. We thought maybe the killer would—you know—return to the scene of the crime."

Eel reached over and placed the tape in Max's hand. Again, it made him feel odd, lighthanded.

"Why isn't it heavy?" he asked.

"Oh, but it is. Very heavy. Metaphorically that is. It's just that time itself is very light, as light as a rainbow. What we've got in there is a small cross-section of time, trapped."

"What time is it in there, then?"

"That's what I'd like to know. What time? What exactly is swallowed up in there? Is it just this moment, or a chunk of time after? And can we get it out? Do you mind if I keep the thing a bit longer, run some experiments?"

"Keep it as long as you like," Max said.

"I might not get to it right away. I'm afraid you've got me at a bad moment. I'm in pursuit of a very valuable jewel tonight, and I mustn't get off track. I'm meeting monsters of very senior status. They terrify me, but I think I've figured out a way to outmaneuver one of them."

"Sure, kid. Think you can unjam it?"

She raised one eyebrow and stared at him intently. She looked like an owl, he decided, judicial. "I think I can."

"That's good enough for me. Leave a message if you get it fixed." But he didn't leave; he took a step closer to the pod. "Need any help?"

"Help?" She seemed surprised. "Sorry," she said, "but no. I can only travel single where I'm going."

"What kind of jewel?"

Eel looked at him. "Is that all you care about, jewels? You really are a baby boomer yuppie, aren't you?"

"I am not."

"Hmm. Not that I care, you understand. If you really must know, I'm on the trail of the sacred spinning pearl."

"Oh." Max scratched his chin. "Is that Moslem or what?"

"No. It's a white pearl, not a black one."

Max shrugged. Let her seek her sacred pearl and slay her monsters. He didn't have to worry about the squirt. She had her immortality in a leather-padded pod.

The movie was just ending when Max got home. A man and a woman were dancing in a crowded café. They came up to their beds drunk, laughing. And then it was morning and the party goers were driving home in the dawn, disappearing at the top of the road into a bright, bright, blinding light—a head-on collision.

The score replayed in his head as he got up and opened the window, letting in a warm breeze, sweet and cloying. He dropped to his futon and slept, fitfully.

He woke suddenly and sat up, his body trembling. How long it had been, he thought as he gawked out the window. The murky haze had lifted and the moon hung like a giant face in the mauve sky. As he watched, something even more miraculous occurred: the sky darkened to brown and then to black, and then a thousand and one stars twinkled on inky velvet like diamonds cascaded across a velvet cloak.

And then, just as suddenly as it had come, the sky clouded over; the gods took back their gift. Dull dun night returned. In the distance he heard the bells chime. Four bells, the hour of the wolf.

At dawn Max had slept just two hours. He rose from his futon and went to the kitchen alcove and drained the last of the bottled rose water; he was still groggy when he took the cover off Paulette's cage.

"Morning, Maxwell," his sole domestic adherent squawked. "Looking good."

He ignored her, stalling the moment when the sensor alarm would warm to his voice.

"Morning, Maxwell, looking—"

"Oh, shut up, Paulette." He opened the fridgecube. Old men get up early for no reason at all, he thought. He pined for the days he would have lain abed, savoring his late Wednesday mornings, the sheets a warm nest.

"Time for vitamins," his clone console sang out.

"Time for vitamins," Paulette echoed.

"Back off, both of you," Max said, surveying the bare fridge: a cup of leftover beans, a few tightly rolled foil packages, one lone Rolling Rock pony. He took the pony, uncapped it, and tipped it back.

"Fill up the glasses with treacle and ink . . ." Paulette sang gaily. ". . . or anything else," she squawked. "Bad boy, bad boy."

Max ignored her.

"Bad boy, bad boy," Paulette shrilled.

"I'll get the *cover*," Max warned.

There was dead silence. Max took another chug of beer and burped. His mind was as blank as the wall screen as he logged on his Navigator: MAC.

The flat-screened computer signed its greeting: THE NAVIGATOR WELCOMES YOU. ACCESS.

He looked at the bird. Not a peep from Paulette. He pressed Systems Messages: No E mail. He accessed the health report, and the wall screen brightened: Projected high: 83. PSI 25—not bad for April. UV-B level, high. Ozone level: 112. The wall screen was showing the sunrise, orange and blue, a desert sky, ablaze from end to end. Sailors take warning.

He chugged the last of the pony. "Time for vitamins, time for walkaerobics," his clone said ever so sweetly and meekly as he plodded past to throw his glass in the recycling compactor. He ignored the music, but he did consent to his clone spraying vitamin mist on his wrist as he passed.

"Time for walkaerobics," his clone sang a shade more hopefully, stepping up the beat and beginning the rousing morning march song. The program was designed especially

to motivate him toward better health and hygiene. Seat yourself upon thy throne and resign yourself to ritual. Time to
perform the morning ablutions. Depilatory applied; odors
neutralized; breath sweetened; skin moistened. Routine—his
life was divided into a thousand and one prescribed perfor-
mances. Get up, drink liquid, take vitamins, check sky, go to
work. Yes, no, off, on, slam, bam, thank you, ma'am. All
whizzing past at increasingly astonishing speeds. It was time
to get off the carousel.

He rubbed his chin. Not today. He'd shave himself. He
reached over and flipped the clone's switch.

"Glork," Paulette said as the clone whined down. "Ah,
sweet silence," she ventured. Max couldn't help marveling
at her timing. He gave her a sunflower seed, and she took it
daintily in her sharp, strong beak and held it. The silence was
indeed sweet, until she started cracking her seed. Max went
back through the Spartan living alcove. No plants, no flowers,
no art, just a few cushions, a low couch, a built-in, computer-
simulated tropical fish tank that had come with the condo. If
he could only find a simulated parrot . . .

When he finished shaving, the screen sky was already
glazed to a crystalline haze. The sun was hidden behind a
dirty dun blanket, not to be seen again till dusk. He stuck bits
of necessary paper on the cuts and admired his handiwork in
the mirror. Not bad for being out of practice.

He put the UV-B screens up a level; while his back was
turned, the message light on his phone began blinking red.

CAINE. COME NOW. EEL.

Now? When did the kid sleep? Max put his "gone bear
hunting" tape on the message unit, got his Ray-Ban Shooters
and his hat, and headed for the second time in hours for Gore
Lab.

The kid was in the crystal pod fighting holographic dragons
when Max entered carrying a white, oily bag. The blue safety
light cast an eerie glow on her shoulders as she sat hunched

in the soft leather podchair. The crystal made her look as if
she were swimming in clear gelatin; she looked fetal, an
embryo in a crystal egg.

Outside of the pod was a soundscape of quiet. The small,
red night-light in the corner by the cot glowed like a flame on
the salmon file above, illuminating in flickers the little cloth
mouse and the sleeping monkey holding it. A handful of
banana pellets glistened on the counterpane.

Max walked up to the crystal pod and looked in. "Morning," he said. "Guess what?"

The kid didn't even look up. Max peered down. Billows of
red smoke were coming off the floor and walls. And then he
saw, suddenly far too close up and real, the jaws of a great
beast—

There was a sharp bright blast of light, and the smoke
turned black and then cleared. The monster was gone and the
kid was safe.

"Sun's up," he said, admiring her artwork. "You told me
to come now," he added. On the wrapped viviscreen a soft
pink subterranean canyon spread out. On the floor of the
cavern were scattered various holographic items. He watched
the kid use her mouse to pick up a compass and a five-colored
banner. Then she hesitated. She looked up at him, then back
at the screen. Her fingers hovered over the directional coordinates.

"I stopped at Pammy K's for donuts. Hope you're not one
of those weird people who don't like chocolate."

"I'm a halfling," Eel said, moving her mouse, following
another staircase down, heading north.

Max grinned. "Anything you say, kid." He waved the
open bag near her nose. "Do halflings eat chocolate-covered
donuts?"

She considered that for a moment, then reached for the bag
and quickly devoured three donuts. Max watched with fascination as she neatly scooped a crumb from her checked

pants and proceeded to lick her fingers. A sudden unpleasant smell made him look up. Oops. Something else liked donuts. On the screen, he watched a large sluglike monster come oozing into the distant dark, a giant white slug, making a little slurping sound, seeking sugar. "Uh, Eel," Max said, pointing.

She sucked off her index finger and pressed a key. The screen froze. The creature hovered. If he looked long enough he could imagine that it was just a giant stalagmite, an ancient limestone formation. "And here, folks, is the statue of liberty, and here's the hippopotamus, and here we have the sea monster." As a spelunker guide summers in Indian Cove he had always had fantastic scripts, great patter to go with the light show. It came easy to him, like looking at clouds.

Eel had another donut while Max contemplated the holographic shape, waiting, curious to see how the kid would deal with it. He looked at the cave floor and saw a knife. Why not pick that up? he thought. Or that can of Mace lying within that small trickle of limestone water? He shrugged. Maybe halflings didn't fight like humans.

"What exactly is a halfling?" Max asked, when she had finished licking the sugar paste and chocolate off all ten fingers. "Half human?"

"I thought you said you played some Moria."

"No, Zork."

"Oh. Well, a halfling is more half hobbit than half human. The game's characters resemble those under the Misty Mountains—only the monsters are my own making."

"What use is a compass down here?"

"A great help if you're looking for the pearl of truth. Unfortunately, the ethmoid bone between my eyes is low in iron. My own directional needle is deficient, even for a female. You see, my placenta was plastic."

Ethmoid bone, plastic placentas. Max stared in amazement at the podtube child that science had wrought. Was she for real? Plastic placentas were not something Max's mother would have let him talk about. This kid had no skin to get under. Eel. What kind of name was that for a kid, anyhow?

She was rubbing her fingers with a compuwrite. Then she took up the mouse in her tiny hand.

"So what's an ethmoid bone?" he asked.

"A primitive compass. In the bone between the eyes, we have an iron eye, a central eye that orients us toward our north pole, a polestar finder. Some people have only to point their noses."

"Astonishing," Max said, rubbing the bridge of his nose, wondering if he had much iron in his. "And the banner? What are you going to do with that?"

"The multicolored silk? You'll see."

"Why didn't you pick up the sword?"

"Spells work better." With a wave of the cloth, she wove a net of invisibility and slipped through the colored panels. The sluglike creature sniffed the air and groaned as it realized its prey had vanished. It slouched off in pursuit of a butterfly.

"See?" she said. "Now I can get on with important business."

"Like what?"

"Following my nose." She reached over and grabbed the last donut. "Thanks," she said, when she had licked out the crumbs in the bag.

As the next section of canyon wrapped around, Max leaned forward expectantly. A smooth marble floor, gem-studded walls—beautiful crystal orbs shining red and green and yellow and white and lavender. Somebody had to be guarding all that. He looked up, but the expected monster never materialized. The kid reached out toward the wall, but she didn't take any of the jewels. Instead she plucked up a small centipede that had been crawling amid the jewels and deposited it in her little bag. She tied the drawstrings tight.

"Just a nano," she said then, looking up and giving Max a big smile. "I'll save this." She exited the program and

saved it. Then she stretched and folded back the arms of her
podchair; when she climbed out of the pod, she looked like a
scrawny chick hatching.

"Did I keep you waiting?" she asked politely. "I wanted
to see you."

"*Now*, you said. Well, here I am. That's quite a cave
there. How deep does it go?"

"I don't know. Deep."

"So, what'd you say this game is called? Wormhole?"
She laughed. "Close. Wormwood."

"Who's the top evil in your game? Is he like Baal?"

Eel put her finger to her lip. "No name. I can't divulge the
evil divinity's identity."

"Why not?"

"For obvious reasons."

"Ever met this nameless terror?"

"No, not exactly. You see, I made him. But I gave him
just a little less power than I gave the powers of good. I could
slay him in a minute if I wanted."

"So it is a he?"

"Yes and no. He is at the present."

"So you made yourself a failsafe switch, just in case he
gets too smart for you?"

"The first rule when you make an AIS."

"AIS?"

"Artificial intelligence system. You leave yourself an over-
ride. A built-in sort of repair service in case anything goes
wrong. I've got two."

"What are they?"

"Why do you want to know?"

"Just curious."

The kid looked at him. He could see her juggling something in her mind, deciding that it was all right for him to
know.

"First a spell to escape from any evil, a built-in protector
wizard. A teleporting device."

"Okay, I follow. Sort of like the escape mode in some of the D and D games."

"Yes, sort of like. I've a wizard mode for escape. And just in case I get in real trouble, I've God mode."

"What's the password?"

"God doesn't have a name."

"What do you call him?"

She laughed. "I don't. So far, my wizard has whisked me out of trouble before I got fried."

"So what can you do with God mode?"

"You can rewrite any lost program, skip over any malfunctioning command. If I needed to, God could revive a dead character."

"Well, that's got to make it a little less threatening. Those monsters seemed pretty real to me. Don't you ever get scared?"

"Yes. But I've got lots of spells and tricks. As long as I play each night, they can't get out of hand. I don't like to play much past dawn."

"I remember, you told me. Nightmode all the way. Kids are supposed to hate night. Early environment, probably."

"I don't know any day kids, just hackers. They bring me Chinese food some nights, and we play chess by E mail, things like that."

"What about play?"

"Play? I play lots of games."

"Games of the mind, yes. But how about running and skipping and playing dolls and dress up and—"

The look on the kid's face pierced him. She had never skipped or jumped; she had missed all that. To her, play meant another monster. "Hey, do you think we could put on a light or two in here? It's like a tomb."

Eel clapped her hands twice, and the lights upped to a dim candle glow.

"Any luck with my tape?"

The kid reached behind her and came up with the brown paper evidence bag. She took out the tape and popped it in the adapter, and the screen opposite the pod lit up; the tape played to the warp and then stopped. The upper right quadrant pulsed, light and dark, light and dark.

"I thought maybe it was some kind of code. Moby says no, though. I can't figure it."

Max stared at the frozen wall screen. His young hand held the doorjamb. Miss Tilly's soft body blocked most of the hall, but he could see her room, her desk. Elephants everywhere. What kind of woman loved elephants? He took another look at the woman's face on the screen. Why was she looking at him like that?

"Like what?" the kid said, picking his question from thin air.

"Damn!" The kid was too young for what he had been thinking.

"Am not," she countered. "I know all about those thoughts. As long as you're looking, take a gander at your own celluloid mug. You're pretty moony-eyed yourself." She cleared her throat and stared at him. "Something here you've neglected to inform me of?"

Eel zoomed the tape, and then Max saw it, his own dopey expression. Miss Tilly had reminded him of his favorite aunt, he recalled. Her voice, her smile—it had just made him feel kindly. But Miss Tilly wasn't Aunt Emma. The look on her face was, well . . . disturbing. Strange he hadn't noticed. She was looking at him with such longing. Desire moldered in those eyes, years of pent-up passion. For him? Crazy. Maybe there'd been someone behind him?

"Of course, your psyche is your own business," Eel said, spinning around on her stool. "I don't care for mushy stuff. All I care about is *how* it got this way. Do you remember anything about that day, aside of course from the murder itself, that was extraordinary?"

Max shook his head. "As far as I know, it was an ordinary day. No earthquakes, no volcanos. Not for me anyhow." He looked back at Miss Tilly. Rose. Had the earth moved for poor Miss Tilly?

"No extreme weather?"

"Not that I recall. Mid-April, neither hot nor cold. Ground was thawed."

"The ides of April. Hmm." She punched a switch and spoke to Moby. "Moby, check Accuweather's databank for nineteen ninety-five phenomena, solar flares especially. Anything out of the ordinary."

Moby hummed and reported: *"NEGATIVE."*

"How about cold fusion experiments?"

"NEGATIVE. NOTHING SIGNIFICANT FOR APRIL, NINETEEN NINETY-FIVE."

"Nineteen ninety-five. I wasn't even a gleam in a test tube yet. But you were there," she said, turning to Max. "There must be something." She pulled her earlobe and leaned forward. "You know what I'd like to do, Max? Okay if I call you Max?"

"Please do."

"I'd like to hypnotize you."

"I can't be hypnotized."

"Never say can't. I can hypnotize a chair. If you don't believe me . . ." She took a shiny purple card from her pocket; its surface was covered with different geometric patterns. Light and dark. She flashed it, and a pattern of light dazzled his eyes.

"Take that chair," Eel said, pointing to a corner Max had not previously noticed.

The soft easy chair of dark red velvet looked so inviting suddenly. He walked over and sat down and the chair folded around him like a fat woman's arms, soft and silky.

"Okay, take off those glasses."

Max lowered his Shooters, folded them, and put them in his top pocket.

"What big eyes you have," Eel said.

"The better to see you with, my dear."

Eel giggled. "Moby told me that one. Okay, watch the light."

The next thing Max knew he heard a snap and his eyes opened. The kid was watching him with a strange look.

"Well?" he said.

"Beta to alpha in thirty seconds, but then zilch. No brain engrams for that section of the ides of April. Boy, this thing is getting strange as a quark. You're a haunted man."

Max rubbed his head. He did feel a little strange. He had been somewhere else when the kid had snapped her fingers. Where?

"In the clouds," Eel answered. "I tried to take you back to nineteen ninety-five. I couldn't get you past the clouds in the film you were watching yesterday. I found the memory engrams for the time following the jam, but the section before has been wiped out. Almost an hour of memory. You didn't get some electrical shock working the tape yesterday?"

"No, it just jammed."

Eel rubbed her knobby knees and lowered her head. She bit her index fingernail down to just above the quick and then started to nibble on her pinky. "Hmm."

"You shouldn't bite your nails."

"It's a most intriguing case," she said, ignoring him. "An exotic force exercising control over that short section of timespace. The tape, your memory. Somehow this giant *thing* seems to be affecting both."

"Thing?"

"A black force. Gravity so powerful that not even light can get out. Somewhere, somehow, someone's been tampering with your electrons."

"That's impossible. I remember that afternoon. Ask me any detail."

"And your conscious mind will supply them, by rote. It's your subconscious memory that's gone missing."

Max blinked. "Mahler Hall. Amanda in the music room, crashing down among the music stands. I certainly remember finding the poor girl."

"What does she look like? Describe her for me."

"She was pretty—and—" Max paled. He couldn't see her face.

"What were you doing before the tape was made? And before you found her that day?"

"Why, I—" Max stopped. "Let's see, it was a Saturday, I'd be just getting off—I was in the diner with Ryan. I walked up the Mall to Mahler Hall; I stopped to watch a stupid squirrel."

"Very interesting," Eel said. "The way you shift your eyes to the left when you relate what should be memories. Your neurosensor expressions indicate a recital, a rote memory of these things, a manufactured memory." She twisted her striped jersey top. "You haven't ever had shock therapy, have you?"

"Hell, no."

"Ever been struck by lightning?"

"Not yet."

"Epilepsy?"

"Not in my family."

"Odd. Seventy trillion memory traces in your brain, give or take a few billion, but nothing for that segment of time. You weren't ill that day?"

"I was fit as a fiddle."

"Odd. It's very much like a concussion. You see, in concussion, you lose about an hour of prior short-term memory. A section of electrical memory is never stored in enduring chemical form. It's a little like pulling the plug on a computer before you've saved a file. Everything that happened before the break is merely energy, pure light. It flies away with incredible speed when the plug is pulled. Unless—"

"Yes?"

"Unless you posit the existence of a great attractor, a very big force, sucking everything in. The electrical memory would still be waiting to be transferred to physical form. Pure memory. If it were a physical memory trace, not even a teaspoon of neutrino material could hold it, but in electrical form, a large segment of timespace could be captured." She stared at the blinking screen.

Max stared, too. In his pocket he found the smooth coin and turned it between his fingers. "But—who? And why?"

"Useless to ask why. Who?" She shrugged. "Maybe it's just the Universal Mind, borrowing a bit of timespace. Maybe next time we look everything will be copacetic."

"You think so?"

Eel smiled. "It happens all the time. Didn't you ever lose something and know exactly where it's supposed to be?"

"Yeah."

"You look a dozen times in the same place and the frobnitz just isn't there. Then you tear the rest of the room apart. When you're totally discouraged, you look for the thirteenth time in the first spot. And it's there."

"How well I know."

"It's just God playing dice with the universe. He needs a prop so He borrows it. He stalls us on Gabriel mode, let's us think we're going la la while He gambles with our trivial little possessions. Then He puts them back, chuckling when we find them and try to convince ourselves that they were there all along."

Max laughed. "That explains it. God *is* a one-legged being. All those disappearing socks. God never takes a pair, just one."

Eel laughed. "No, that's a different monster. God always returns His props."

Max stared at the screen. "So how long do we wait?"

Eel shrugged.

"Is there any other way to get it back?"

"An excellent question." Eel turned to her keyboard and performed a series of nimble calculations. " 'A teaspoon of sugar makes the medicine go down,' " Eel sang as she worked. After a short moment, she smiled and eyed Max. "There just might be a way. Want to play guinea pig?"

"With a black hole? You're serious, aren't you?"

"It's *your* black hole. You do want to use it, don't you?"

"It was never on the top of my must-do list."

"You like being haunted?"

Max gripped the faceless coin in his pocket and tried to picture Amanda. "You really think I'm haunted?"

"Where is the self to be found except in the deepest enchantment you've experienced?"

"Enchantment? I wouldn't exactly describe that time as enchanting."

"No? You're a man who held a dying woman in your arms and yet there is not even a trace of that memory in your brain. I've been down to the bottom of your barrel—you're a true amnesiac. They are the most haunted of all men."

A sudden stab of angst. Maybe he was hiding the past. Max picked up the evidence bag and smashed it with his hand. Air whooshed out.

Eel was staring at him as if he had just performed a miracle. She jumped up and grabbed the bag. "Caine, that's it! What if I penetrate the bottom of the bag with a subatomic stiletto laser beam, make a kind of box camera projector. Light is coming out, exotic light. I make a microsize hole and project a neat orderly single file of electrons. I project them to your brain and you store them with the flanking patterns for the timespace. We recapture the memory, pure nineteen ninety-five grafted onto twenty twenty Max."

"You can do that? Get back the past?"

"I think so. You see, when you study very small particles, you realize that time is just a sophisticated illusion, a human invention. The forward march of time isn't sacrosanct."

"What is, these days?"

Eel smiled. "The universe is really very simple—it's just composed of such ridiculously large numbers. I can't guarantee I'll be able to get the entire memory back. The fifth force is by nature random so hypercharge deviations are to be expected. You might get more than you bargained for. If you do get the whole segment back, you might have to see her die again."

"Amanda?" He stopped and thought. His memory was clouded. Had she really died in his arms? He couldn't separate the real from the imagined. He'd worshipped the ghost of Amanda, courted her with devotion. And somewhere along the way the ghosts had taken over. His life had been filled with her death for twenty-five years.

Max lifted his head. "Maybe I need to see it."

"Need—" Eel started to say something but stopped herself. "Speaking of needles, you afraid of needles?"

"Needles? Sewing needles?"

"No," she said, holding up a long needle attached to a vial.

"What's that for?"

"Your blood enzymes and memory proteins."

"Hey!" He backed up.

"I need to make a receptacle that will attract the memory. I take the DNA from the referent engrams and then, using polymerase chain reaction, I brew a batch of memory large enough to analyze and make predictions from. A kind of fishing hook."

"That's an awfully big needle."

"Trust me."

Max laughed. "Okay, I'll bite. What have I to lose but my sanity?"

"Good." She prodded for a vein, injected the needle, and drew out a sample of blood. Max suddenly felt a little queasy. It had been a game till now, letting the kid experiment with him. Now he wasn't so sure.

"I'll have to work out a few bugs, but that will be the fun

part. Working you into my program. Then we attach you to the machine and play a few games.''

"I'm actually going to see it?"

"See it, feel it, smell it. You might experience a little bit of déjà vu when those memories are revived, but remember, as I explained, déjà vu is always out of context, trivial, spontaneous, and unstable. You can't hold that channel, especially if you try.''

"I've got one question. Is it possible that since I'm older and wiser now, I'll see something I didn't notice the first time?''

"Hmm. A most intriguing thought. Your filing system has changed. Yes, very intriguing. Since timespace isn't linear till you file it, you might be able to refocus. I'll look into it.''

"Maybe I'd see the mystery man, be able to chase him.''

Eel laughed. "Now you're getting silly. You can't alter your path. Don't start thinking you can play Engine Tootle and get off the track. No, Caine. You won't come back with buttercups and daisies in your cowcatcher. You can't change history. History's fixed in timespace; it's just our view of it that changes. There is, I'm afraid, only biography.''

The question is, thought Max, as he walked to his office, can you write your own biography?

Eel had told him to give her two hours to get her equipment set up. Who knew, maybe the kid could do what she said. Max reviewed what she had told him; it wasn't all mumbo jumbo.

Short-term memory was electrical energy, light. And it was complete, nothing had been filtered out. Yet.

Memory, that stuff humans filed in their brains, was not electrical. It was not a connection but a physical thing, like a molecule, coded over a large number of cells in the nucleotide sequence of RNA, a result of genes and neurons and experience. Alter any part and a different engram will be recorded. Memory is a thing. A less than perfect arrangement of symbols, representing a perfect whole. A thing.

A thing he was missing.

He sighed, thinking of last night's movie: *The Unbearable Lightness of Being*. History. What was it Voltaire had called it: a pack of tricks we play on the dead.''

The first thing he did when he entered his office was to take a long look at Amanda's face. Such a fearless face, unmarked by time, always smiling.

They could make baby rats fear the dark by injecting them with the fear enzymes produced by older rats who had been taught to fear the dark. They could make grown men smile and feel happy by feeding them with love proteins. What radioisotope markers had been robbed from his brain? Would putting the macromolecules back make any difference?

In fear of the dark? He'd replay the lost hour with a revived electrical spark. He wouldn't have to mince his brain. He'd have a chance to relive that fatal afternoon in stereophonic panavision.

He looked up Miss Tilly in the directory. Had her memory been wiped out, too? He felt his neck prickle as he jotted down the number. Déjà vu. He'd done this before, just here. He tried to hold on, remembering Eel's explanation, but as soon as he concentrated, the imagescape dissolved. Looking at it consciously made it go away. As Eel had said, it seemed entirely without consequence, of interest only for the oddly transparent feeling it produced. Just a trivial moment. He sat on his sponge-seated swivel chair and leaned back.

Just slide through a hole in this little thing, he thought, pulling the Möbius strip from his pocket and looping it around and around. The end and the beginning hole were the same hole. One could take the high road, or—with a teaspoon of energy—one could take the low road. Who was to say that he had not come full circle, back to stand over the buried past?

Alpha and Omega. No more half-life.

The monkey was awake when Max returned to Gore Lab. He felt a sense of excitement, anticipation. He was going to walk his beat again that day in 1995, up the Mall to Mahler Hall, under clear blue skies. He was going to approach the music building, go in, and find Amanda. And see it *all* with 2020 eyes. He could choose which view to remember.

Eel had chalked up an entire wallboard with her calculations and was deep in conversation with the Cray. When she looked up at Max her eyes seemed a little glazed. "You ready, Max?"

"Ready as I'll ever be. Where do you want me?"

"In the pod," she said, pointing to the ovoid crystal.

"Is that the program?" Max said, indicating the board.

"No, just some preliminary notes." She went to her desk and lifted up a stack of computer paper and let it accordion down and down onto the floor. "This is the program for the memory graft."

Max whistled.

"It's written in C. I've used some of the optical projection structure from my Wormwood game program. It's linked to the NIMH Mishkin simulator and creates lifelike introphysic landscapes. We send you down several levels into subterranean territory. Then we use the teleport mode to make our tunnel. As the light show hits your sensory banks, your brain will code them. But, as you yourself remarked, the 'you' coding the pictures won't be the you who would have coded them in nineteen ninety-five. You'll be using your twenty twenty self to do the filing. That's the most intriguing thing. Max, I think I can direct your consciousness to retrieve a different aspect of reality, i.e., change what you bring back. Tell me, how do you feel about squirrels?"

"Squirrels?" Max shrugged. "They're okay, I guess."

"Good, no strong feelings either way. I can work with ambivalence."

"Work with it?"

"It's in the records. You looked at squirrels and missed seeing the mystery man. But your electrical memory will be omnimemory—it will have the whole picture from periphery to center. We just have to direct you away from the periphery. Give you frog vision."

"Oh, great. Do I get to jump around on lily pads?"

"I was speaking metaphorically. Frogs have isolated and limited memory—keyed to recognize flying flies. Of course, they can't see a still fly to save their life. Serve 'em up a whole plate of dead flies and they'll still starve."

"Ugh, so would I."

"We've got to key you to look forward."

"How?"

"Just hold on a second while I try an adjustment. Yes, that should do it. The Max who goes back is going to have a strong aversion to albino squirrels."

"Huh? You didn't tell me I was acquiring any racial prejudices."

"Just albino squirrels, Caine. We fix it so you don't look at some measly little squirrel's antics—you look away."

"So?"

"We get you looking dead north, up the Mall toward Mahler Hall. We send you back so you can see the mystery man."

Max grinned. "No sh—" He stopped himself. "But if I see him I might be able to identify him. I might be able to catch him."

"Yes," Eel said. "But don't get your hopes up. Even if we can adjust the focus, we can't guarantee that you'll be able to *see*. Yes, you may go back and get a glimpse of the joker but learn nothing. Besides, he was probably wearing a disguise."

"Why do you say that?"

"Hat and glasses and floppy coat. Come on— Hey, you want to be an elf or a halfling or a half human or what?"

"What? You mean I have to play a game to do this?"

"I thought I explained that. The Wormwood game program is the only thing complex and powerful enough to handle all the variables and produce the needed range of graphics. We give you an identity and start you off underground. Then, when you get into a jam, we use wizard mode to teleport you down the wormhole. You'll be in the fourth dimension, so you'll have all the time you need then. Just take your memory banks down, trick the electrical spark into rejoining its own track, fuse memory to memory. Mind taking off those glasses again?"

"Why?"

"We don't want to block your compass."

"Sure, anything you say." Max folded his glasses; he shut his eyes when Eel raised the silver tentacled electrodes.

"Now we just hook up your hippocampus and amygdala to the electroencephalograph, and you'll be off to the picture show. So, what's it to be? Halfling, elf—?"

He took a peek. Wires were coiled like serpents from his temples. "Half human, please."

"So be it. What class? Priest, Fighter, Rogue, Paladin, Mage. I'm a Rogue myself."

"What's a Paladin?"

"Sort of a hero. A fighter-priest, a champion."

"A champ—I'll be that."

Eel smiled. "A wise choice. Some magical powers, a good measure of intelligence, charisma. Never underestimate charisma. Now, select your weapons."

Max selected armor and mail and sword, then added a laserlight.

"Feel like taking a trip, Paladin?"

"Have sword, will travel."

"You don't have high blood pressure, do you?" Eel was holding a little spray bottle.

"What is it?"

"Vasopressin. A synthetic peptide hormone that stimulates the recall of old memories."

"Why am I doing this," Max said, but he took the bottle anyway, and sprayed both nostrils.

"*Why* is not the question. Now," Eel said, "just sit back and relax." She began reciting a ditty: "There was a young lady named Bright . . ."

"I feel like Frankenstein," Max said.

"Frankenstein was the doctor, not the monster, Caine."

"And this is Mary Shelley Building. Aren't you going to finish the ditty?"

Eel started over. "There was a young lady named Bright. She went out one day, in a relative way, and returned the previous night." She smiled. "Now, Paladin, just play. When you get into trouble, type Control W. The screen will ask you for the wizard mode password. The password is Thuban. Then use Control T to teleport. Do you have all that, Paladin?"

"What if I need God mode? I bet I can guess the code."

Eel smiled. "Be my guest."

"Sey-mour. Right?"

"Wrong. I told you, he doesn't have a name. Or if he does, it's been washed in a black whirlpool. Don't worry, you won't need God. This is just a very tiny jump. Ready?"

"Thuban. Where'd you think up that?"

"Thuban?" She sighed. "And to think once everyone knew its name. Thuban is a three-point-six magnitude pale yellow binary star in the constellation Draco. It was circumpolar when the pyramids were built. It would still be circumpolar but for the precession of the equinoxes."

"Come on, true north is true north."

"Yes—and no."

"You're saying Polaris wasn't always true north?"

"Precisely. No, our earth clock is faulty. We wobble as we spin in space, arriving each year at the same point twenty minutes early. Five thousand years ago, the Dragon ruled the universe. Simple temporal displacement. We're still approaching Polaris but in less than a decade we will have passed it. For centuries then we will be lost without a star.''

''What's it mean? Thuban?''

''Judge of Heaven.''

''Thuban it is then.''

''We'll try you with the test graphics first. A chair.''

Max watched as the chair appeared before him on the holly screen, a blue chair that had once sat in his grandmother's kitchen against black-and-white linoleum. He reached out—he could almost smell the watery plastic scent of the padded seat. If he looked closely he could see himself in the gleaming chrome of the fluted trim.

''Okay, it's working,'' Eel said, checking Moby's readout.

A shiver ran up Max's spine. How was she doing this? He had fed the machine that chair without realizing it. The machine had picked his brain, the way the kid was always doing. If it could do that . . .

Max looked up and saw Eel watching him. He swallowed. Better not to ask. ''I'm ready—I guess. Lead me to the dungeon.''

Eel smiled. ''It awaits you, Paladin.'' As she spoke a staircase appeared before Max. A spiral of worn, blue flagstones, set by ancient hand.

Max sucked in his cheeks in anticipation. ''Back in a flash, I guess.'' He moved down the steps with the mouse. Presently he came to a plateau in the turning stone. A doorway. There was writing over the lintel ahead, carved holographic letters, a palindrome:

LEWD I DID LIVE & EVIL DID I DWEL

Max looked for a keyhole and found one very low on the door. He bent down and peered through.

"Who's there?" a voice whispered.

He answered without thought, as a Paladin should. "Madam, I'm Adam." The door swung open, and he stepped forward into a giant blue-green, smog-filled chamber. A flesh golem with a putrid stench was waiting.

He used the sword of words to counteract its spell, a spell stronger than putrid stench. Thrusting it aside, he took the flight of stairs that led to the second level. A large evil-looking rabbit was waiting as he reached the last stair; he blinded it with his lightsword.

Three levels down, the Paladin encountered a small yellow dragon. Just a young dragon, without its full fire, but when the dragon opened his mouth, Paladin was nearly fried for breakfast.

"Now," Max heard a voice whisper.

CONTROL W, he typed.

PASSWORD?

THUBAN.

WIZARD MODE ON.

CONTROL T.

Paladin's face was bathed suddenly in a radiant chromatic light. He looked out the pod's window, but all he saw was Seymour Cray's homely mug looking down on him. Was it his imagination, or was Seymour winking?

Then time soared over and around him in a roaring stream. His face, then his whole body, seemed squashed. A circular window appeared in the wall of the cave. Paladin climbed over the sill and vanished.

Although he disappeared from sight only briefly, becoming as ultraradiant as the little brown evidence bag for only the barest fraction of a second—and though his jaunt on the other side was comparatively short—occupying only forty-five temporally marked minutes, a lot seemed to happen. As soon as Max got there, he could see the denseness of it. Unfiltered, the world was a mass of information. It could take ages to wade through the levels.

1995

Saturday, April 15, 3:45 P.M.

Down the long, long back of time he floated till he came to a place where there was a door shrouded in green phosphorescent mist. The mist came in thick clumps, whiting out his progress. At last the door's handle was within his grasp; he looked up. There was writing over the lintel, strange writing he couldn't read. A crack of purple lightning struck behind him; he smelled ozone. He grasped the handle and a wave of time washed away the dreamer. He was falling.

He landed with a wrenching thud; the whole world seemed to tremble and shake and roar. Bells and whistles and shrieks. Who am I? Where am I? When am I? Everything seemed to be moving at astonishing speed: people, things. Only the clock hung limp, its numbers cracked and broken. Shifting, confusing gusts of fleeting memory. Aromas unlocking his brain. Primal memories. Consciousness. Yes. Ten fingers touching thick, white, mug china, bringing it to lips. His lips. The rim was old and softly pitted. His lips parted and sipped: hot nutty ambrosia. He swallowed, tasting the beans. He opened one eye. Strange. Crooked walls. When he moved his gaze, the walls moved too. A buzzing in his ears. Where am I? He opened the other eye. Mica-flecked counter, a paper napkin: Ye Olde Ivory Tower. He lifted his head and found his body in the mirror. A smooth-shaved self hunched atop a vinyl stool that swiveled when he turned, a perfect fit. The bean aroma wafted up to him again. His hands moved and raised the cup again to his lips. He heard the ring of the cash register and the swish of Plexiglas swinging doors. A tingling began at the back of his neck. He blinked and then his eyes seemed to focus more clearly; some inner eye opened. It was like a veil being lifted—sounds and smells and sights were all magnified, immensely. A knife rang against a china plate, and he jumped. His nerves seemed situated abnormally close to his skin. He could hear a dozen conversations from the booths beyond the counter.

2:00 A.M.

Tears on her pillow. She had been crying silently, deep in sleep. Her pillow was drenched in warm salty tears mixed with sweat. She turned it over.

Sleep, Mandy. Go back to sleep. Gradually, sleep unknotted the clenched fists. Her hands folded up under her chin and Amanda slept a dreamless sleep.

The baton snapped with great force. Amanda recoiled and opened her mouth to scream . . .

She woke falling, the scream frozen on her lips. Her body beneath the flannel nightdress was bathed in a cold sweat. "Jenny?" she whispered. She looked over at the sleeping form of her dorm mate. Jenny was sleeping soundly. Damn, what an awful dream. Out damn spot, she cursed, closing her eyes and licking the salt from the back of her index finger. The man had been small and misshapen. He had been limping after her, and she had run, only the road had been sludge. She couldn't see his knife, but she knew it was hidden in the folds of his raincoat.

Her flannel nightgown was damp; still it was comfort for her face and fingers as she tried to nestle safe in bed. Soft like

the blanket her gran had made her as a child, soft as her
gran's voice:

> Backward, turn backward, O Time in your flight,
> Make me a child again, just for tonight.

The bells rang out the hour melody, then tolled: Doom,
Doom, Doom. She closed her eyes tight and buried beneath
the coverlet. From somewhere far off, she heard the mournful
call of the whippoorwill. Cluck whip poor will, cluck whip
poor will, a slow steady rhythm. The bird paused half a beat
and raised the tempo a quarter: whip poor will. Keep still and
the terror will pass.

Whip poor will. The bird dropped the tempo, and its song
blended with the sounds of the frogs and canyon birds in a
mindless chanting cacophony. She might have been sleeping,
as she started once or twice as if she were falling, but if one
bent near and listened very closely a faint conscious melody
could be heard, the most ancient and bloodiest of cradle
songs:

> Rock a bye baby in the treetop
> If the wind blows the cradle will rock
> If the bough breaks, the cradle will fall
> And down will come baby, cradle and all.

Only when the bells rang again did her hands fall away from
the cover and rest like white doves on the pillow.

3:46 P.M.

He swallowed, tasting the rich, bitter coffee in his mouth.
There was someone next to him wearing Old Spice: Pat Ryan
in a blue serge suit, his friend. He held up his hands: strong,
ringless, no-nonsense hands; the hairs aglow in the afternoon
sunlight.

He looked down at the paper in front of him: *Shawneeville Times*, April 15, 1995. INCOME TAX DUE AT MIDNIGHT, the headline read. Taxes, he hated even thinking about them. He scanned down the page, reading by rote: a piece on the spring soccer melee, Panthers over Indians 3–2; an article about the changing of the campus bell tune; a photo of the college president shaking the bell ringer's hand and presenting him with an onyx panther. The old familiar "Blackwell's Tune" was to be replaced by something called a "Parsifal Tune." Wagner.

Wagner. He had never cared for Wagner. He folded the paper and looked at the photograph of the new Miss Shawneeville walking down the rainbow ramp. Why did women cry when they were happy?

Strange. He had been here before. Exactly at this spot where all is always now and time is not. There was nothing special about the spot, nothing special at all, just an ordinary day, but it all seemed suddenly charged with import. Miss Shawneeville, blue-eyed and rosy-cheeked, standing in a pink ball gown at the end of a rainbow-shaped runway, beaming a broad smile. 1995? It could be the 70s. Or the 50s. Decades cycled and recycled. It was all a mix now. On the kitchen radio the Beatles were singing: Paul, Ringo, and George, singing about John: "John, we hardly knew you." It could be any time, couldn't it? He looked out the glass of the revolving doors. April and the sky was gloriously, marvelously blue, a deep cerulean cloud-bearing blue. The signature of our world, our planetary flag.

"You coming back, Max?" Pat's voice was sardonic.

He felt himself grin. So strange. Max, of course, that's who he was. He looked down at his brown sleeve. Detective Max Caine about to speak.

"God, the sky's blue," he said, hearing his voice echo off the crooked walls, knowing as he spoke what Pat would answer.

"Ain't you the poet today?"

"Blue as you, and almost as delightful."

"Ruskin, don't ya think?" Pat said, kidding him.

"Yes," he replied. "Blue is everlastingly appointed by the Deity to be a source of delight."

"I won't tell the guys down at the station. Next thing you know, you'll be quoting Shakespeare."

"No," he said. "It's Rossetti: 'I have been here before/but when or how I cannot tell/I know the grass beyond the door/ the sweet, keen smell . . .' "

"Yeah, yeah, but how about them Pirates."

Max looked up at the clock. He could see the electricity flowing through the wire leading to the round face, could hear its crackle as the long hand moved slowly and inexorably up, all of it utterly irrelevant. Time? All he knew was that there seemed to be plenty of it.

He felt pins and needles in his legs. Suddenly he jolted, up from his seat. "Pat, I forgot, I've got to do something. I'll see you at the station." He grabbed his hat and did protocol with the check. On the way out he looked up at the wall; there was a shiny new token sitting in the phone till. He reached out to take it but stopped himself. After all, he was supposed to set an example. Let someone else phone home. He was out the door by the time the cashier had stuck the receipt on the spindle.

9:45 A.M.

The quarter-hour bells woke Amanda. She had overslept. The day was bright; her roommate's rumpled bed lay empty. I'll never make it on time, she thought, swinging out of her dorm bed and zipping into leathers. Why hadn't her wrist alarm gone off? The toon face read 4:00. Judge Doom was chasing Benny the Cab in Toon Town, but his hands weren't moving. She lifted it to her ear and shook it: the digits didn't budge. No time to buy a battery—she had to make that class.

And Gino would absolutely fire her if she were late one more time. She would have to use the bells for time today.

Grabbing an Umbro jacket, she hit the cool air. It was only then that she remembered the dreams. Pigeons lined Strauss Hall's peaked north roof, silhouetted by sky. Amanda's sharp heels ricocheted off the flagstone, quick reports echoing into the dense jade courtyard ivy. As she passed the quad's cornerstone, she looked back up at the gargoyle. "Hi, ugly, bye, ugly." She cut across Union Lawn and jogged north.

It was a clear, brisk day, with blue sky and flat-topped sheets of clouds. She could see pink buds on the little mountain a mile away, and up where the highway cut above the neighboring village of Juneville, one red car was parked on the overlook. People up there looking down on her looking up. She took the shortcut, off the beaten path, through soft-floored pine woods. She made her class with a minute to spare, slipping into the back aisle just as the attendance count lights went on. She opened her book and read the highlighted passage on John Cage. He had composed by the *I Ching* method: the next note depended on the toss of a coin.

She closed the book. Something was bothering her. It was only when she yawned and her eyes closed involuntarily that she heard the music and felt the dream still lurking. She looked at the clock above the stage and then back at the door. It was still open to admit tardies. She didn't think, just gathered up her books and slid out of her seat, a fraction of a second before the professor took the lectern.

In the hallway she stopped and opened her purse. She rubbed a dab of ocher paint high on her cheekbones and pulled up her boots.

3:47 P.M.

The sky was so utterly buoyantly blue as he crossed the street and passed beneath the arched stone gateway and under the elms. They stretched high and barely leafed above him, like the charred ribs of a burned cathedral. Mosaic light scattered the pavement; his black shadow whipped in and out of light and shade. There was nothing of volition about him, no question of where or how far—no thought at all until he reached the crosswalk and a flock of pigeons erupted like a deck of cards being shuffled by a magician. He heard the distant shouts of a soccer game and the nearby chatter of a squirrel.

Smelly little rabid rodents, I hate squirrels, he thought. He was thirsty suddenly. He had reached the spot where the Mall widened like the end of a telescope. Out of the corner of his eye he saw a white flash and he caught himself, almost stumbling, noticing as he tripped the jagged outline on the sidewalk. "Step on a crack and you break your mother's back," his mother used to tell him, and he had dutifully missed every crack. No time to look at the heart carved in the pavement: Sally loves Billy, 1969. Ancient history.

" 'I have been here before/but when or how I cannot tell.' "

The Mall telescoped before him; the trees moved in the wind high above, their branches creaking like old memories.

He strode out from under the elms and began to ascend the three-step tier leading up to Mahler Hall. The building loomed above like an ancient temple, its arched facade etched against a blue vault of sky. The deep sound of bells punctuated the air. Wagner. It wasn't a pleasant melody. Then the gong tolled the hour: *doom doom doom doom*.

His eyes scanned the high staircase, up and up to the tall green bronze doors. He was still thirsty, and the water inside would be cold. He took the steps two at a time and pulled open the heavy door. The hallway was deserted. He took a sip of water, tasting his metal fillings. Too cold. The door to the music room was open; he went in. It was a big room, with a grand piano and drums, assorted music stands, a bookcase along one wall, a blackboard along the other, and a high arched window with a north view. Empty. It seemed wrong somehow.

4:00 P.M.

Tears came to her eyes. It hurt. Damn it, and she couldn't breathe, there was a sharp pain constricting her chest. She clutched her hand to her chest. "You're crazy," she said, as the bells began. "You hit me!" As she pushed past him the yellow flier fluttered: forty swallows. She ran, the heavy coin bouncing in her pocket. Why couldn't she breathe? She clutched the coin as she started down the steep steps. She should have thrown it in his face.

Then the vise hit her. Christ, something was wrong. It was like the time she had jumped from the sidewalk to reach the highest rung of the school jungle gym and fallen. She had been at the far end of the playground, alone. No one had seen her gasping. She had thought she was dying.

Stop running, catch your wind. Use your head. Stop and let the world catch up. She stopped. Jagged blazes of light ate across her vision, buzzing like a chain saw. As she started down the last stairwell, she saw, through the wired glass window, the heels of a man, entering the music room. Get help. Jag, jag, little blue lightning bolts. She winced, and her hand gripped the silver. Hold on, don't fall.

4:01 P.M.

Max's hands froze on the ivories. He heard noise outside. He went toward the door. Steps, someone running. He looked out into the hall and saw the girl.

The music room. Help there. And then she felt the blood rushing and knew she was drowning. Falling in a slow gyre, she saw him coming toward her, his hand raised.

She opened her mouth, and the vice gripped her tighter. It wasn't fair. The lightning bolts that zigged around her didn't have her number on them.

"Help me," she mouthed, and then the silver cord at the back of her neck snapped and she was falling, a pillar of light bathing them both, a beautiful, warm, golden light. She let go then. Let go of the anger and the fear. She heard the music then like wind and saw the tunnel bright before her, and though the man was holding her, calling her, she felt herself flying away, the music swelling around her. The finale began with its downward tones. D major. A sustained hymn, *Adagio*. Now a semitone away, to D flat, all of it coming at once, a great sad sweetness, *Weltschermz*, nostalgic and yearning, not backward-looking, but forward-looking, into the abyss and beyond.

She was running toward him, her face anguished, a pre-Raphaelite sort of face, pale and glowing, two hectic spots of red on her cheeks, and the most amazing wild hair and purple eyes. She let out a little low-throated cry when she saw him. Her breath was jagged and staccato.

Then her legs buckled. "Help me," she gasped, slumping forward into the music room, upsetting the snares and music stands. He caught her and lowered her to the floor. She was crying, and then her eyes fluttered closed. In the background he heard a hissing sound.

He kicked the door full open with one foot and shouted loudly for help. Then he knelt and with shaking hands felt her neck beneath her ear. His chest seized up. For a space, his heart was as still as hers. Then he knelt and pressed his lips to hers.

The man with the fox-colored eyes stood frozen in the doorway. The pounding was all around him now. With a start he realized it was his heart. He took a deep, jagged breath and collapsed in his chair. Precious oxygen flooded his clogged brain, and the world swelled back around him. Sweet Mother of Christ, the music didn't matter. He was still holding the metal blade!

He almost dropped it, almost smeared the blood on his stiff white cuff. Only with great effort did he catch himself and, grabbing the yellow flier from the bulletin board, blot the silver scabbard. Where now? Where would a Jeffersonian man hide? In his library, of course. Five thousand books, nothing but the finest papers and prints, nothing but canvas and leather. There, on the bottom shelf, back in the last century, beneath the ladder where a man would have to stoop to reach. He thrust the paper-wrapped blade in the folder and stooped down, wedging it tight between Dickens and Poe.

Oh God! He had forgotten the pictures. He grabbed the aquatints and thrust them in the bottom of the filing cabinet.

The music's spell had faded when he went to the men's room and ran cold tap water on his wrists. In the mirror, he looked into his eyes. They seemed ancient, devoid of remorse.

Maestro, maestro. Encore, encore. He was a virtuoso; everything he touched turned to perfect gold. And now he had touched murder.

He blinked a saurian eye and smiled. Amber eyes, white pearly teeth. Blood as cold as winter mud.

He adjusted his cuffs, then wheeled to the stairwell and headed down the ramp. We are all capable of evil thoughts, he mused, but so few are capable of evil deeds. At least he was not common. Below people were gathered in little clumps: men with hats and notepads and electronic equipment, a group of blue coats, a man running a camcorder. He saw a young man standing with Miss Tilly, deep in conversation. He felt his brow glistening and realized that Miss Tilly was looking strangely at him. She knew.

His face flushed, and he felt a trickle of sweat run down his back. He saw her glance at the metal detectors leaning against the tile wall. She was warning him.

He went back upstairs and shut the frosted glass door. He sat at his desk and put on a tape of Mahler's Ninth, his eyes growing darker and more intense. Two small, blue, lightning-bolt veins swelled on his temples. His features contracted and glowed. The second movement began in C major. Death as the fiddler. His fingers tapped the rhythm on the arm of his chair. The fiddler picked up the beat, a scherzo with two trios in F major, first a fast, gay, parodistic country waltz; then the music twisted into a sardonic bitter dance, grotesque and mocking.

And now he had Rose Tilly. In her eyes had been his future, a future bounded by banal, artsy-fartsy knickknacks and cloying perfume. Belladonna—every loaf, stem, and berry fatal—staring at him with poison-widened eyes. He could see it as plainly as if it had already happened: Years and years of lifting that plain blue smock to quiet Rose. Pink, soft skin, arching up to meet his rough beard as he parted her pliant petals. Hoist with his own petard. He had underestimated her, miserably. All those years she had served him in mouselike silence and all those years she had been watching, prying, waiting for her chance.

She would save his skin today. As she had done just then, warning him to disappear. People trusted Rose; she was so mousy no one could mind her or notice. He closed his eyes and imagined her carrying the killing blade past the metal detectors.

He stopped the tape and fast-forwarded it past the A minor double fugue with its manic tempo—the master at his worst dementia—to the D major interlude, an oasis of peace.

She didn't have him for life. He looked down at his hands. A man could do many things. He couldn't help wondering about the blood, wondering what it would feel like to see it spurting. Would it coat his fingers with a tiny minuscule spray, shade his cuff the color of an autumn maple?

*   *   *

The next time Max stopped to think, he was standing before the surveillance camera.

"Testing, one, two, three. Testing, one, two, three . . ."

Miss Tilly appeared in the doorway. "It's probably not important, but—"

He leaned forward to catch her words, watching her like a young devotee in a front-row seat, and in that instant felt himself falling, falling back down the long corridor of time, into the perfect black of space, into the future.

2020

Wednesday, April 15, 8:30 A.M.

"Testing, one, two, three . . ." The camera panned around to the door, toward the rosy-cheeked woman. "It's probably not important, but—" Bright light. Everywhere. Noises and static.

Max opened his eyes and stared at the larger-than-life celluloid that had just spoken. The baby-faced man had stopped moving; he was frozen on the screen.

"Just a nano."

Who had said that? He tried to sit up.

"Give the cobwebs time to clear." A hand pushed him back down. "Not yet."

Far-away voices, then bells, colors dancing. A haunting little tune playing over and over. Sweet strings and rose water.

"Try opening your eyes now." A kid's voice.

He blinked. Laser lights glared overhead. Behind him he heard the noise of a fan. He breathed in and smelled ozone, banana, and Chinese food. He reached up to rub his eyes and met the coils of the wires at his temples. He still felt cobwebs inside his head—thick, dusty cobwebs. Everything seemed to be bathed in a dull film, and rubbing his eyes didn't help. He closed them again.

The veil lifted and the textured world appeared again. His fingers, the touch of the girl's skin, a pulsing smell of roses.

"Max, try opening your eyes again."

He pondered the request. What did the kid want?

"Maxwell Caine, I know you're here. Come back right now."

He floated to the top and raised one eyelid. The kid was standing there with her little monkey, cute as pi. Then he remembered what she had been trying to do.

"Did it work?" he asked, his voice coming out gruff and unoiled. He cleared it, and his eyes blinked open and shut, then seemed to work.

"You glowed red, then blue. I think you made it down the rabbit hole. Let's see what we got." She rewound the warped tape and pressed PLAY. The tape was still frozen. Quadrant eighteen still blinked off and on: elephants, white elephants, dark elephants.

Eel turned to Max. "What do you remember?"

He frowned. "I was in here with you, then—"

"Yes?" Eel's expression was expectant.

Max's face paled as memory congealed in his mind. "I was drinking coffee in the diner and reading the paper. There was a strange quality to it all. I left the diner and started up the Mall. I heard the bells, had this strange feeling of foreboding. They seemed to be tolling doom, doom."

"So, how do you feel about albino squirrels?"

"Stinky little rodents—huh?" Memory came oozing back. Two memories. Some other Max who once or twice had sat on the park bench under the elms and fed them peanuts. Yes? No—squirrels had rabies, rabies made you thirsty, gave you lockjaw. What had this kid done to his brain? Made a mush? His memory of the last two-score minutes seemed clouded, as if he had woken from a deeply imagined dream.

Then his head cleared and he remembered what he had gone for. His mystery man. But there was no mystery man, was there? "Eel, I saw the steps. There was no one there. I went inside, and there was no one there, either. There was no mystery music man. She wasn't killed in the music room. How blind I've—"

He stopped, dizzy. There were two Maxes now. All those years he had been chasing a phantom. Miss Tilly had lied. Why? Just the attention-seeking behavior of a middle-aged spinster? Had he dismissed her too quickly?

"I was all wrong," he said. "And you were right. I'm no closer to catching the killer."

"I thought something like that might happen. You got a better view this time—there just wasn't anything to see." Eel was studying a printout Moby had just delivered. "Here are the temporal results. The graft occupies a space of approximately forty-five minutes, just about middle of the curve for electrical shock loss. You seem to have come up slightly behind the target. That's the temporal displacement effect. There's a few jerks on the memory tape. And some oddities." She swallowed loudly.

"Oddities, Eel?"

"Of course, that's to be expected when dealing with such ephemerality. There's a fuzzy area of memory at the beginning, an overlap of perhaps a hundred seconds. And your reaction to the albino squirrel carried over to all the squirrels. You started thinking rabies, and that subconsciously made you thirsty. You hurried up to Mahler from that point. You appear to have arrived at Mahler Hall just a shade earlier than expected."

"The timing was off. I knew that. I felt it as soon as I entered Mahler. Up till then, I'd been floating. Suddenly I felt like a puppet on the wrong stage."

"You got there before you did last time. If that's the case there should be evidence." She turned around to Moby. "Moby, can you run the engrams for temporal input? He must have noticed the time on the hall clock. Can we get a readout on that?"

She turned back to Max. "You don't have to go under. Just close your eyes and relax. Moby'll be done with you in half a nano."

He did as he was told.

"Okay, thanks Moby," he head Eel say. "You can come back now, Max."

He opened his eyes. Eel was reading the printout.

"Interesting, very interesting. There's not a single shot of a clock from the moment you enter till you go down the timehole. But the bells."

"What about the bells?"

"According to Moby, there's a discrepancy in your previous testimony and your present memory graft. Earlier you said the bells were chiming as you approached the Mahler steps. But your memory has them chiming as you mount the steps. The acoustic calendar is off."

Max closed his eyes, and the memories welled up like music. Amanda, running toward him, opening her mouth. "Help me." Her voice wasn't as he had imagined it. It wasn't light and melodious but deep and sultry. And there was some other sound in the background: a low, distinctive hiss.

Max's face paled. Or had he imagined it? Two sets of memories. The Amanda he had found on the floor of the music room, and the Amanda who had come running into his arms, the silent Amanda and the one who had spoken. He looked at the clock. Only seconds had elapsed, but his world had changed immeasurably. Two memories, two sets of sensations separated by the thinnest of molecular veils. His head spun and his heart began to flutter. He felt hot and cold.

"Hold on," Eel said. "You can handle it."

"But—"

"The test of a man's intelligence is his ability to hold two opposing facts at the same time without going crazy. Courage, Caine. You're not crazy. You haven't changed anything but a few engrams. You haven't changed the basic fabric of the case. You arrived a little earlier on the scene, got a different angle of the track. Nothing's different."

"She didn't speak to me before—I remember being surprised when she did. Her voice wasn't as I'd imagined it. I know her voice now. If only I could have helped her."

"Perhaps she spoke before and you just didn't hear it. Before she was a tree falling alone in a forest. This time you were in the forest with her. Too bad she didn't tell you her killer's name."

Max shrugged. "If she even knew it." He took out a handkerchief and wiped his brow. "I'm okay now. I think I understand. Reality hasn't changed, just my view of it."

"Exactly. Like I told you, I don't think paradoxes are possible. You can't change history. Time's a river and you're just a small reed being carried along. You might end up with a different view from the bank, but you won't change the course of the river."

"Not even if I'm the reed that completes the dam?"

"Pretty grandiose thinking for a reed. No, it's not likely you'll find any of Bradbury's butterflies to step on here. From what I can see, you can only change things that don't matter. Call it a kind of principle of least disturbance." Eel laughed. "Just plug it into the old physics formula and peel off a new layer of reality. It's aleatoric, life is. Time's like white light, primordial."

"Prime what? Mind bringing that down to a level I can more clearly misunderstand?"

"Time is ubiquitous; it permeates every pore of the universe. Time is like an engram in a brain—it's coded over a vast section of cells. It's linked to our language/memory system. Our perception of it as reality is just a probabilistic illusion, linked to the decay of subnuclear particles. At the deepest level, in the center of the black hole, time and space don't exist. And now I know what I've suspected," Eel said, clasping her hands. "God plays dice with the universe."

Max smiled, and in his head a picture appeared. Ivory dice, with red and black numbers. Strange dice. He had an idea. "Eel, back that up again, will you? Run it in slo-mo."

Eel went over to the video and reversed the tape. "I'll be back in a moment. Want anything from the vending machine?"

"Thought you had your own supply."

"Cleaned out. I'll just go to the next level."

"Nothing for me, thanks." Max watched his celluloid self walk jerkily backward across the wall against the cloud-filled, blue, vaulting window. High, white, cumulus clouds scooted across the sky. It didn't make any difference which way clouds blew. A perfect day. The screen Max smiled a smooth-shaven smile and moved back to indicate the chalk outline. Max froze the frame. Was it his imagination, or had the outline shifted?

He had gone back and replayed life, replayed it with subtle discrepancies. A different perspective in time, and now this feeling of great waste. He had spent a quarter of a century chasing a ghost. History itself had not changed—only the chalk outlines had been shifted.

Eel came back in carrying two cans of soda. The door hissed as it closed itself.

"That's it!" Max yelled.

"It's only Coke."

"No, the noise. I heard a hiss. It was the door closing. The door Amanda came from. It was on a spring; it hissed as it closed. I heard it."

"Which door?"

"I don't know. I didn't look up. I was too intent."

"How many doors were there?"

"Three galleries. Three."

"You could eliminate two-thirds of your suspects. Too bad."

"But couldn't we go back again? We've still got the time-hole, don't we? Do a double exposure on the exotic light. Get there just a tad earlier, see which door it was. One more shot at the truth—how about it, kid?"

"Hmm. The truth. I've been thinking, Caine. What if you're just the worm on someone's hook? What if someone is using you?"

"For what?"

"To catch something."

"Like what?"

"I wish I knew."

"So what's to worry? We've proved I can change my focus and my speed. Just rig up some more tricks. Get me there a little faster, a little closer to the door. Make me hate coffee and order milk. It won't be so hot. I'll get out of the diner sooner."

Eel laughed. "I told you, Max, you can't change the fabric of history. You may be able to change the design on that one small square of timespace, but your personal history is woven across many layers of your mind. You won't be able to change anything of consequence. You can't save her, Max."

Max stared at Eel. He knew she was right. One couldn't rip up twenty-five years just like that. Amanda was buried on the mountain. Her body had moldered long ago. He was here in 2020, burnt out, frustrated, beyond revival. "I know all that. I just want to catch the guy who did it."

"You are sure it is a man?"

"Had to be."

"Maybe I could work on the thirst response. Inject you with a mild memory of hydrophobia to increase your thirst."

"What?"

"It would be quite harmless."

"You're going to give me rabies?" Max stood up and delivered his opinion with a gnash of his teeth.

"You don't need to start foaming at the mouth. I can't inject premotivation. Only base desires."

Max sighed. "Couldn't you just give me clap?"

"Clap doesn't make you thirsty."

Max shook his head and slumped in a chair. "Do what you have to do. Rabies, squirrel phobia. While you're at it, why don't you throw in a little snake phobia—get me looking for where that hiss is coming from."

"Oh, cheer up, please," Eel said, throwing a ball of paper at him. "You got back your memory, be glad of that. Go confront Miss Tilly. Maybe she was covering up for the killer. She might be ready to confess. Call her."

"You think the answer's in the present?"

"I do now."

Miss Tilly's yearning face. Had she been looking at the same door? "Then what?"

"If we don't get anywhere, we try the timehole again. Send you back and see what else you can see. Maybe you can get there earlier. Maybe Amanda will tell you the killer's name—if she knows it—if she's not shielding him. Maybe you'll see which door she came from. Who knows, maybe you'll see the murderer."

"Well, let's get on with it. The early bird catches the worm."

Eel looked up at the clock.

Max followed her look. "I keep forgetting it's so early. Maybe we'll give her a little time. So, what do you Nightmode folk do now?"

"Eat Chinese, play chess."

"For breakfast?"

"Why not?"

"Then what?"

She shrugged. "Feed Lucy."

"Sleep? Nap? You ever do those things?" He looked over at her beaten pillow.

"Not till noon."

"Does anybody—I mean, no one comes and tells you to brush your teeth and turn out the lights?"

"No." Her voice was disdainful.

"No?"

"Moby reads to me sometimes. Or sings."

"The Cray? I suppose he tucks you in, too?"

"Tucks?"

Max shook his head. "Don't need anyone, do you? Old Moby there takes care of it all." Max glared at the machine and stuck out his tongue.

"Now look who's anthropomorphizing."

"I bet he gives you whale music for lullabies."

"What if he does?"

"Probably the song the bulls sing to lure fish to their baleen, variations on killing songs."

"I told you they were love songs. Courtship songs."

"Same thing, eh?"

"And you think *I* have an adjustment problem. It's not the same thing at all. You married?"

"What do you think?"

"How would I know? You've never thought about it one way or the other."

"Believe me, if I had a wife, I'd have thought of her by now, one way or the other."

"Really?"

"Kid, there's a lot they never tell you in books. Moby can't teach you everything. So do you want some breakfast, or not? Yes or no?"

Max didn't give her time to think. "Yes," she spilled out, laughing.

"Let's go then. Hot cross buns are waiting." Eel jumped off her stool and was halfway out the door before Max had taken his first step. He stepped carefully, half expecting the ground to come up to meet his foot. It didn't.

"Well, what do you think, Eel?" Max licked the last morsel of buttered hot cross bun from his finger and looked at the clock. "Don't old folks get up early?"

"You should know. But don't you have to go to work?"

"Wednesday's my late day. A long-standing tradition with my secretary. Besides, this is work."

"What will your boss say?"

"I am my boss. So, ready to perform a little mind reading?"

"If we can have the top down."

"I didn't mean *my* mind. Stop that, will you? It gives me the willies. But you can have the top down—unless it starts to rain."

"But it was such a nice picture. It's primordial, isn't it?"

"Huh?" Damn the kid, at it again with her fifty dollar words. Well, she wasn't going to get his goat. "You'll see," he said.

"Does it have HDTV?"

"Nope."

"A holly navigational system?"

"Nope."

"Must be like you."

"How's that?"

"An antique."

"Like her?" he asked fifteen minutes later when he opened the door to his garage.

"Like it? Are you kidding? Can I touch it?"

"Her." Max nodded. "Be careful though. Name's Lady." She was a white boxy BMW, an '88, sort of a graduation present to himself.

"She's in better shape than you, Maxwell," the kid said.

"Thanks a lot. Hey, what's your real name, anyhow?"

She made a face. "Eloise Elysium Lacoste," she said, running the words together.

"Who thought that up?"

She shrugged. "Some bigwigs. Moby gave them some help."

"That figures," he said. "Go on, put the top down."

Eel eagerly pressed the button, and the top reared up noisily and accordioned slowly back. "Wow," she said, and then sneezed.

"Allergies?"

"Yeah, but that's okay." She sneezed again and her eyes watered. "I'll get used to it."

Max handed her a handkerchief, which she folded into a makeshift filter. So they hadn't removed all the genetic deficiencies.

Max took the overpass to Juneville, the village on the

plateau at the foot of little Mount Shawnee. Lone Eagle Mountain and Old Indian Mountain could be seen east and west in the distance, but the valley was wide at Juneville, and the little mountain loomed larger than the distant peaks. Eel was strapped into the black, glove-leather bucket seat, playing with the musical dial. It was a dour, humid day, reminiscent of ancient watery times. The road gleamed blindingly before him. Stringy yellow clouds whipped past; steam rose from the dank canal.

"Find an oldie," Max said.

Eel found a western, a lusty Dolly Parton love song, as old as the rounded hills. Max found himself humming along. The scenery was enthralling—his jaunt into time had rejuvenated him, left him with a fresher vision. Ridge and valley, valley and ridge, the roots of ancient mountains that once soared higher than the Himalayas. Grand majestic peaks of ancient rock thrust up and folded when continents had collided, deeply grooved by rivers long dead. Twenty-five thousand years earlier ice a mile high had gouged and rasped the mountain's core.

Did Eel know all that? Probably.

They passed a talus slope; the rounded stones gleamed in the yellow light. Billions and billions of years—and his own life was bounded by days and hours. He caught a glimpse of movement in the woods flanking the rocky slope. "Hey, Eel, did you know there used to be black panthers in these woods?"

"*Panthera pardus*. I know new world cats were common to this area, but they weren't black."

"You ever see a real one?"

"No."

"Well, I did. One night when I was six. And boy was it black."

"Hogwash, Max."

"I bet you never heard the story about how the black panthers got here."

She sniffed. "I don't believe Moby has told me that fable."

"And you a valley girl. Well, you see, Shawnee—that was the name of the Indian princess who used to live here. She was sort of a Joan of Arc princess, the leader of all the braves. She never married, and she lived to be a hundred."

"When was this quaint person supposed to have lived?"

"Well, I don't have a date. She lived long ago, when the Gitchie-Manitto still visited the earth, before the mountains were born."

Eel raised an eyebrow. "You mean, 'once upon a time.' "

"Yeah." They had reached a fork in the road. The little road to the left led up to the mountain cemetery. To the right were lanes lined with old three-story houses. He turned right.

"So, you see, this princess named Shawnee—Shaw-nee really—well, she was a great personal friend of the Gitchie-Manitto, and he watched over her and helped her plant and hunt and protect her tribe from her enemies. He gave her this beautiful little cedar forest. And she lived there with her tribe, and the only time anyone was unhappy was during certain cold months of the winter when the north winds would blow . . ."

They had come a quarter mile; Max pulled up to a tin mailbox and killed the motor. The flag was up.

"Better put the top up. Same button." He latched it in place. "I'll finish your story later."

"I can't wait," Eel said, giggling. They walked up the driveway to the big necco-wafer-brown house with pink gingerbread trim. SHAWNEEVILLE RETIREMENT HOME, the peeling sign proclaimed. The house was going, a centurion, the victim of age and weather. Max saw a trace of greasy slime protoplasm mold growing on the naked porch rail. There was a duck mat in front of the door. "Wipe your feet," it said. They both did. Max let Eel sound the old-fashioned knocker-bell. A cascade of flowery notes sounded inside, and almost immediately the door was thrown open by a white-coated nurse.

"We're here to see Miss Tilly. I called."

"Oh, yes. In the third suite on the left. She's expecting you. Don't expect too much, this isn't one of her good days." She whispered, "Alzheimer's. And the light hurts her eyes."

They walked through a hallway flanked with cheaply upholstered eye-searing plaids, down a green striped carpet.

When they entered, Miss Tilly leaned forward from her wheelchair and pushed her blue butterfly and rhinestone mauve-tinted glasses back on her nose. The curtains were drawn; a dim rectangle of light from the open bathroom provided the only illumination. She scowled up at them. "Do I know you?"

"I'm Detective Caine," Max said. "We met on the Zephyr case in nineteen ninety-five."

"Nineteen ninety-five?"

"Long time ago. And this is Eloise. I wanted to ask you a few questions, Miss Tilly. You are Miss Tilly?"

"Hardly get any visitors, so nice to talk to visitors." She indicated the two wing chairs, and pressed the call button on her bedside table. "I'll just have the girl bring in tea."

Max smiled. "No, please don't bother. I just wanted to ask you a few questions. Do you remember the case?"

"Some pinup, wasn't it? Didn't ever find the boyfriend."

"What boyfriend?"

"It's always the boyfriend. Don't you watch Jessy the Robocop? Always always."

Max looked at Eel. Hopeless, wasn't it? Eel shook her head just slightly: No, go on. Ask her the questions.

"I understand you've just moved here. It seems a nice place."

Miss Tilly leaned forward. "I'll tell you. There is no such thing as a nice hotel anymore. The service is terrible here."

Max smiled weakly, feeling sorry for the old crone. "Miss Tilly, I'd like to show you something. You mind if we use your media center?"

"Help yourself."

Max loaded up the tape and played it forward to the warp. He left the audio on. "It's probably not important, but—" He let it repeat three times and then cut the sound. "Do you remember saying those words to me?"

"I just heard them, of course I remember. I'm not senile, you know." She wheeled closer to the screen and broke into a large smile. "I remember that dress. My simple blue smock."

"I wasn't suggesting, Miss Tilly. I would just like you to tell me again, in your own words, what you told me that day—as best you can remember."

"I—" She stopped. "I'm afraid I don't remember."

"Okay, just one more thing. Look at the screen. In the corner there."

"Yes?"

"Do you remember who you were looking at?"

"Is that you? Why, you of course."

"Wasn't there someone behind me?"

"I remember that dress," she said. Miss Tilly stared at the screen. A small smile crept up the side of her face. She half turned and seemed to be talking to the fireplace. "Remember that blue smock. You mocked me for it."

"Miss Tilly?" Max reached out and touched her sleeve. She seemed to be carrying on a conversation with another universe. A little malevolent light shone in her eyes.

"Miss Tilly?"

She swallowed. "Who are you?" she asked, wheeling around. "Did I meet you?"

"Yes, Miss Tilly. You invited me to have some tea."

"Of course I did. And that lazy girl hasn't brought it yet. Did you say you were a detective?"

"Yes, ma'am." Max looked over at Eel and sighed. Miss Tilly reached out and grabbed the dish at her side. "Have some Gummi Bears? Come on, Eloise . . ." She shot a triumphant look at Max.

Eel shook her head.

"Don't be shy. Cat got your tongue?"

Eel screwed up her nose and looked at Max. He motioned for her to help herself. She reached in and took a purple one and put it in her mouth; her mouth promptly puckered.

"Perhaps you don't like purple."

"Tastes like worms."

Max handed his handkerchief to Eel. "Sorry about that, ma'am. Not used to that candy, I guess."

She held the dish out to Max. "Detective?"

He shook his head. "Not while I'm on duty."

She turned to Eel, who was staring intently at a small, plastic snow dome. "Eloise, do you like that? Go on, pick it up and shake it."

Eel picked up the dome and shook it, and a smile spread on her face as the glittery fragments flew up and rained down on the globeworld within. A snowman with blue mittens raised his arms to the snow; little flecks alighted on the miniature green pines.

"Eloise, you may take that if you like."

Eel looked up at Miss Tilly and she backed up a bit. "No, thank you." Eel set the snow world on the table.

Max gave Miss Tilly his card. "Any time, night or day. If you can remember anything about that day, please call."

"What day?" Miss Tilly asked, a worried look on her face.

9:45 A.M.

When they had gone, Miss Tilly took off her glasses and wheeled to the window bay. Nosy, nosy man. Not very smart. She had heard the nurse whispering to him—her hearing was keen, even if her memory suffered gaps. He had been easily fooled, lulled. He still thought her a nice old lady. She had brought him coffee once a day for six weeks following the investigation. They'd had a surveillance camera on the room—the "scene of the crime," he used to call it, and he would lock himself in there for hours, tinkering on the piano and doing a monitor of the tapes. The killer never showed up in the camera, never returned to the "scene of the crime."

She laughed. She had fooled him then, waiting on him like a servant, never receiving a level glance of interest. And she had fooled him today.

She saw the man and the kid climb in the car. That Eloise, though. What a strange child. She had given her the chills.

She turned to the mantle and addressed the urn. "Remember that blue smock, Luther? You mocked me for it, but you couldn't wait to get it off that night. My wedding dress."

She turned back to the window. Why hadn't they gone yet? Were they sitting in the car, talking about her? Did they suspect? What if they had seen the knife?

She wheeled to her desk, lifted the lid, and started searching through papers. There had been a note from Luther's sister when she sent the ashes. She knew about the two of them, she wrote; she sympathized. There was a number on the note she was to call if she were ever in trouble. She had the number here somewhere; if only her hands would stop shaking she could find it.

She calmed herself as she was wont to do by going again to the flames. Wheeling toward the fireplace, she looked up at the ceiling fixture. She would have to find another hiding place. All these years, and *now* they came snooping.

At the hearth, she forced herself to her feet and took down the urn into her lap. She took only a tiny pinch, rubbing the ash into her forehead as if it were a sacrament.

"Well?" Max asked Eel when they were back in Lady.

"She was lying through her false teeth, Max. No micro tremor in her voice at all—she was obviously extremely stressed and on guard the whole visit. That was all an act. Wish I could hypnotize her."

"Pretty convincing act."

"Oh, I'm not saying she's not afflicted. That's a lady with very random brainwaves. But she was still acting. When you asked her if she was looking at someone behind you, she looked up and to the right, the neurolinguistic eye movement for memory. I caught a glance of a face. There *was* someone behind you."

"You got a picture?"

"Half a picture. She's got very solid defenses—the man was behind a lead veil and wouldn't stay focused."

"But it was a man?"

"Yes."

"No face?"

"No face. Even if I got a face, it would probably be too distorted to use. Women, you know, invent their memories, fabricate men."

"You mean lie."

"Not just Miss Tilly."

"I know. Believe me, I know. I just don't know why."

"You asking me?"

"I didn't really expect an answer."

"But I had one ready. It's your fault."

"Mine?"

"Men encourage women's exuberant excess of subjective propensities. At least that's what Moby says."

"Moby again. What's it mean, anyhow?"

"That women have to be all things to all men. Men don't permit them a true nature. They lie to order, in order to please."

"Or not to please."

"I think it's just part of our cyclical nature. The world begins anew each day. Women are more dependent on the structure of the whole field of perception; they accept that field as a whole without question. Just listen to us talk. Women use present tense; men are more likely to use past and future. It's not pure falsity—it's just our nature."

"To lie."

"When necessary."

"For the fun of it. I tell you, you're foreign creatures. My father always told me that. A different species."

"I won't deny that. A decidedly more adaptable species than man."

"Fickle."

"Actually, women's 'variability' is an asset, Max. It's what keeps marriages together."

Max laughed. "You're saying lying keeps marriages together?"

"As I was saying, yes, it obviates the crude requirement of polygamy. To be one woman is to be all women. Therefore, one good wife can act the part of a harem. Keep her man happy. It takes imagination to lie."

Max shook his head. "Boy, I've got to meet the guy you marry. Watch out."

"I'm not a boy."

"I know that."

"You said, b—"

"It's just an expression, okay?"

"I'm never getting married. Boys. Ugh."

"Never, eh?" He smiled. "I wouldn't bet on it." He turned the key in the ignition, and Lady purred to life. "So, we go back and try again?"

"As soon as I work out the temporal coordinates. Won't take me too long." She reached up and adjusted the rearview mirror. "Don't look now, but Miss Tilly's watching us through the front parlor window." Eel slouched down in her seat.

The hair rose on the back of Max's neck. The air was laden suddenly with electricity. Beyond the mountain, a wash of yellow-gray clouds banked and rose. Lightning flickered in the distance.

"Better get home," Max said, stepping on the accelerator. They outran the storm, pulling into the narrow garage just as the first drops of acid rain dotted the white enamel. The storm began then in earnest, pelting the garage's tin roof with a barrage of black hail. A typical April storm, it would blow over soon.

"What do we do now?" Eel asked.

Max reached in the glove compartment and took out two chamois cloths. "We fix Lady's face," he said, tossing Eel a cloth. "Get all the drops."

They finished drying Lady and walked to the doorway. The rain and hail had stopped, and a wind was already blowing the pavement dry.

"I'll walk you home," Max said.

He walked her to the front of the AI Building and watched as she drank water from the outdoor spigot. "You going to do the program now?"

She yawned. "Probably."

"Maybe a nap is in order."

She shrugged and took another drink. "So," she said, wiping her mouth on her dirty sleeve, "how did the panthers get there?"

Max smiled. "Well, once upon a time— How far did I get?"

"Up to where everything was great except for the cold north wind."

"I'll just walk you upstairs," he said, picking up where he had left off. The monkey came flying into Eel's hair when they went in. He started again.

". . . and on the night she died, a titanic storm blew up, more terrible than even the oldest person could remember." He walked to the cot and turned the pillow and fluffed it. "The winds howled and shrieked, and the trees bent double, on and on, all through the night. Not until dawn did the fierce storm abate. And guess what? When the sun rose, in the center of the cedar forest plain stood a new mountain, a sylvan princess covered with dense groves of cedar and pine and birch, a shelter from the cold north winds. And on that night were also born the Shawnee lions."

"I bet the PR office made up this story."

"Shh . . ." He shook his head solemnly. "An old Indian told me this, Indian Joe. Scout's honor."

"Really?"

"Ask Moby."

"I believe you."

Max smiled. "Well, did you like it? The story?"

"It was okay."

"Just okay? I suppose Moby does better?"

Eel giggled.

"Well, does he?"

"Remember, you asked. No going off in a blue funk." She turned to the white computer. "Moby, I'm tired."

A deep and sonorous silvery voice filled the entire room, invading every pore of his being: God and Moses and every Elizabethan actor who ever graced a stage rolled into one. Even the little monkey was still, listening.

"ONCE UPON A TIME . . ."

Max slammed the door on his way out.

He took a long, slow walk across campus, thoughts reeling in his brain like clothes in a tumble drier. It was past noon when he started back.

He tiptoed into the lab. Gentle lapping music ebbed and flowed from the megaspeakers. He looked at the kindly reflection of Seymour Cray.

"SHH," Moby said.

"Yeah, yeah," Max whispered. He took a step toward the game console and peeked in. The screen controls were aglow. She had not gone straight to bed. She had played Wormwood by the light of the sun—the kid was brave, wasn't she? How far had she gotten, he wondered, answering his own question by flipping the control to IMAGE. A hydra-headed dragon was approaching in the distance.

The bells played the quarter-hour melody. Max dimmed the screen and started to tiptoe out.

"I wasn't asleep." Eel's voice rang out. "Just napping. I dreamed you were William James."

"William James?"

She laughed. "You brought me a jam tart and were wearing a pork pie hat. We discussed the etheric structure of timespace. Guess I must be hungry. Bring any donuts?"

"Couldn't you dream I was Kevin Costner?" Max smiled. "*More* donuts? But you had three hot cross buns for breakfast."

"Who's Kevin Costner?"

It was his turn to laugh. "Ancient history obviously. So what else did I say in the dream?"

"You were telling me about a train, the Flying Scotsman. You said it was going to jump the bridge."

"But that's a true story. It happened, didn't it? North of the Firth of Forth. Some man dreamed the dream, and then, five months to the day later, the train jumped the track at the end of the bridge."

"James Dunne, of course. I confused the two Jameses in my subconscious." Eel rubbed her eyes. "The point is, effects exist independent of antecedent causes."

"The point is this," Max said. "James Dunne was not on the train that jumped the parapet. He was able somehow— perhaps at the moment of his death—to go back and warn his younger innocent self. He avoided the future."

Eel smiled. "Just as I said. But he didn't change history, only his biography. He couldn't stop the train from jumping the track." She got up and yawned, smoothed her black-and-white striped top, and shuffled to the crystal pod.

"Just a few final touches and we'll have you out of here. Come on, you may as well get hooked up."

"Just a sec. Give me a capsule summary. How *do* you do this?"

She pointed at a diagram in the corner of the board. "Think of the black hole as an electrically conducting, spheroidal membrane. We set up an interacting magnetic field and use a simple generator to extract energy and produce a voltage differential between the poles of the sphere and its equator. The wires and brushes make electrical contact at the axis and equator, and we get power. We wormhole through the membrane and prop it open with exotic material. Just simple mechanics.''

"Oh, I'm sure. I won't even bother to take notes.''

Eel smiled. "As I said before, the universe is really very simple—it's just composed of such ridiculously large numbers. In timespace itself the concept of linear movement is nonsensical. Synchronized past is always present. So, at least in theory, you can visit any section of timespace you please—with one exception of course.''

"What's that?''

"No rainbows.''

Max laughed. "Why no rainbows?''

"Because they're not there, really; they're like time, an illusion. There are no illusions in timespace. That's why clocks don't work in the fourth dimension; why knots won't stay tied.''

"But rainbows are real.''

"If rainbows were real, they would appear differently from different angles; they wouldn't always look perfectly symmetrical. A rainbow is just a shared illusion. A phantom like a mirage. A rainbow doesn't reflect in a mirror. Rainbows and vampires belong to the other dimension. No, rainbows are merely God's covenant that the fourth dimension is still within us, God's promise not to take away our *psi* sight.''

"Hmm. Only humans chase rainbows. Lucy can't see them?''

"No, Lucy can't see them, no animal can see them. Only the highest primates have the circuitry built in for going beyond Euclidian three-dimensional space. The rainbow is proof of that, our covenant.''

"Well, were there any rainbows the day Amanda died?"

Eel shrugged. "If there were, I'd never be able to prove it."

Max sat back and watched Eel complete the final calculations; he didn't even wince when she attached the electrodes.

"Promise to come right back?" she asked.

He looked at the clock: 1:30. "I'm here, aren't I?"

"Yes."

"And I'm not actually going anyplace, right?"

"Right enough."

"Okay, I promise."

She gulped. "It's just that if you somehow suddenly weren't here, I'd probably just think I was dreaming."

"Would you miss me?"

"How could I miss a dream?"

"Well, I'll just have to come back and bother you then."

She smiled. "Cross your heart and hope to die, stick a needle in your eye?"

He raised two Boy Scout fingers. "Cross my heart and hope to die."

Eel cocked her head. "Yeah, *this* you promises."

"This me? What's that supposed to mean?"

"It's ironic how the Creator made a creature with the capacity to both promise and lie. No other creatures make promises. It's irrational to even ask you. Did you know, none of the atoms in your body now existed twenty-five years ago."

"Oh, yes, they did. I've got you there. My new engram, my nineteen ninety-five memory trace, it's physical, an atomic presence. I've got that, don't I? A quarter-century-old patch of that younger me."

Eel studied him. "You're right, old man. Well, you ready to play Wormwood, Paladin?"

He settled back in the chair. "Why do I keep thinking of Madame Curie, playing with her fatal uranium?"

"Probably because you're about to glow in the dark."

"It made her immortal, didn't it? And if someone could have warned her, she might never have been famous. Which do you suppose she would have chosen?"

"I think her uranium. You ready?"

"Would it make me immortal, if I violated causality?"

"Eternally. Only no one would ever know. It wouldn't make any difference to anyone. It would be like the sky turning yellow overnight and everyone knowing it used to be blue but not being able to prove it to the little tykes seeing the sky for ever after yellow."

Max nodded. "I see what you mean. You'd just forget I ever existed?"

Eel shrugged. "Maybe we'd have met anyhow." She stepped back from the pod. "Ready?"

"No ditties for me today?" He grinned. " 'There was a young man from Tass . . .' "

"Who was most terribly crass."

"No, who went to the head of the class."

"Sure, Caine. You know, I didn't come down with the last shower. Here's one Henry James dreamed."

"Not my Henry James?"

"No, that was William."

"I could have sworn you said Henry."

"William. He dreamed this poem and woke thinking he had discovered the secret of the universe. 'Higamus, hogamus—' "

"Higamus, hogamus?" Max reached in his pocket, took out the coin, and clasped it in his hand.

"Higamus, hogamus, women are monogamous. Hogamus, higamus, men are polygamous."

Max laughed. "I think I'm in the proper frame of mind. Now let me get this straight. I just start playing, let myself get into a jam, and then press Control W and type the password. Thuban, right?"

"That is correct."

"You sure I won't need God mode? What if I get fried before I can transport?"

"You won't."

"What is the God mode password anyhow?"

Eel shook her head. "No need to know what you do not need."

Max shrugged. "It's your game. Wormwood. Where'd you get that name, anyhow?"

"The Bible. Just sort of a revelation."

"Sure."

"I did." She pointed to a book on the mantle. "It's in there."

"Okay, the Bible. Well, wish me luck, I'm out of here."

"Good luck, champion."

Max wrapped the sensory screen full round and began the game. He played with a reckless abandon, knowing he was supposed to fail. Ten minutes and two small trolls to his credit, he saw a steep staircase spiraling down before him. He went down and found himself in a small room with a large and lethal undead being. No way out—he had come too deep too quickly. The scaly beast opened its mouth and roared fire. Time to teleport.

CONTROL W.

PASSWORD?

THUBAN.

WIZARD MODE ON.

CONTROL T.

Max felt the tingling begin at the base of his neck. Then time wrapped around him like water. The world flowed past, a busy river of sound, rushing to an electric ocean of consciousness.

1995

Saturday, April 15, 3:43 P.M.

Max felt the tingling begin at the base of his neck and swiveled around on his stool to face the swinging door. He was dizzy suddenly, flushed and hot, his cognitive map askew, no way to navigate.

Two words formed in his brain. I am. Hold on, he told himself. I am. I am.

But he couldn't hold on. The world was disintegrating, coming apart in little pieces. His mind, too, was unraveling. The music of the spheres spun around him. He tried to tune in a station, but the soft paper below his fingers had the fabric of a dream. Hold on. He struggled to stop the spinning. Am I dying?

He was very hot suddenly and acutely aware of the sounds around him. Hot, then cold. Adrift in a world of random noise and vibrations. A buzzing like a million bees, hard smooth marble beneath his hands.

He was there. Inside the Ivory Tower.

10:15 A.M.

Amanda sat in the deep, soft, leather chair and faced the clinic receptionist. The woman put down her knitting and listened. A shaft of morning light turned her hair chestnut.

"I've been having these dreams. Recurring dreams."

"You want to talk to someone about it?"

"Yes. If I could. Now?" She looked at the clock just as the bells chimed the quarter-hour melody.

"We'd have to do an intake interview first with one of our supervisors. Then you'd be assigned a therapist."

"I understand. And it would all be confidential?"

"Yes, certainly. There's just one form you would have to fill out. You can use that table if you like." The woman indicated a table in the alcove. "Take your time."

After Amanda filled out the form she was taken to a room with two doors and asked to have a seat at the round table. Amanda did as she was told, observing the room. There were no mirrors and no clocks. A wall mural of the ocean was the only decoration.

Amanda kept her hands neatly folded on the table so whoever came in could see that she wasn't shaking. The tall bony woman who entered the room and greeted her seemed harmless enough.

"I'm just here to sketch a brief overview of your problem," she explained.

"I've been having these recurring dreams."

"You had one last night?"

"Yes. Several times. It upset me—I don't know why."

"Recurring dreams are a way our subconscious has of letting us know our buried wishes. The unconscious has only one tool: repetition. Dreams are like art—they use symbols that evoke feelings. They're never rational. Tell me, how did you feel when you had the dream?"

"I told you, upset. Scared. Powerless."

The woman nodded. "Perhaps you would like to tell me about the most recent dream. Just get comfortable and then speak out. If you can, just forget I'm here."

"Well . . ." Amanda took a deep breath. "The bells were ringing, and I was walking toward Mahler Hall. There was a man following me; he was limping. I had my cello case, and it kept tripping me. The trees were heavy with leaves, and it was dark. I tried to hurry, but the case kept bumping my knees and the canopy of trees started closing in. The boughs cracked and long switches raked my face . . .''

"Go on."

"Suddenly I was in the music room, taking a counterpoint lesson from the maestro. The maestro had turned into a cello."

Amanda looked up, but the woman had her eyes closed; she was listening intently. "It doesn't make much sense, I guess. He was playing himself with his bow. And then he lifted the bow and hit me. I started crying."

Amanda felt the salty tears run coolly down her cheek, trickling little sullied rivulets into her mouth. "It was just a dream," she said. "I don't know why it makes me so scared."

The therapist handed her a tissue. "That's what we're going to find out, aren't we? Do you have a preference for a male or a female therapist?"

"A man," she said, hurrying because she could hear the quarter-hour bells through the glass and knew she had promises to keep.

3:43 P.M.

Something caught. A sound. The click of a second on the clock. Not that it mattered, but still somehow he realized that matter was ticking away. The people around him had aged. He heard the clink of a spoon on a china mug. With it came the smell of coffee and burnt caramel and Old Spice. I am here, he thought. I am. Drinking my afternoon coffee in the diner, smelling the grilled hot cross bun that someone is eating. He reached beneath the counter, and his fingers touched newsprint; he pulled it up and spread the newspaper on the mica-flecked counter: *Shawneeville Times*, April 15, 1995.

He knew before he looked what he would see. The Panthers had won the spring melee, hadn't they? Yes, 3 to 2. He scanned the page: old news. A picture of the newly crowned Miss Shawneeville—not a bad-looking woman; an article on the retirement of the carillonneur and his bells, the switching of the bell tune to Wagner. A damn shame, he thought. Wagner! A bloody Teutonic tune, and rung by a machine at that. No sense at all. A million-dollar set of American bells and you use a $10,000 Braun machine to make them ring Wagner. Ever since the reunification the Teutons had been taking over. He cursed the day in '89 when the wall had come down and the blue-eyed tow-headed youths had begun singing "Deutschland über alles."

He looked up past the swinging Plexiglas doors at the blue vaulting sky. White clouds like elephants scudded past.

11:00 A.M.

"Boscoe's," the sign proclaimed, "only minutes away—depending on where you live." Amanda rushed up the stairs just as the carillon bells began to chime eleven. The lunch crowd had arrived early. "Sixteen Candles" was playing on one of the Seeburg 200 wall-omatics. She made her way across the black-and-white tile floor, past the chrome and marble soda bar, and through the metal swinging doors. She hung up her jacket and changed her boots for black-and-white saddles and short lacy anklets, put on her crisp frilled white apron and Boscoe's button and belt coin changer, and clipped on her black bow tie. She unwrapped two chunks of Bazooka and worked up a nice bubble before going out.

"Blue Suede Shoes" was playing on the juke when she relieved Angel. Surveying the scene, she saw that two booths had their food, and a couple were waiting for menus. She took the menus over to the date table and did her bubble-gum routine. "Hi, how ya doin' today?" she said, tossing down menus and cracking her Bazooka.

A jock with a massive build looked up and gave her a

dazzling capped smile. He looked over at the doe-eyed dish next to him. "Great."

Amanda recognized him from the previous fall's pep rally at the panther shrine. He had been talking to a reporter. "Was fatigue a factor in your defeat?" the reporter had asked. "Who?" the jock had answered.

"I like your pins," he told her now. " 'Eat at Boscoe's, 'cause you can't bowl here.' Great stuff."

Oh well, he could kick a ball. Nothing wrong with his looks either, although she preferred men with necks.

She popped a bubble. "Just take your time," she said. She left the menus and checked the other two tables. "How ya doing here? Need change for the box?" A skinny red-faced boy in a panther sweatshirt handed her a bill, and she made change from her waist.

"We'll take another basket of fries, okay?" He punched his selection: "Love Potion #9."

The first table was ready and she took their orders: Boscoe burgers, string fries, and six-and-a-half ounce original Cokes, authentic down to the script logo, made with sugar and magic ingredient Merchandise TX. The real thing.

Boscoe's, famous since 1989, their slogan read. It had been a joke then, the brainchild of a local high-school dropout who bought the old railroad diner on the wrong side of the canyon tracks and brought back the fifties. Now Boscoe's was franchised in all fifty-one states. EAT, pink neon proclaimed outside. BURGERS AND SHAKES. The shakes were the best, made with a foam green Hamilton Beach Drinkmaster. She didn't know much midcentury history but she liked Populuxe music and artifacts. It was so vulgarly and candy-coated confident, so naive. And it all still worked, would probably be working when all of the malt machine imitations made in the nineties had gone to their planned graves. And to think her parents had actually received one for a wedding present—and returned it to the store.

Old metal cigarette signs were posted next to every De-

partment of Health NO SMOKING sign: LIGHT UP A KOOL, CALL
FOR PHILIP MORRIS. Men in low-slung slouch felt hats draw-
ing on slim filterless sticks. HAVE A CAMEL. THEY'VE GOT
WHAT IT TAKES. Didn't they, though.

"Do wa diddy, diddy," she hummed to the juke as she
surveyed her tables. Wish it had been my idea. She looked up
at the red-neon hexagon clock. The blue crescent hand crept
slowly around. She had a long time to go still.

The woman at the second table was beckoning to her. A
Dresden blue blouse with a frilly collar and bow tie, ruffles
down the front, a page boy—probably one of those fifties
children on a nostalgia trip who liked to come in here. She
ordered a triple-thick chocolate malt and punched in two
Johnny Mathis croonies.

"Child," the woman said, as Amanda was refilling her
water. She put her hand on Amanda's wrist and gave her a
fond, doughy look.

"Yes, ma'am?"

A small furrow appeared beneath the woman's eyebrows.
She beckoned her closer. "Dear, you're a beautiful young
woman, but I thought you should know. Your hair, it's standing straight up."

Amanda smiled. "It's meant to."

The woman clucked softly. "Doesn't your mother have a
fit?"

Amanda grinned. "Hardly ever." She ran her hand
through her spiked cut. "Anything else you need?"

"No, just the check. I'll just go powder my nose first."

Amanda pointed the way, grinning as the woman walked
to the door marked REAL LADIES. She added up the check and
put it down on a saucer with the Boscoe trademark: a piece of
penny Bazooka. A laugh and a bubble for every customer.

"Hey, Amanda," the cashier said, motioning to the back
booth. "Trade."

She turned around and grabbed a menu. She almost
dropped it when she saw who was sitting there.

3:44 P.M.

The carillonneur took a last glance at the right-for-left twisted world; then he positioned himself at the keyboard, and waited. As the clock hand swept toward 3:45, he raised calloused fists to the wooden levers. "Sisters of succubi," he whispered, looking up at the flanged E bell in the belfry. "I'll miss you." He looked down at the deep-throated behemoths that would ring out the new tune. Wagner's "Parsifal's Tune," mostly footwork.

The sun slanted at a low angle through the faience, casting an Oriental pattern on the floor. Through the cutouts he could see the top of the Mall. A long-limbed coed with spiky black hair slept on the library steps, her head atop a cello case. The quarter hour arrived. A salty tear ran down the man's creased cheek as he struck Blackwell's chords for the last time. After this, his grand piano in the sky would be nothing more than a Wagnerian player piano.

3:45 P.M.

Amanda was half-asleep when she heard the bells. She sat up and rubbed her eyes. Damn. A quarter to—she had overslept. It was time to see the maestro. Maybe if she ran she could make it. She closed the book on her lap, lifted her cello case, and climbed down the marble ledge.

The bells sounded the quarter hour, the last time Max would hear the old melody. Such a simple little tune, high and sweet, American. He watched the clock hands circling.

"You coming back?" a male voice asked.

"God, the sky's blue today," Max heard himself say, looking to his left. It was Pat Ryan, eating a hot cross bun. Of course it was Pat, looking at him a bit strangely. No wonder.

"Like a poem," Max said then. "I have been here before, but when or how I cannot tell. I know the grass beyond the door, the sweet, keen smell—'' He looked at the clock on the crooked wall. The hands seemed bent and broken.

"Yeah, yeah, but how about them Pirates?"

It was his cue, wasn't it? It seemed to jolt him from the seat. He seemed suddenly in a great hurry, but on the way out the door he stopped and stared at the phone token in the slot of the wall phone. "Phone home," the voice in his ear said, but he shook it off. His parents weren't home, they were away on vacation. Pocket the token? He lifted it and looked at the elephant head stamped on the metal. An elephant never forgets, he thought; without thinking, he returned it to the coin slot. A recorded voice announced that the unit was ready to make a call. He kept going.

Ah, yes, he murmured, as his feet hit the pavement. I remember. Here I am. Here where the sky is so immensely and flawlessly blue. Here where clouds as big as buffalo roam. It's so light. Everywhere.

He walked beneath the arched elms, listening to their murmurings and sighing. Yes, here I am. Here, where all is and time is not. He stepped up the stairs to the second platform. The last step came up to meet his feet. He smiled. Up the Mall, up the long back of yesterday. Consciousness coming in fits and starts. He saw a squirrel and shuddered. Squirrels gave you rabies, made you hydrophobic. It would be terrible not to drink. He was suddenly thirsty, violently and burningly thirsty. He looked up at Mahler Hall. The water inside would be cold, cold and quenching.

So thirsty. Max's teeth chattered then, as if he had just bitten into tin foil, and a wave of angst hit him. There was Mahler Hall, sitting so quiet as he came up the last platform onto the piazza. The bells began the Teutonic melody, blatantly metallic. More of a malady, he thought.

Doom, doom, doom, doom, the gong sounded as he took the stairs two at a time and wrenched open the heavy door. Four o'clock and something was not well. His ears felt as if they had grown; the blood vessels within surged and sought.

Echoes were dying off among the sleek buildings. Then there was silence.

Deep, deep silence.

The hallway was empty, thirsty for sound. The water was cold. A sip sufficed to quench his thirst. He straightened and walked to the music room. A clutter of music stands stood like black stork skeletons. He stood there a moment, senses straining. The white ivory piano keys gleamed; they seemed to be asking him to play them. He stepped to the piano, lifted one finger, and started ''Chopsticks.'' The C needed tuning. The ivories were lively, though. Poor elephants, he thought, plucking out the melody. Not a bad rendition. He started again. Even better.

4:01 P.M.

The man with the fox-colored eyes stopped with his hand on the frosted door pane, listening intently. Somewhere, far below, someone was murdering ''Chopsticks.''

Epiphany.

He had been listening for something, and now that it had come he knew he was finally worthy. Only now, after tragedy, could he fully appreciate the fiddler on the roof, the organ grinder. Now the madness took hold with all its glory. The sacred and the profane, the brutal dissonance of the trivial with the tragic. He was seized with a joyous rapture. Yes! He had come this way before, heard the elves singing at his door. And now they had come again to serenade his heat-oppressed brain with their voluptuous, languishing music. The past didn't matter, only the music.

He licked his cracked lips. Behind him the raptus of notes stood waiting, waiting for him to play. He turned, and with the tool he held in his hand raised like a lance, he moved toward the crystal notes. They threw themselves at him with blind obtuseness, flaunting their perfectness like painted women: Use me. He grabbed one roughly. The music was his alone, all his. He had fought death and won. He had been appointed God's holy vessel. He wheeled toward the Sonus keyboard and played, letting the music flagellate his flesh, not thinking of the outside world, not caring, swept up in the raptus, tempting fate.

Max's fingers lingered on the ivories. He heard something: footsteps, someone running. He stepped from the piano to the door. The music began as he did, a cello's sweet, wincing melody.

A girl with short black hair was rushing toward him. It was the hair he recognized, how it stood up like the back of a Halloween cat. The Halloween Wind, her caption had read. Amanda Zephyr. Zephyr meant a west wind. He got a hollow feeling in the pit of his stomach then. Precognition. He saw, clearly as day, the next morning's paper: it would be her picture on the front page. Not for winning a prize but for losing. She would be dead tomorrow.

His eyes caught hers. He raised his hand to her. She kept coming, her eyes shining brightly, her face scarlet, frozen in a tearless cry—a face of anguish. For half a second he thought she was going to strike him; instead she stopped, and he saw her waver on her feet. Her eyes widened, such intense violet eyes, the damndest, crazy color eyes he had ever seen. She held out a clenched hand, then tipped backward.

"Help me," she said, falling; whatever she had been holding in her hand rolled rattling to the floor.

Catching Miss October, he saw the small medallion of blood on the white blouse cuff below the leather bomber jacket. "What happened?" he asked. Had she cut her wrist?

"Dr. Garver . . . hit me . . . dirty pictures," she said. "Forty swallows." She clutched her chest, and then her head fell back and her knees went out completely; her eyes fluttered and opened, then rolled back. One arm flew out.

Dirty pictures? Forty swallows? Some sort of deep-throat perversion? He heard a hiss and looked beyond her. The silver coin was still rolling down the marble floor. He watched it topple and fall, heads up, as he lowered her gently to the floor and cradled her head. He heard a squeeze of sound and then a longer hiss, just beyond the coin. He looked up as with two fingers he found the pulse. The door to gallery three was just closing on its spring.

He knelt and grabbed her wrists. They were clean.

4:20 P.M.

Only when the raptus had subsided did he lift his fingers from the digitizer and look at the bow. He was amazed to see that it had become a blade. And Nero thus fiddled while Rome burnt. Only Rome had not fallen. He had the symphony in hand. The prize would be his. And no one had come to accuse him.

There was still time. Time to hide the blade.

It was only minutes later that Miss Tilly had told him breathlessly about Dr. Scutari's phone call. He remembered looking down at Kennedy's shaggy hair as he took the call at Miss Tilly's desk. Heads. He was at the desk looking down, but he could feel Miss Tilly looking at him intently. Tails. In God We Trust. He looked up. Her look was strange, almost expectant.

Then Phil Scutari's voice came on the line. Max looked down as he listened and noticed a little Oriental ivory letter opener in an elephant pot, shuddering to think that the elephants had all died because their tusks were so beautiful. Horridly beautiful, that little carved handle. He was almost tempted to touch it.

Dr. Scutari was impatient. "Listen, detective, this ain't no social call . . ."

And then there was a great gathering of men and women and energies, all flowing forward. He remembered smelling coffee brewing, nutty and fresh. So much to do, so little time. Memory crashing in. Miss Tilly hovering nearby. And then the camera men had arrived and he was marking the chalk outline on the hallway floor, directing the telcam. The chalk was dusty and milky smelling on his hands.

Miss Tilly approached him and opened her mouth to speak. Her eyes were wide, both tender and frightened. There was a message in them, but she wasn't looking at *him*, was she?

"It's probably not important, but—"

He felt an urge to turn around. Then he was falling, back to the future. Down the long back of yesterday, helpless to help her, the coin pressed in his hand, the music raining down from above.

└ 2020

Wednesday, April 15, 1:45 P.M.

He landed with a wrenching jolt. He could see stars spinning in circles above. He took a deep breath. Something was wrong. He inhaled again. Not chalk. Banana. The tingling began at the back of his neck.

He opened his eyes.

"Have a nice trip?" the kid asked.

Above him, a celluloid self peeled away and went sparking back across the abyss toward the square white screen. His half-life self stepped into the hall and was showing them where to mark the outline of the fallen body. Not in the music room but in the hall. Amanda's chalk outline had shifted again.

And then the slow turn, the camera panning the doorway, a shot of clouds against a blue sky, time and direction passing only in relation to the imagined shapes. West wind that day, and then two people appearing within the frame as before, a man and a woman, the shot of an office and desk across the way. Elephants. Primordial elephants.

The tape was still blinking; the little ivory letter opener was pulsating with energy. A sort of Morse code, a little tune of energy. Final credits and theme song again, please, he thought. That's all folks, just crashing waves of music pulsing into the wormhole. Or is it out of the wormhole? Which me is Caine? When he closed his eyes the pulsing remained, shrinking to a single string, like a laser's beam—

shrinking to a small spot, just a kernel, just a grain, then darkness, inky darkness, not even the last sweet string to caress him.

He kept his eyes closed and let the music return as he nursed the small, inky darkness to light. The touch of her hair lingered on his senses, the smell of her.

"Max." Someone was calling him.

"No!" he shouted.

Someone touched his shoulder.

He opened his eyes. It was the kid. "Eel—" He tried to sit up. "I can't."

"What happened, Max?"

He shook his head. He didn't want to fall again. He was afraid he would close his eyes and be back there. He sighed in a lungful of air. It hurt, right there, in his center.

"You may be experiencing a kind of time-lag bounce. Just take it easy and take deep breaths. You were remembering what Amanda told you. 'Dr. Garver and dirty pictures, swallows.' "

"But it doesn't tell me anything. Dr. Garver was miles away. I knew that the first time."

"What else? Did you see the door?"

Max closed his eyes and then he smiled. "Eel, it worked. I heard the hiss. It was gallery three. And there was music this time, coming from above." He squeezed his eyes further as memory flooded in. "I felt a pulse—and—" His eyes widened. "There was blood, Eel. There wasn't any blood before. Eel, what's happening?"

Eel didn't say anything for a minute. "I'm not sure, Max. Some sort of quantum effect perhaps. Once particles have been near one another, they continue to affect one another. You appear to have crossed some epistemological barrier. Amanda's caught up in the crisscross. I've got the temporal coordinates here. We've come up behind the target again. Your new engram appears to begin at three forty-three, approximately a hundred seconds sooner than the old graft. It's like there's a thicker scar tissue this time. And this time we have a hard copy backup of the bells. You definitely arrived sooner.''

"I did, didn't I?'' he said, opening his eyes and focusing. "It's on the tape. Look at the chalk outline. It's shifted. The evidence has changed to fit my memory of it. Eel, this thing just gets more and more bizarre. Listen to this. I swear I felt a pulse. I'm sure of it. She was trying to tell me something. Everything's changed again, hasn't it?''

"Yes. And no.''

"Don't give me that old nut.''

"It's not as if we've changed reality. You intersect Amanda's energy field slightly earlier than before, so you're seeing and hearing things you didn't before. Maybe the intersection was prolonged enough to change her biography slightly, as well; you reach her before her heart seizes up and she bleeds a drop. Or maybe there was blood before. Maybe you just didn't see it. Let's see what else Moby has recorded.''

Eel was tearing off a printout. She whistled. "Interesting. According to Moby, there's been a change in the case records as well.''

"What sort of change?''

"Your mystery man's moved. Somehow the nineteen ninety-five Max managed to access some of the twenty twenty memory. It adjusted for the fact that there was no genuine suspect fleeing the scene of the crime. There is no 'portrait of mystery man' in your final case file; it's been relegated to a background file.''

"You mean the page is blank?''

"No, it's been replaced. There's a report in its place.''

"What?''

"A copy of a Psych Clinic therapist's intake record. An interview with her during the time she was supposed to be attending her aleatory music class.''

"Therapist?" Max remembered the moment the words were out of his mouth. "Oh, yeah." He rubbed his chin as the memory seeped in. "I interviewed her. I think. A repressed old maid—the report was hogwash."

Eel was staring at Max with fascination. "Did you or didn't you?"

Max fought the dizziness.

"Zymurgy's First Law of Evolving Systems Dynamics," Eel said.

"Zymurgy's?"

"Yes. Once you open a can of worms, the only way to put them back is to use a larger can."

"Give me that stupid thing," Max said gruffly, reaching for the therapist's report. Had he seen it before? Of course he had. Then why didn't he know what was in it? Of course he knew. He didn't make grand mistakes. He was no slipshod novice who would take Amanda's signature on a class list as proof. Only a buffoon would have failed to check the clinic records for that day.

Then why did his brain feel like worms crawling through cream cheese?

Max took a deep breath. Handle it. Knowledge is truth and truth is beauty. Just discrepancies of memory, nothing more. He gripped the silver coin in his pocket; gradually, a little of the dizziness left. Still, something was unsettling him, some memory not placed, some dark shadow behind the altered memories. When he blinked, he got flashes of memory mixed with music.

He opened the file and read:

Subject: 19-year-old Caucasian freshman. Music Major. Subject experiencing recurring dreams. In dreams, woman is stalked in dark places by a man. As dream proceeds, the stalker attacks and the woman panics and wakes herself up. Her defenses break, and she seeks consciousness.

Analysis: Oedipal turmoil. The woman's secret desire is to be penetrated by a man (father), but her code of ethics will not let her accept this secret wish. Not even in her dreams. To hide that wish she creates a dreamworld where her secret desire takes the body of a stranger, a stranger who has, not a penis, but a knife (or cello bow).

Her real wish is to have a father figure (man) penetrate her, but a dark fantasy has attached itself to her normal desire. Her secret buried wish is that the penetration be deep and brutal, perhaps fatal. Like similar subjects, she is more than willing to talk about the fantasy but denies its sexual content.

The rest of the report was informal, the therapist's personal notes.

Course of therapy: 1. Delve into past? Has subject encountered and buried the memory of a menacing abusive male? Alcoholic father? 2. Help her to develop her defenses. Teach her to change the course of the dream and render the attacker impotent.

"Amanda knew, somehow, sought help," Max said. "If the stupid woman had only told her to trust her instincts, avoid Mahler Hall."

Eel looked up. "But she didn't."

"If only we could warn her." Max turned the report over, thinking of the white terry robe on the hook at the back of Amanda's dorm door. What, really, did he know of her?

Max stood up, suddenly agitated. It wasn't that anything was changed, not really, and yet everything was changed. The girl had fallen before; the door had swung closed before. It was only his biography that had changed. And hers. He and Amanda were entwined somehow. As Miss Tilly was somehow entwined. Who else? What else had changed? Who else was caught up in the crisscross?

"I feel strange," he said. "Like I'm still there somehow." He rubbed his fingers softly together. "I can feel her hair, Eel." He smelled his fingers. "I was with her longer this time, wasn't I?"

Eel nodded.

"I should have known—given chase."

"You had no choice, Max. You can't get off the track. You can't ever speed things up enough to get off the track, even if you could arrive twenty minutes earlier. It's like stretching a rubber band. Everything's elongated. Caine, you're wound up with the dying of that woman, not the living. You were there when her spirit departed the world— who knows, maybe on some higher realm, you're responsible for her—but you can't save her. She's in you. You couldn't let her go just to catch a killer."

"Eel—"

"What, Max?"

"I think she was trying to tell me how to find her killer. Something about swallows and dirty pictures. Some clue. She just needed a little more time." Max stared at Eel. She didn't have to read his mind to know what he was thinking.

"Again?"

"Please."

"You're so determined?"

"I am. I think the third time must be the charm."

"Always beware of third and final wishes."

"Who said third was final? What's to prevent me from going back and back, at least till I see the killer? He was right behind me, just outside the warp. He got away. All you have to do is make me turn around. I've seen interviews of everyone in that wing. I'll know his face. Bet you it was Cartland."

"Who's Cartland?"

"A donnish professor who jumped off a bridge during May break. Then there's Bates, the graduate student oboe player who we found in the men's room hiding from the cameras; he was put into the orchestra after Amanda's death to balance the sound—it might have been the motive.''

''Any of these jokers still around?''

''Hmm. Good question. I think I'll go over to Mahler Hall and do some prowling around, check out the faculty rosters.''

''You mean Relham Hall.''

''Huh?''

''You reversed the name before, too. It's Relham, not Mahler.''

''Relham?'' The name seemed wrong somehow. Saying the name out loud didn't improve its sound, but Max realized his mistake.

''Yes and no.'' He was beginning to sound like the kid. ''Same thing to me. It was called Mahler then, that's all. Guess I'll never get used to the new name.''

''New? It's been almost a quarter century. More than two of my lives.''

''Has it really? When did Luther Relham leave his millions to the college? The year two thousand?'' Luther Relham. Saying the full name out loud brought it back. Of course, Relham Hall now. ''Holy cow.'' Max closed his eyes. As suddenly as it had ceased before, the music began, the sweet aching string melody, a cello more ethereal than he had ever heard.

He opened his eyes. ''Did you hear that?''

''What?''

It was mixed up with his memory, buried somewhere in his jaunt into timespace. The music had been loud, not muffled by a closed soundproof door. Someone in the hall above had the door open. Had Amanda fled from that door?

Max closed his eyes. The music began. ''That music. Where'd I get it?''

''You didn't say anything about hearing music when you left a few moments ago. It must be wormhole music. Something you heard but didn't file the first time.''

Max blinked. The music twisted at him, blending with the

touch of Amanda, entwined with her, wrenching his memories. And then it was joined by another tune, so simple it defied naming. Two tunes: one complex, one trivial.

"Eel, do you play any musical instruments?"

"Just the didjeridoo."

"Huh?"

"An Aborigine flute. It sounds sort of like a horse snorting. Not much range, but it suits me. They make them out of a root that's been hollowed out by termites."

"Lovely. You're weird as a brush, you know that?"

"How weird is a brush?"

"Never mind. Listen to this." He tried humming the easier of the two tunes.

"Never heard it," Eel said.

Max shut his eyes and tendrils of music grabbed him. Even when he opened them, the music seemed to impinge on his vision. He saw the notes as he heard them, dark, whispery, shadowy wraiths that brushed at his temples and nipped at his ear.

A lot had happened to him in the last hour. He had to absorb it. He closed his eyes. Instantly, she and the music were there. Wormwood, he thought, that's what I've become.

"I need some fresh air," he said.

"Take a walk. Do you good," Eel said. "Get the cobwebs out."

The bells began the hour melody as Max walked down the Mall. Wagner. It sounded worse and worse all the time. The bells tolled the hour, and in their echo he heard the faint little tune. He cocked his ear, stopped walking altogether, and listened, but he was too far away. Just a little tune, easy, familiar. What? Something he had heard in which past?

The tune faded and he walked on, keeping his eyes wide open, not letting the melody impinge. Beneath the frieze engraved TRUTH a student slept on the marble platform.

Amanda had slept there the day she died. He looked at the lanky coed, then up at the lacerated clouds and yellow ultra-violet sky. The folly of youth.

The truth is, he thought as he climbed the library steps, these stairs are a hell of a lot steeper than they were then. The revolving door stood waiting. He took a deep breath, then plunged within and tiptoed past marble busts of learned men. The music nettled at his brain, tormenting him, then flitting away with a little flounce, only to return to take up the skirmish, bow scraping painfully. And then, just as before, he heard the simple little melody: point and counterpoint. He took out his pad and jotted down the notes. The key was too high for him to carry, but he tried the tune anyway. "Da, da, da, dum . . ."

What was it?

YOU ARE HERE, said a sign next to the woman at the checker scanner. She was a student probably, earning extra credits.

"Excuse me," he said. "Can you tell me if this sounds familiar?" He hummed the tune.

She gave him a blank look and rolled her eyebrows. "Sorry."

He tried the middle-aged woman at the reference desk. "I've been here ten years. Certainly not something familiar."

"How about this?" With more than a modicum of difficulty, he hummed the more complex tune.

She smiled. "Why, that's 'Alma's Song.' Everyone knows that."

Everyone. Of course. "Alma's Song." Relham and Ravisky had shared an Oscar for Best Score for the music. The movie had been on the tube the previous night—he must have heard a snatch of it in passing. The wormhole music wasn't something he had brought back from 1995. It was something he had sent back to 1995, from this present. Or was it?

Luther Relham had an office in his namesake hall.

*   *   *

In gallery number three. Max stood outside the frosted glass of the office, which had been long since vacated by the maestro. He knocked on the door, but no one answered. He walked slowly back down the hall, down the ramp that led to the second level, and down the ramp that led to the main level. But the killer had been a tall man, striking from above. Luther Relham had been a cripple.

The mystery is the music, he said out loud, cutting across the Mall. That's what the Blue Lady had said, wasn't it? He said the words as he approached the panther shrine at the end of the path. He walked up the knoll slowly, approached the beast, and ran his hand down the cool sleek stone to stroke one massive paw. It was like Egyptian sculpture, idealized. Not true to life, but a symbol of some measured perfection, living stone. Princess Shaw-nee would have approved of her totemic mound.

Cat and mouse. Maybe he was the bait in some larger experiment, the music luring him into the labyrinth of time. He didn't feel like bait. It was just happening, that was all. "The dark backward and abysm of time." It was all around him, invading every pore. He could no more stop now than a man could step in the same river twice.

Two melodies, one complex, one trivial, both wound up with him and Amanda. And another layer of onion was peeled away; fresh tears were shed. Reality boiled down to a shadow of itself.

The music seemed to fade a bit when he entered his office. Gallery three. He reached in the video box and took out the tapes marked Interviews. The interviews had all been conducted the same day. Someone there was the killer.

Gallery three, wing A. Detective Pat Ryan, long since deceased, had gotten that plum, one geriatric female, a man in a wheelchair, an overweight assistant professor, and three graduate students. There were four other offices there, but they had been vacant that day. Seniority meant having to keep the fewest records. Max watched the tape with only half an eye. Ryan was interviewing the maestro in the wheelchair, Luther Relham. Ryan had his notepad out and was taking Relham's statement. There was a knock on the door, and Miss Tilly entered.

"Afternoon mail, sir. Oh, excuse me, I didn't know you had company." She set the mail down in front of Relham and looked at him. Adoringly? Max backed up the tape and replayed it. No, more as if she had a question in her eyes.

The top envelope was blue overnight delivery, marked between red stripes: Priority 1.

"Don't let me stop you," Pat said. "You take care of that, if you like."

Relham picked up the letter.

"Go ahead, see to your mail." Pat was looking around the room, not at the pile of neatly slit envelopes in Relham's musical notation letter holder. On the desk was an ornate onyx desk set. A pen with a Toledo-steel engraved cap occupied the recess next to the Excalibur letter-opener sheath. Just a faint imprint in the stone for a knife hilt, a suggestion only. A handsome piece. Only there was no letter opener.

"I— I—" Relham was nervous.

Ryan looked up, suddenly wary. Max knew that look. Pat was suspicious. Any second now and he would notice Relham's shaking hands, would see the missing letter opener.

"Oh, for heaven's sake," Miss Tilly said suddenly. "I'm sorry. I forgot I borrowed your opener. What a ninny I am. Just a sec, I'll have it up in a flash." She jumped up and bounded out. Ryan eyed her as she went. He always did prefer soft women. She was back in two minutes, handing Relham a letter opener.

"Ivory, eh?" Pat said.

"What?"

"Your opener. A damn shame, there being no more elephants. I always loved elephants."

Max jotted down the tape coordinates. A dark thought was lurking in his mind. But Luther Relham was a cripple—he couldn't walk. And the killer had struck his killing blow from above, downward. Max leaned closer to the screen.

Luther Relham took the letter opener in his hand, and a thin smile curved over his face. He looked up at Miss Tilly, just a hint of question in his expression. "Actually, this is Javanese ivory, a *kris* knife, an extremely rare piece." He ran his finger down the carved elephants and then turned and gracefully sliced open the blue envelope.

"Always admired people like you," Ryan was saying. "Me, I'm a slob—just rip them open."

The hardest things to hide are those things that are not there, Max mused. He should have known when he had misnamed the music hall. Luther Relham, too, was caught up in the crisscross.

The widow Relham lived in a small tudor mansion on the edge of campus. It was set next to an experimental field, accessible only by a long funnel of a driveway.

Grace Relham herself answered the door and ushered him in. The house immediately gave the impression of culture and good taste. And books. Everywhere, even in the entry hallway decorated with what he guessed was an Austrian crystal chandelier, there were floor-to-ceiling, wall-to-wall books. Max noticed the staircase and the elevator in its golden cage beside it. The room they were standing in smelled like lemon oil and old leather. Grace Relham smelled like baby powder. She was a sweet-faced seventy, plain and simple, neatly dressed in a shift that matched her blue forget-me-not eyes. Max liked her at once. He wasn't in the door two minutes before she was showing him her late husband's butterfly collection.

"That one's a Mourning Cloak," she said, pointing out a maroon-and-yellow banded butterfly with blue spots. She didn't seem at all concerned about getting to the purpose of his visit.

"And this is a picture of us on our honeymoon, in front of the pensione in Toledo." She was standing proudly by her husband, her arm on his wheelchair. "Luther took me to see the bullfights, and I hated it." Max stared at the picture. Luther was frowning; Grace smiling. She seemed happy with her lot.

"Toledo?"

"I meant Spain, of course."

"Of course. Afraid what I don't know about Spain would fill a bullring."

"Toledo's a great Moorish city. El Greco was born there. It's built on a granite hill, surrounded on three sides by the gorge of Tagus. What a view. It used to be Toletum, an archiepiscopal see and Visigoth capital."

Max nodded. Finally, something he could relate to—he had played Visigoth Warriors once upon a time, and thus knew quite a bit about Visigoths. He chatted easily with her about battling the Huns.

"Candy?" She was offering him a silver bowl of Gummi Bears.

"No, thanks," Max said, wondering. Twice in the same day.

"They were Luther's favorite," she told him. "Probably that's why he had to have so much dental work." She took one herself and chewed it thoughtfully. "Never touched them when Luther was alive."

"Did your husband have any interest in coins, ma'am?"

"Coins? Why he was secretary of the Numismatical Society, as well as president of the International Mahler Association. Sometimes I wished he'd stuck to his coins. I've still got his collection—perhaps you'd like to see." She led the way to a small blue-wallpapered dining room. "And there's his Medal of Commendation from President Robb," she said, pointing to a gold medallion on a plaque. "And there's the prize trophy for the Mahler Prize."

"And there— May I?" Max approached the familiar gold

figurine and lifted it up. The Oscar was heavier than he thought it would be. He set it down carefully. Mrs. Relham opened a teak case and turned on the display light. "He claimed to be embarrassed by that, but secretly I think it thrilled him, more than winning the Mahler Prize for the score. Mahler's life on screen, his hand in the background."

"It suited the story," Max said. "Any Kennedy half dollars?" he asked, coming over and standing next to the case of silver dollars she had just set out.

"My word, yes. The finest collection in the country."

"Something of a Renaissance man, wasn't he?"

"He was a master of many things, detective. We put most of the Alma money into good works. Most of it still goes there." She wiped her hands on her skirt. "I don't need much. Luther's half sister has a trust fund. There is no other family."

"The Alma money?"

"My maiden name. I wish Luther could have heard the memorial that Robb preached."

"I'm sure it was touching. A sister, you said? Where does she live?"

She shrugged. "The college has her address. They weren't close. In fact, Luther didn't even know she existed until quite late in life. But he provided for her, all the same."

"And solar gliding? When did he take that up?"

"Just before he died. Seven years ago. Just one more world to conquer. Ever since the Daedalus flight from Knossos to Santorini he'd been fascinated, but those last few months he became obsessed. He might not have been able to walk, but he could fly. He bought the graphite fiber Pegasus and—" She indicated a stationary robotic bicycle under a plastic shroud in the rec room off the dining room. "He trained so hard. I don't know, maybe he was too old. I was told the crash killed him instantly."

"I'm sorry," Max said. "I didn't know how he'd died. I'd been away from campus, heard only that he had passed on. I

assumed—'' No, that was crass. Just because he was a cripple.

He didn't quite know how to ask. "Look, I don't want to
be rude, but may I ask, ma'am, what happened to your husband to put him in the wheelchair in the first place?"

"Luther was born with a club foot," she answered matter
of factly. "As a child his parents hid that fact by treating him
like a cripple. Over the years, he atrophied, and his brain
began to believe he couldn't walk. So he couldn't. I tried
when we were first married . . ." She fell silent.

Max coughed. "Could he stand?"

"Stand? Once, when he was angry at me, he forced himself to his feet. Just for a second."

Max nodded. A second was all it would take. "Mrs. Relham, there's a favor I wanted to ask."

"Anything for the State."

"I was hoping you might have kept some of the things
from his office. There's a—a book, er, that I noticed he had
when I was reviewing the tapes. It seems now that it might
have some relevance to the old Zephyr case. If you wouldn't
mind?"

"A book?" She looked around her. "Luther had five thousand in his office alone. I don't know how many he's got
here—probably however many there were in the Alexandria
Library when it burned." She laughed.

"Where are the office ones?"

"His Jefferson Monticello library is in the Safari Room,
with his nickel collection. Frankly, I don't think he'd read
half of them, he just picked the same number. I haven't
shelved them, that's the rub, but if you want to look, it might
be in one of those boxes that were brought over after the
crash. They cleaned out his office in a hurry, I remember. The
boxes arrived before the funeral, and I just stacked them in
there, never opened them. You're welcome to look. Was it a
big one or a slim one?"

"Quite small."

She led the way down the hall and opened a door. "His private secretary Miss Tilly delivered these. She labeled them I think. The books are over there," she said, indicating them with a broad sweep of her arm. "I think." She sneezed.

"Private secretary? I thought she was the department secretary?"

"Oh, that was years ago. Rose was Luther's alone for years. A devoted little ninny. I don't know how he put up with her." She sneezed again. "I'm afraid there's too much dust and cobwebs."

"I'll get by, ma'am. Don't worry."

"Sorry, my allergies. If you need any help, just holler. You'll find scissors in the top drawer." She took out a handkerchief and blew her nose. "I could get you a surgical mask."

"I'll be fine." Max watched her walk quietly back down the hall, and then he found the scissors. It was not the box marked books, but the box marked "Crufties" that he opened first.

He went through the box carefully and found, wrapped carefully in one piece of tissue, the pen that belonged to the desk set, but no Toledo steel letter opener. In a shoebox at the bottom of the box was a cigar box sealed with four rubber bands. These, under a small stack of blank envelopes, lay the white ivory letter opener. And under the tissue-thin paper that lined the bottom of the box, lying among old shreds of tobacco, was a set of hand-colored etched photo postcards. The photographer had been expert and the model beautiful. She lay on a zebraskin rug, bare bottom exposed. A fat man stood over her with a whip and a lascivious smile.

He tried three boxes more and still did not find the base to the desk set. He started looking around the room. In one corner of the desk lay a pile of old clippings atop a blue book. The onyx Excalibur mound was anchoring them.

The clippings were recipes, fish soufflés and chocolate mousses. He tore off a four-inch column of type and slipped it in the knife slot. It disappeared, just a jagged tear of paper protruding. Luther's Excalibur was exactly four inches long.

He slid the blue book from the pile before replacing the letter opener: *Aleatoric Music*. He took it down and looked inside. There was a folded piece of lined paper stuck within: a page of foreign script. German. It was tucked in beside a color picture of John Cage, tossing dice as directed by the oracles of *I Ching* in order to produce music devoid of melody, harmony, and rhythm.

"This will do," he said, slipping the book under his arm and the little pictures in his coat pocket. He carried the knife and book into the cool, dry drawing room.

"Good, you've found your book," Grace Relham said when he came in.

"Yes. If I could just borrow it?"

"Oh, keep it, what do I need with one more book on music? And what's that?" she said, indicating the letter opener. Max handed it to her.

"It's not Luther's," Grace Relham said as she examined the ivory piece. "It's quite a fine one, anyone can see, but I'm afraid it wasn't one of Luther's passions. Or possessions. You see, he was a member of Greenpeace and the Sierra Club. Ivory, no. He might covet it, but he would never own such a piece. Perhaps it belonged to Miss Tilly. She was mad about elephants."

"Would you like me to ask her?"

"Oh, would you? I'd offer, but I just—" She stopped herself. "I'm sure she'd appreciate your gesture." She pressed the ivory in his hand.

Max nodded. "I appreciate your cooperation. Your husband, he was a Mahler expert, I understand. I wanted to ask you about 'Alma's Song.' "

"Yes?"

"This is it, isn't it?" He hummed the tune.

She listened. "Almost. Yes, that's from the Tenth Sym-

phony, Luther's award piece. A very difficult passage in Purgatoria. B flat. A mini scherzo, part of the restoration.''

"Written when? Can you pinpoint it?"

"Purgatoria? I remember it well. I was going through my
own private little hell with Luther. I think he was in love with
someone else. I don't know. We never spoke of it and it
passed, but I felt it in the music he was writing. He'd betrayed me.''

She looked out the window as she spoke, but when she had
said her piece she looked back, square in Max's eyes.

"Betrayed you how?"

"Don't be naive, Mr. Caine. Even a man in a wheelchair
can make love. Besides, love is not of the body but the mind
and tongue. It's words that matter in the end, what you say to
one another that counts. Yes, spring and summer of nineteen
ninety-five. Not that it was the first time."

He changed the subject. "Do you like Mahler?"

She shuddered. "Way too gloomy for me. His first work
was a fairy tale about infanticide. A flute made from the
child's bones exposes the killer at his wedding. Macabre
stuff. The Tenth Symphony is among the worst. He's the
devil to play, sheer musical purgatory, but I suppose he has
his rewards, if you can stomach a whole universe of reality.
Of course, he was Luther's whole life."

"Did your husband know how you felt about his work?"

"He knew. Of course we never spoke on those terms. He
made out that I was antirestoration, and I let him. We fought
our war on a musical plane. Mahler wanted the music burned;
he abhorred unfinished work. 'He who tries to go beyond the
ninth must pass away,' he wrote."

"What's so magical about number nine?"

"Beethoven, Schubert, Dvorak, Bruckner. None com-
pleted the mystical tenth." She laughed. "Luther wasn't
afraid of the ominous horizon. He used to tell me he liked
standing so near the thereafter." She sighed. "I don't miss

him, not anymore. Sometimes I think he married me for my name and not the money."

"Grace?"

"No. My maiden name. Alma was Mahler's wife's name."

"I'm afraid I never much liked Teutonic music. But I'm no musician." He shrugged.

"I was a musician myself, a cellist. Of course I gave it up when I married Luther."

"Why is that?"

"He demanded it."

"You said that Mahler is purgatory to play. Can you explain?"

"What did someone once say: 'Mahler's music is like visiting a wild and secret stormy country with eerie chasms and abysses. Once every blue moon you get a glimpse of idyllic sunlight meadows just beyond your reach. Then the storm descends.' I believe Mahler was quite mad when he began the death symphony. You see, his wife was having an affair. It's savage music, accompanied by cryptic notes to his wife Alma, avowals of love." She shuddered again. "I've always hated 'Alma's Song.' ''

"I think I know what you mean," Max said. He brushed cobwebs off his trouser legs. "I just wish I could get this snippet out of my head. It's driving me nuts. Mahler, foo— I'm ready for a glimpse of sunlight." He turned and flipped the book, so that the paper in it would fall as if by accident. He retrieved it and held it face up.

"German?" he asked, handing it to her.

"Yes," she said, glancing at the page. "It's Luther's writing." She read a few lines. "But those aren't Luther's words. He's only copied them."

"Whose words are they?"

"Why, Mahler's, of course. Luther sent that to me the day after we met. Anonymously. I can't imagine what it's doing there. Maybe I tucked it away and forgot it.'' She took the sheet and read:

"It happened overnight.
—I was awake throughout—
So when there is a knock
My eyes fly immediately to the door

I hear: Word of honor!
It rings always in my ears—
Like every sort of cannon:
I look to the door—and wait!''

She sighed. ''I found it romantic when I was twenty. All I'd sworn to do was to promise to think of him that night.''

''Do you have a picture of Mahler?''

''Oh, plenty.'' She took down two or three thick square books and piled them on the table. ''Please, take them if they'll help.'' Max opened the largest to the photo pages, stared at the taut thin-lipped face. Mahler had a high furrowed forehead, dark intense eyes, and uneven teeth. There were also pictures of his wife and his sister and his mother. Oddly, the mother and wife had a strong resemblance. A strong sensuous face. He stopped—take away the dress and caps, and the woman also resembled Amanda.

Max was looking at the text beneath Gustave Mahler's photo. It showed him in a cap with a dark coat and spoke of his facial tic and staccato speech and his jerky, limping gait. Children jeered him when he passed.

Max was looking at the face of his mystery man. Miss Tilly's joke: Gustave Mahler had taken the rap that day.

Max sat on a park bench and read the book's text. A quote from Mahler: ''Whenever I am in a bad mood, I suddenly think of Wagner, and cheer up again. That such a light could penetrate the world! What a spirit of fire . . . He was born when the circumstances were precisely right for the world to receive his message . . . The essential is birth and the ray of light that touches the newly born. What a terrible role in posterity is that played by the *epigoni* born after great spirits such as Beethoven and Wagner! The harvest has been entirely brought in, and they are only a few little ears of corn to be gleaned here and there.''

''A man possessed,'' Max said aloud. In the distance two black squirrels chattered; he paid them no heed. Mahler's words were prophetic: three blows of fate. ''The last blow fells the hero.''

Eel was eating noodles from a white paper carton when Max entered Gore Lab.

''Guess what?'' he said, throwing the tape of Ryan and Relham on the desk.

''What?''

''I know who killed Amanda.''

''Professor Plum in the library with the candlestick?''

''Almost.''

''Who?''

''Luther Relham. He was under my nose, all along. And I let him get away.''

Eel was silent. Max tapped the letter opener against his palm. ''I'm sure there's a way.''

''A way to do what?''

''To trip him up. Maybe even to warn her. Help her to save herself.''

''Amanda? How?''

''That's what we have to try to find out. I don't know. What if you could program me to call in a bomb threat? To evacuate the music building.''

''How would I make you do that? You're a cop. An honest cop. You're not about to make a prank call. It's just like in hypnosis—we can't make you do something against your grain. I doubt if you even kill your house spiders.''

Max shrugged. "Spiders eat flies. I kill roaches."

"Roaches are the scum of the earth. Okay, so you're not Mother Teresa. But there still wouldn't be time. It takes time to evacuate a building. No, too drastic. It would have to be something much more subtle and intrinsic. Something that really might have happened, but for some other coincidence. It would have to be something already lurking in your subconscious."

"Send me back with an obsession for ivory, make me pick up Miss Tilly's knife and get her to acknowledge ownership. I remember staring at it last time. She wouldn't have a knife ready on a platter to serve Relham."

"You think he'd crack?"

"Yes. Hoist with his own petard."

"Or rather lack of one. You might be right. It's not a bad idea. We do have the actual artifact. That helps."

"You think you can do it?"

"I can try. I program the letter opener's coordinates through your tactile and olfactory and visual and auditory senses. I saturate your memory with the sense of the knife and send you back to look for it. Yes, it's possible."

"And put in some auditory focus. I want to hear the music and whatever Amanda might have to tell me. I didn't tell you about the Blue Lady, did I? 'The mystery is in the music.' "

"Okay, let me see the evidence."

Max loaded the tape. "There he is, the dragon in his lair."

"Knows his ivory, doesn't he?" Eel said. "Well, let's see." She walked over to the console and called up the command program. "If we glitz these grims and throttle these zotzs, it just might work. You following this?"

Max was reading over her shoulder. It wasn't such a complex program. Ultrabasic was infinitely sensible and friendly. Just program in an optical stimulus for the ivory letter opener; make his "then self" more sensitive to its animal qualities; up the audio vigil.

The question was, could he effect a change in the timespace

following? Could he strike a glancing blow that would send Relham hurdling off his safe little track?

And if he could do that—couldn't he warn Amanda?

Except for one thing. He was here, wasn't he? Here with this kid in this room that smelled of banana and ozone, looking to catch a criminal. If he'd already caught him, he wouldn't be here, would he?

"No, you wouldn't, Caine." Eel tapped the white letter opener against her palm. "I'm doing this because you think it might work. I just hope we're not overlooking something here. This *kris* letter opener. It's not some mass-produced Indian thing. It's a very special carving. Luther Relham recognized that."

"So."

"In Java and Sumatra, one learns special ways of killing. The concentration is on silent bloodless killing. What if Miss Tilly is a Javanese orphan transplanted to America, trained in the art of death?"

"Eel, you've been watching too many movies."

"We can check quickly enough. Moby?"

Moby ran the trace and gave them a fax of her birth certificate and school records. Shawneeville Hospital, Shawneeville High School.

"I told you it's Relham," Max said. "But it would help my case if Amanda were to tell me, too."

"Or Miss Tilly."

Max nodded.

"Do you think it was love or blackmail?"

"Love, of course. A sick love. And I think it's time I paid her another call. Want to come along?"

"No, I'm going to work on the program. I've been thinking."

"Uh oh."

"Your idea was good, but you got it twisted. You stared at the ivory knife because you were repulsed by the idea of the carving. But that helps us. Obsessions and desires are harder to induce than repulsions and aversions. They require more focus. I was thinking of Hansel dropping bread crumbs so he could find his way out of the labyrinth—only a murder of crows ate them. Maybe I can arrange to have you drop the knife in the trash where the old crow won't find it.''

"That would be a neat trick."

"Tricks work well against evil forces."

Max walked slowly up the steps. In the lobby, he stopped, confused suddenly. In a moment the feeling of jamais vu faded and reality returned. He had just come up from Gore Lab. He was on his way to see Miss Tilly. Why did the thought make him suddenly queasy? He took a deep breath, and the feeling passed.

Miss Tilly was sleeping, the nurse told him when he arrived. Would he leave a note? He should have called before making the trip for nothing, he reflected. The nurse gave him notepaper. He wrote his name and number and was about to leave it when the nurse beckoned him over.

"She's not very well, Mr. Caine. Only a few moments, if you will."

He went into the darkened room and approached the bed.

"Who's there?" her voice came.

"Maxwell Caine. I came to ask you about Luther."

"I've nothing to tell you."

He drew out the white ivory opener and turned on a lamp.

"Where'd you get that?"

"From his house," Max said, noticing the streak of ash on her forehead.

"Did she—" She stopped herself.

"Mrs. Relham thought it might belong to you."

She reached out and touched it fleetingly. "No, it was Luther's." As she said his name, she turned and looked at the mantle; Max followed her gaze. She was staring at the metal urn. In a moment of insight, he saw the whole picture. She

had somehow gained possession of Relham's ashes. Did she
have the killing blade, as well, he wondered, knowing that he
would never get a judge to give him a warrant for a search.
He would have to follow through with the plan and hoist
Relham with his own petard.

He dug into his pocket, took out his handkerchief, and
reached over to wipe Miss Tilly's forehead before she could
protest. Maybe having some trace of the man would help
him. Eel could make him a little voodoo doll.

3:15 P.M.

Miss Tilly found the letter from Luther's sister at the bottom of her desk. It was typed on an old manual, signed in red
ink: Lola. Perhaps it was time finally to hand the knife over,
before she forgot where and what it was, before it fell into the
wrong hands. Her hand hovered over the phone, and then she
lifted it and dialed.

4:30 P.M.

The afternoon light was fading when the call came. Max
was sitting with Eel in the lab, watching Moby analyze the
ash results. They left Moby working and drove back out to
Juneville.

"I'd rather wait on the porch," Eel said, looking toward
the large, green, slatted swing.

"Come on, then." He led the way up the path. The lights
were on inside the house. The slime protoplasm on the railing
of the nursing home's balcony seemed to have spread. Max
lifted the knocker and let it fall heavily against the brass
plate. Bells sounded within, but it was several minutes before
the door opened. It was the same nurse who had received him
before, but her cap was askew this time and her face flushed.

"I got a message Miss Tilly wanted to see me."

"Heavens," she said. "Come in. You'll have to—" She broke off and started down the hall toward the door now occupied by an emergency oxygen unit. The man in the doorway was shaking his head; he stepped aside to let the stretcher out. The stretcher was covered with a white cloth.

"I'm sorry," the woman said.

"What happened?"

"She went in her sleep, God bless her," the nurse said.

"What?" Max stepped toward the stretcher. "May I?"

He took a last look at the kindly motherly face, the square jaw, the thin little mouth. Some men looked for women like their mother. He let the cloth drop back to veil her face and turned and faced the nurse.

"May I look at her room?"

"Certainly. It's a bit of a mess—"

He went into her room and turned on the overhead light. He sighed, looking around the room at the white elephants. A white elephant sort of life, nothing quite new, nothing that had not belonged to someone else before. The sort of person who lived her life through proxy. Pictures of nieces and nephews and animals, no children, no people of her own.

She might have told him. He stooped to pick up a sheet of balled paper and started to throw it in the trash. It seemed to be some sort of flier. On second thought, he unballed the crumpled yellow paper. It was a flier from the birdwatcher's club, no date. It gave the count of chickadees and swallows for April. Forty swallows. So she had been interested in birds. He balled it and—

Swallows. Forty swallows. He stopped in his tracks.

The paper in his hand was brittle. He spread it out. There was an old dark stain in the corner. A blood stain. He held the paper to his nose. Some aged scent.

There was something else he smelled in the room that he had smelled before. The sick cloying smell of hospitals and old-age homes: the smell of dying flowers and Lysol. He took a step toward the bed and leaned down and smelled the pil-

low. Something else, too. A smell he hated. An evil smell.
Ether.

He looked around the room again, noticing at last that
drawers had been left open at odd angles, that bits of lace
spewed out here and there. The room had been pin neat that
morning. Had someone been there, looking for something?
Had someone held an ether-soaked rag to Rose Tilly's face?

He looked at the flier in his hand. Amanda had tried to tell
him where to find the killer. He wet his finger and touched the
spot. The ink didn't bleed. He put his finger to his tongue and
closed his eyes; his head fell back. When he opened his eyes,
he saw a strange shape. In the light fixture Miss Tilly never
used was the shape of a dagger, a dagger with a hilt.

Someone had come looking for the dagger and hadn't found
it. He moved the chair and with his handkerchief lifted up the
piece. It was Toledo steel, not as in Ohio but as in the Visigoth kingdom, a lovely piece of craftsmanship. The blade
was four inches long.

He stepped down and laid the knife next to the candy dish
on the glass-topped table. Then he stopped and stared.

The Gummi Bears were gone.

He came out and found Eel swinging, a tear running down
her face.

"It was her, wasn't it?"

"Yes, Eel."

"Somehow I sensed that. Heart? Stroke?"

"In her sleep, or so they say." He held up two plastic
bags.

"You found it?" Eel's face paled. "Oh, no, you don't
mean she was—"

"No, she wasn't stabbed," Max said. "Not Miss Tilly.
But I suspect she didn't die in her sleep. Eel, someone's been
there, before me. They were looking for this, and maybe this,
as well." He thrust the bag with the yellow paper at Eel.
"We'll have Moby check these for latent fingerprints, then

run a match on this stain. I've a hunch it's O negative, Amanda's blood.''

They drove around a bit before starting back to Shawneeville, putting a lot of distance between them and death. They returned in silence, buffeted by a muggy breeze. Max pulled into the garage and killed the engine.

"You up to eating, kid?"

"No. Well, what you got?"

"What you want?"

"I'd like a steak the size of a policeman's leg."

Max laughed. "Settle for some down-home cooking?"

"Define that, please."

"Cooked by me in my kitchen, nothing fancy. My specialty is mock anything. Don't ask me what's in it."

Eel smiled. "I might bite. Give me energy to do your program."

As he unlocked the door, he remembered his bare cupboard. "Uh oh," he said, "I hope you like your mock steak made from beans."

"I love beans," she said.

Max heated the beans on his omniregulator and opened a can of rice pudding. Gummi Bears, he thought. Wonder who ate the Gummi Bears. For a split second, a thought came to him, but he dismissed it. He was starting to believe he had imagined the ether as well.

"I love beans," a woman's mocking voice sounded from the kitchen alcove.

Eel stopped in her tracks. "You told me you weren't married."

"Meet Paulette," Max said.

"*Squawk!* Pretty Paulette," the bird shrieked. Eel took a few steps forward and saw the cage. She smiled a wide, toothy grin, and in that moment Max had a glimpse of her grown to maturity. She was going to be a lovely woman.

"Hey, don't get so close!" Max shouted. "She hates females. Hey, watch out!" The kid had her damn nose almost up to the cage. Paulette was going to— "Well, I'll be danged." Paulette was giving her a kiss, politely.

"She likes me," Eel said.

"She likes me," Paulette echoed. All three of them laughed.

"Now I've seen everything," Max said, setting out the meal. "Like parsley pepper?"

Eel nodded. Max seasoned the beans and slid them onto Eel's plastic plate.

"Eat up," he said. "Want to watch the news?"

Eel looked at the clock. "I should run these analyses. Then I was going to work on that program. Get you to hate the ivory lovers."

"Suit yourself." He got up and turned on the set, then propped himself down on some pillows. Eel came in and looked at the empty couch; in a moment, she had climbed up and stretched out. By the time the commercials came on, she was sleeping.

Max yawned. He had slept only two hours in the last thirty-six. Maybe he would just catch a few winks himself— right after he went outside and put Lady in the garage for the night. He was thinking of doing just that when his head hit the floor.

6:00 P.M.

The snoring woke Eel. She had never heard a man snore before, and it took her a few moments to convince herself that Max wasn't dying. She balled her fists and rubbed her sleep-encrusted eyes; her eyes began to water. Paulette stared at her with beady eyes when she got up. "Shh," Eel said, tiptoeing over to Max. He was sound asleep. She left a note for him on the kitchen counter: *Gone to lab.* Then she gathered up the evidence bags and slipped out the front door.

*　　*　　*

When Max awoke it was pitch dark. He had slept too long and couldn't quite shake the cobwebs. He groped his way in the dark and found the light.

"Eel?"

"Glork," Paulette squawked.

"You still up, Paulette? Where's the kid?" He checked the bathroom and spare room. Then he saw her note. She had gone back to work.

He got his keys and went outside to Lady; the car was gleaming under the street lamp. He stepped off the curb.

"No!" he screamed as he saw her slashed tires. He should never have left her out. Damned hoodlums. Too late for service. He risked the rims and put her in the garage, driving slowly and locking the door behind him. Then he set off for Gore Lab.

As he passed the library clock tower, he looked up. His watch hand stood at the hour. He looked up and waited for Wagner. No bells. He looked at his watch. It was still running, past the hour now.

He stopped a stranger on the Mall for the time.

"It's seven-oh-one-eighteen," the student said. That was odd. Max walked to the library steps and looked up at the door. The library was still open. He went inside and took the elevator to the top floor. The stairwell door was open. He started up the spiral steps to the clavier room.

There was a phone on the mirrored alcove wall just inside the door, an old black standard model. At first he thought the room was empty, but then he saw the man just beyond the twelve-lever clavier keyboard, below the floorboard. The man was as ancient as the phone and just as black.

"Hello," Max called down. "Some trouble there?"

"I was just starting to work on this bourdon bell. Have to rotate it."

"Rotate?" Max looked down at the mammoth bell.

"You have to rotate the bells every twenty-five years or the clappers wear the metal thin; the bells stop producing perfect chords.''

"You said twenty-five years," Max said. "I seem to remember. It was you who saw Amanda Zephyr that day before she died. I thought your face—''

"Rang a bell?" The man laughed a deep warm laugh. "Yes, that was me. Sam Stick.''

"Your last day, wasn't it?''

The man nodded. "Not much of a job that. They'd waited too long. I tried to warn them, but they wouldn't listen until it was too late. The overtones in the harmonics had gone.'' He looked up toward the row of bells far over his head. "Thirty-seven years these had gone—damn shame—couldn't save them. Had to find a new tune without sharps and flats. Retired them the same time they retired me.'' He patted the behemoth bell. "We use the big bells now—just the white ivories, no ebonies.''

"What did the bells play before?" Max said, knowing as he asked what the answer was.

" 'Blackwell's Tune,' '' the old man said, humming the high melody.

Max jumped up. That was it. The whole picture. The simple tune and the complex, the sacred and the profane. The mystery was the music. "That's why I couldn't remember," he said. " 'Cause I was hearing an absence, not a presence.'' He smiled. It was all coming to him now.

"My farewell piece, so to speak. They went electronic after that. Understand the college got a slew of complaints. People liked the old tune better.'' The old black man shrugged. "They got me out of retirement for this—it's a big job rotating these deep-throated beauties. You won't hear the bells for a day or two.''

"Thank you," Max said. "Everything's a lot clearer now.''

He took the steps down slowly, his hand brushing the rail. He was thinking of a Chinese tale about a cup: The usefulness of the cup comes from empty space, the part that is *not* there.

Yes. In the interval between heartbeats lay the secret of helping Amanda. He couldn't wait to tell Eel. He took the rest of the stairs two at a time, nearly losing his balance.

6:45 P.M.

Eel tried calling Max with the ash results: the ash wasn't human, wasn't even animal. As near as Moby could determine, it was fiberglass and canvas. There were no prints on the knife, not even Miss Tilly's prints, but on the paper, she had picked up a latent. It matched Relham's. And the refractive index results were positive. The blood matched Amanda's down to the finest gen code set. The disturbing thing was that the print wasn't ancient.

The print was recent.

The implications were enormous.

A dark thought tugged at her. What if the forces of darkness had taken over her program, infected it with an evil virus, were even now manipulating the game toward their own evil purposes? The blood worried her. Out damn spot. She had tried not to let Max see she was worried, but the spot of blood terrified her. If the forces of evil were at work; if they wanted a blood sacrifice— If she bleeds this time, there will be a trail, she thought. Blood can't be swept up as easily as bread crumbs. Caine will get his wish.

She wrapped herself within the confines of the crystal pod and gripped the ivory letter opener. She held it to her nose, smelling the tusk, communing with the benevolent spirits of elephants. An elephant never forgets, she told herself. If one held enough pieces of the past one could pick up the vibrations of the past. If one could tune in on good strong vibrations, the ghosts of the past would walk the halls. Shut out the Toledo Visigoth steel: focus on the ivory.

There was enough evil out that night. Moby could make no

voodoo doll out of Relham's dust. Luther Relham was not dead. Luther Relham killed Amanda. And he killed Miss Tilly. Perhaps even as she sat and put the pieces together Luther Relham was on his way to kill for that very knife.

She had no choice. Max would have to use God mode. She would have to give him the number.

Eel called up Max's temporal program and studied his last "trip" backward from Control T. Paladin had progressed three levels farther than on his first trip, but he tended to concentrate too much on weaponry and not enough on experience and spells. To reach the pearl, certain imaginative powers were needed. It wasn't enough to just pick up the swallow and the needle of iron if one didn't know that dragons were afraid of centipedes. One had to know how to use them. She programmed in the small willow basket, carefully thatched. It would do to carry a small swallow. On the next level, she gave the Paladin a choice between a love spell and a compass. She knew he would pick the practical.

It was funny how she and Max now held all the props: the chinese ivory, the murder weapon. All the clues, and she could now name the killer: it was Colonel Mustard in the library with the candlestick. Just go through the timespace tunnel and accost him with the facts.

Eel be nimble, she chided herself, sending her fingers scurrying over the keyboard. She had it now. She just had to follow Hare's Law of Large Programs, remembering that inside every large program was a small program struggling to get out. Just a little change: a sacred/profane emotional response. Nothing too sophisticated or reasoned, more of a broad-based primal reaction. She inserted the stimulus and set it for automagic. Subtle, very neat.

She filed it and saved Max's character, then loaded her own halfling and went subterranean. She traveled quickly, more quickly than she had in many games, taking with her only the things Paladin would need. She left them in the deep tunnel, at the entrance to the final wormhole.

She had only just come back to ground level when she saw the warning light blinking. Someone had entered the room without knocking or saying hello. The light wasn't red, so it might be Max. Eel sat up and peered through the crystal. She could just make out a tall figure limping toward her.

"Hello, Eloise."

As she climbed from the pod she saw that the man was old and his skin very white. His golden-brown eyes skewered her to the wall.

"I came for the letter opener, Eloise."

"Which letter opener?" she asked.

"The one the nurse saw your friend take. It's not there, so it must be here."

"You didn't hurt him?"

"Not yet." He came toward her. He had an awkward limp, but he moved quite quickly. She saw that he was wearing tight leather gloves. She tried to move to block his view of the blade sitting on the lab table, but he saw it and grasped it. "What did you find on it?"

"Not a thing."

"I don't believe you."

"Check the printout yourself," she said, picking up the printout on the knife, drawing his attention away from the blood- and print-stained paper, which she kicked off the table into the trash. "You're clean as a whistle."

The man read the printout, then laughed. "So the bitch lied to me, telling me she had the evidence. She wiped the blade clean years ago, I'll bet; held it over me all those years."

"That's why you killed her?"

"You're not too smart, little girl, are you?" He raised the knife. "What makes you think I killed her?" He smiled a craggy smile. "Maybe your detective friend killed her. Maybe he killed them both."

"You could walk, couldn't you? Only no one knew."

"No, not one step. That came later. That day was my first attempt."

Eel took a few steps from the pod and made a wincing sound. She had seen a mother bird do that once, limp and wince her way away from her brood. Relham had been warned that they were snooping, that's all. He didn't know about the wormhole. But if he figured it out . . .

A dark thought swilled in her brain. He could send himself back through the wormhole into the past. He was there, off camera, but present, at the precise moment. He could send himself back, before the murder, and relive it, savoring new details. Rise up from his chair in 1995, put on his cap and glasses, and limp out the front door. No one would recognize him; he could escape into an already invented past and actually become the mystery man. She watched him tap the knife against his palm, and for the first time she was afraid. She could read his thought, the picture of blood swirling in his head as the mad music played. One corner of his mouth lifted, and a lurid light made his fox-colored eyes gleam gold.

"I think, Eloise, that you will come with me, too. Just in case." He took a step toward her and touched her yellow hair with the tip of the knife.

"Can I leave my houseparent a note? She might worry if I don't."

He looked at her, thinking, then nodded. "Perhaps that is wisest. I'm watching, mind you, don't try any tricks."

"No, I'll just tell Mrs. Trevanian that I'm going to the library."

She slipped backward, went to the mantle, and got a stylus and pad. The trick was writing quickly enough for him to think it was spontaneous. She thought a half beat and then plunged in.

Mrs. Trevanian. Gone to help friend at library. We may go to dinner after. I'll be back later. I didn't lose my key, so don't prop door open. I will phone if I'm going to be late. Keep the home fires burning. Love, Eel

"Okay?" she said, showing him the note.

He read it carefully, backward and forward, she noted. He nodded.

"I'll just leave it in the usual place, in the Bible." She walked quickly to the mantle, opened the Bible to the dog-eared page in Revelations, and inserted the note. Then she followed the man up the stairs.

There was a rusty turn-of-the-century Banshee idling outside. He thrust her in the back and locked the door. "On the floor and stay down," he ordered, starting the engine. She didn't argue. There was an old woolen rug on the floor; it smelled of dog. She pulled it down and made a pillow. They drove in silence. She oriented herself by sounds and smells, and used her pulse to keep track of time. He wouldn't speed, just go at a regular pace. They had gone about three miles north when the car stopped and he opened the back door. She stole a glance at the holographic navigational screen floating above the hood. They were facing north on the Juneville airstrip, in front of a small white jet.

The trip lasted twenty minutes—he kept her blindfolded for the last five. They landed between a row of green and yellow lights. Eel was led into an ordinary twenty-first-century underground home.

The living room looked like a museum, filled with tribal masks, rare Persian rugs, and jeweled scabbards. "My humble abode," he said, leading the way into a stainless steel kitchen. He tossed the steel knife onto the counter. "You must be hungry," he said, pinching the flesh on her arm. "Skinny little thing, we'll have to fatten you up a little."

"I'm not hungry," she said. He tied an apron around his waist and began to take food from the refrigerator.

"To taste good, Eloise, fish must swim three times," he said, spooning a glob of yellow butter into the saucepan.

"I hate the name Eloise."

"Three times, Eloise. Once in water, once in butter, and once in wine." He uncorked a bottle of chablis and set it next to the saucepan. Then he took out a knife and whetstone and began to whisk the blade back and forth. He tried it on the string of the white paper parcel, nodding when the string parted without a snag. He set the knife carefully on the counter and looked at her and sighed, then took out a fish, placed it on the board, and gently slid the knife under the oily skin. He dipped the clean filet in flour.

"Couldn't you call me Eel?"

"Eel hatch as larvae and have scales," he said, turning on the fire beneath the yellow butter. "Do you have scales, Eloise?"

She had been scanning his mind, skirting around bits of emotional flak, past demented corners. He had not started to think about killing her yet. He was still thinking about food, concentrating on neatly sliding the filets into the sizzling butter.

"Do you, Eloise?"

"Do I what?"

"Have scales?" His tongue flicked out, wetting his lips. "I bet your skin is soft."

"I have scales," she said. Better change the subject quickly, before he decided to skip dinner. She turned her stool quickly and brought her elbow back against the wine bottle; it careened off the counter onto the Spanish tile floor. He didn't say a word, just got a cloth and cleaned up the mess. He took club soda from the refrigerator and blotted the rug. Then he took a bottle of wine from the rack: red.

"You see, Eloise," he said, uncorking the bottle, "the true test of a good host is how he reacts to emergencies. A good host is like a general. It takes a crisis to reveal his true genius."

He tipped the bottle and poured a bit into the shimmering liquid. Then he got down two glasses. A bit of wine splashed on the countertop when he finished pouring; he stared at it abstractly. Blood, he was seeing blood. A medallion of blood, enameled like a Red Cross pin. A saucepan of blood, boiling, covering the walls.

He looked at her suddenly. She pretended to bite a cuticle.

"Don't bite your nails, Eloise," he said. Then he turned to the cutting board and began to slice a melon. His hand trembled as he cut.

"You like musk melon, Eloise?"

"If it's ripe."

He lifted a wedge and smelled it. "This one's good. Yes, that's important, Eloise. Some foods must be eaten at ripeness: melons, beef. Others must be eaten before: asparagus, pigeons, suckling pigs, swallows."

Eel gasped.

"And some," he went on, "as they begin to decompose: woodcocks and pheasants, game birds."

"Peacocks?" She had to shift his thinking.

"Peacocks, as well," he said. "As they decompose." He looked at her, then turned, got out a bone china plate and silverware, and set them on the dazzling white linen tablecloth. He lit the lone candle, transferred the fish to a salver, and brought it in holding it aloft. "Presentation is important as well, Eloise. You don't spread butter with an old razor or serve wine in a soup can. These are Czech crystal," he said, giving her wine.

"I don't drink."

"One won't hurt you," he said, lifting the glass and pressing it in her hand. His voice was hard. "Drink it all, Eloise."

She took a sip and made a face. It was drugged. She took a bite of fish and chewed slowly. "It's a lovely sauce," she lied. "Aren't you going to eat?"

"Later."

"You're just going to watch me eat?"

"Yes," he said, licking his lips. He seemed to have such large eyes, magnified by the round glasses. "You're quite lovely," he said, arranging the knife handles neatly along the counter. "Have another sip of wine to wash that down." He reached out and touched her with a dry finger. She forced herself not to shudder when the finger traced down the stripe on her shirt. But he was waiting. Eel would be his dessert.

7:20 P.M.

The door to Gore Lab was open, and inside the little monkey was screeching in panic.

"Hey kid! Yo! Eel!" Max called out. There was no sign of the kid. As he passed the mantle, he noticed the paper in the Bible; it had not been there before. Had she left a note?

Max flipped open the Bible. Revelation. He took out the note and read it. Don't prop door open—what did it mean? There was no keyhole in that door. And who was Mrs. Trevanian? Trevanian? Hmm?

He turned to the Cray computer and swallowed his pride. "Okay, big guy, so who's Trevanian, the housekeeper?"

"TREVANIAN IS THE NAME OF A BRITISH SECRET SERVICE CODE."

"Eel left me a message in code? I'm supposed to figure it out? Let's see." He read the note again, then shook his head. "I don't have the key, do I?"

"IF I MAY ASSIST?"

Max bowed his head. "Be my guest."

"READ EVERY THIRD WORD AFTER PUNCTUA-TION."

"Okay. Let's see: help . . . go . . . back . . . lose . . . prop . . . phone . . . home . . ." Help. Go back. Lose prop. Phone home.

Help? Was Eel in trouble? Whose home? Stranger and stranger. The nagging doubt that had been forming in his mind like a squirmy, viscous Gummi Bear suddenly became real. "Moby, did Eel do the analyses on the evidence?"

"YES, CAINE. WOULD YOU LIKE TO SEE THEM?"

"Please." Max read the results and saw, as he did, the yellow paper where Eel had dropped it.

Suddenly reality came crashing in. Luther Relham was

alive. Max had the evidence to convict him in hand. Relham had fooled them all—his wife, Miss Tilly, the entire community. He had created a new self through exercise, a walking self, and faked his death. Max had a hunch there was no sister. Relham was the sister, living off his own funds. Free.

Miss Tilly had somehow threatened that freedom. And Relham had bought himself a little more time.

Time. The question was, did Max have enough? Eel was in danger, that was all he knew. She had left him instructions.

Go back. Lose ivory letter opener. Go back and force a confession in the past with knowledge gleaned out of the future. Now.

Now? What if he hadn't come till tomorrow?

Go back. Lose prop. He prayed Eel was still alive.

Go back. Now.

He walked toward the sensorama booth. Eel was in trouble. And she was gone he knew not where. He had to go back and try to slip the knot.

He climbed in the pod, called up ultrabasic, and scanned the program. It looked fine. Only there was something he wanted to change. Just one small thing. If Eel's calculations were right, this time he would arrive at the diner at 3:41. That would give him just enough time. Eel had programmed in a repulsion to ivory. It would be easy to make the small change. The Paladin who set forth on the next journey into the wormhole would carry simpler baggage. He held neither the silver coin nor the ivory knife but a smaller, lighter psychometric object. A passionate hatred of Wagner.

"Trust me," he told himself as he picked up electrodes. He attached the electrodes as he had seen Eel do, red wire into silver connection, black wire into gold.

"Want to hear a ditty?" He answered himself with a nod and began: "There was a young lady of Chichester/Whose beauty made saints in their niches stir/One morning at mass, the curves of her ass/Made the Bishop of Chichester's britches stir.''

He loaded Wormwood and retrieved his file. The pod filled up with green light, and his Paladin's subterranean world wrapped around him. A staircase lay ahead, descending. He took the steps, around and around, down into a large, blue, fog-filled room. An evil dwarf blocked his passage. He used a fireball to topple it. On the floor lay a compass; he picked it up and hung it on his belt and headed north, toward the steep stairs.

At the top of the stairs he felt a breath of warm air and a sudden flutter. He looked up. Above his head was a swallow singing a simple little tune. He held up his finger and the bird alighted, still singing. Suddenly he felt a pang in his heart. He looked down at the floor strewn with weapons. He had room in his pouch for only one item, but in that moment of sadness the bird's song was the only thing that warmed his heart. He slipped it in his pouch and proceeded to go down the deep stairwell.

Halfway down he knew he had made a mistake. The approaching sounds of a dragon were unmistakable.

CONTROL W, he typed.

PASSWORD?

THUBAN.

WIZARD MODE ON.

CONTROL T. Hold on, he thought, here I go . . .

He found himself in another room in the Black Pit, a room whose roof was covered with all the stars of the ancient night skies. Great winged horses, beautiful women and muscular men, sailing ships, a huge gyrating dragon: Draco.

His heart skipped a beat. There, lurking above, the great beast of the constellation drew a breath of air, drawing all the warmth from the spaces around him and chilling the air. He saw the beast stirring, unwinding, beginning to sense him. Its red eyes glowed in the darkness.

Something was wrong. Wizard mode should have removed him from danger. Instead it had brought him closer.

It hit him suddenly. Eel had used God mode. He needed the password to escape. He looked up at the beast gyrating above him—the great worm, the evil serpent who had once overshadowed every astrolabe and celestial globe. He had no weapon, only his compass and swallow. And then he realized his mistake. Dragons liked to eat swallows. The dragon must have been drawn to the scent.

He tried the simplest thing he could think of.

CONTROL W.

PASSWORD?

GOD, he typed.

INVALID PASSWORD.

The room changed from hot to cold, depending on whether the creature above him was inhaling or exhaling. It was an exceedingly wicked demon-of-power, more loathsome than any Baal. Max took a deep breath and tried the mail net.

TO: GOD MODE.

GOD NOT FOUND. ENTER TLX.

TO:

The Bible. Eel had said something about getting Worm-wood from the Bible? Revelations? He raced back to the mantel. It had been a clue. "And the third angel sounded and there fell, a great star from heaven, burning as it were a lamp—And the name of the star is Wormwood."

Yes, it was coming back, his days of Bible school: "Here is wisdom. Let him that hath understanding count the number of the beast: for it is the number of man. And the great dragon was cast out, that old serpent, called the devil."

Satan's number was 666.

Max typed the number.

INVALID PASSWORD.

But that had to be the clue. He looked up at the astrolabe, at stars that formed the dragon's body, at Thuban and the others, at Draco winding above him, as three thousand years before it wound above the polar sky. But Draco's powers were a thing of the past, weren't they? As if in answer, Draco moved one of its heads in his direction and hissed like a python. Max froze. A great stench of cold evil chilled his blood.

He had to have the password. Without it, all was lost. Draco would devour him, fry him to a crisp with his hot breath. The dragon stirred, and Max scanned its body, looking for some weak point, a missing scale perhaps. An iron sword, wasn't that what one used to kill a dragon. Why iron? Then he recalled the compass on his belt. North. True north. Great elephants, that was it! His iron sword might be small, but it could find the spot.

POLARIS, he typed.

INVALID PASSWORD.

Maybe some other polestar? But which? He found the ring of polestars on the ceiling. Thuban, Polaris, Vega.

And then he saw the pearl, resting under Draco's chin. The north pole of the ecliptic. The star map sky indented slightly there, and in the dimple was a planetary nebula, the gaseous ring around a star one hundred times bigger and hotter than Earth's sun. The only true north. The star was located where artists for centuries had depicted it, down the throat of the dragon, directly above the heart. It was the sacred pearl, the center of centers around which all pole stars revolved. Thuban and Polaris and Vega and the others, past and present and future, all lay equidistant from that spot at 18 hr RA arc.

A planetary nebula, appearing to Earth as a hazy blue-green star, 3,200 light-years away. No name. Just a number.

Number 6543. The kid had created a cabalistic universe. 666 added up to 18. So did 6543.

He realized with a start that that was his phone number.

PASSWORD?

Phone home.

6543.

GOD MODE ON.

CONTROL T.

He seemed to be in a swiftly moving dream. The world rushed darkly by, and voices sang in his ear. Billows of dark octopus ink rippled out, covering his face, and he smelled ozone. The River Destiny flowed past, smooth as a sheet of satin.

It came to him as he found the fabric of the dream that he had landed oddly this time. The threads that met his fingers weren't warp and woof threads. They were seam threads. He saw it all then. Past, present, and future—synchronously. All time is now, he thought. You create your own reality every moment you exist. When you need a long shot, really need it, you can find it. Providing you are at the right time at exactly the right place.

With a song and a sharp iron needle, he set about tearing the seam. At his side, the sparrow regurgitated a centipede and burst into song.

1995

Saturday, April 15, 6:00 A.M.

Toward dawn Amanda began screaming.

There was blood everywhere, blood on the gray tile floor, bright red medallions of shiny blood. Mahler picked up a medallion and handed it to her. It was cold as ice.

"Murderer!" She shouted it twice.

"Amanda, wake up!"

She opened her eyes. Her roommate was over her, shaking her. She was in her own room, safe, alive. There was no blood.

"Boy, did you scare me," Jenny was saying. "That dream again?"

"Yes."

"You want to tell me about it?"

Amanda shook her head. It was over—she had to put it out of her mind. It was just a dream. Mahler was dead. He hadn't stabbed her with his baton; she hadn't bled all over his floor. Just a dream. She lay back on her pillow and closed her eyes. It was almost dawn; she would be safe now. She fell back into sleep and dreamed she was taking a cello lesson.

The teacher was a blue bottle-nosed dolphin.

"Don't forget," he lectured. "it's not you and the cello versus the music, it's a holy trinity. The plucking of the string must come like a smile, from the heart, not the mind. Feeling must draw out the bow."

"But what about memory?" she asked.

"Forget memory. Let yourself be created by the music.

209

Use your training as a springboard—use it to dive to new depths."

The dolphin dove and disappeared into the blue. A second dolphin stood where the first had sat, cello positioned between its flippers.

"It's like blowing soap bubbles," he said, pointing the bow at her. "You don't calculate the pounds of pressure and speed, you just blow."

The dolphin puckered up and blew her a kiss. The kiss blossomed into a rose. The cello bow turned into a stalk of limp asparagus. "Remember, the flowers are easy to paint, the leaves difficult."

She looked at the rose, full-blooming and fragrant.

"I don't understand," she said.

"You will in time," the dolphin said, and dove into the cool, blue water. She dove after him and swam effortlessly, fluidly as the dolphin ahead of her, bubbles streaming in her wake, the music of the spheres guiding her deeper and deeper. The "Fiddler's Dance," point and counterpoint, a perfect polyphony.

3:41 P.M.

The smell of coffee washed past, immersing him in bittersweet warmth. Music was everywhere. Slowly, like a great panther rising, the past came to life. He knew this one. He took a deep swallow, savoring the coffee taste head-on; then he took the newspaper from under the counter and spread it out. April 15. He swiveled on the stool and focused keenly past the swinging glass doors: big blue sky, galleon-sized cumulus clouds.

He started humming "Waltzing Matilda."

"You coming back?" He knew that sardonic voice. Max focused his eyes and smiled at his friend Pat.

"God, the sky's blue today." He felt suddenly lucid; he was riding a supercharged envelope of energy. Inside his head, "Waltzing Matilda" played on: '. . . and his ghost may be heard, as you pass by that road . . .'

"Springtime," his friend said.

Max smiled. "And a young man's fancy turns." He swiveled back to the counter and looked down at the remains of his hot cross bun. One last raisin. He popped it in his mouth. Yes, he thought, looking at the clock. I know this one. Let it come.

11:20 P.M.

"Trade," the cashier called, rousing Amanda from her reveries. She got a Boscoe's menu and took it to the customer in the wheelchair.

"Hi ya—" she began, then saw who it was. She set the menu down next to the navy fisherman's cap.

"Hello," he said. His eyes burned into her. "So, what do you recommend I try?"

"The burgers are very good. The malts are terrific." She forced herself to recite the spiel, but her palms were sweating.

"I'll have a cup of coffee, hot and sweet." He didn't take his eyes off her as she backed away. She went to the counter and poured the coffee into a thick china mug, then set it down without spilling a drop.

"I wanted to talk to you, about your music."

She didn't reply, just waited. He took out his slim black appointment book, took his glasses from his pocket, and looked down at the page. "Today is a busy day . . . I'm free at three forty-five."

"I usually practice then. And I've got a counterpoint lesson after with—"

"Oh, but didn't you know, Bannon is sick today. You can practice during your lesson time." He pulled the pencil from the spine of the black book and licked the tip. "Quarter to the hour. Don't be late.'' He smiled and she caught a glimpse of gold on one tooth. What strange eyes he had, sort of golden-brown behind those glasses, entrancing eyes. She felt herself flushing. He liked her. He wasn't so scary when he was smiling.

"I'll try, sir."

"Sir?" He laughed. "You'll have to do better than that." He took a sip of coffee and made a face.

"Oh!" Her hands flew to her mouth. "I'm sorry." She had forgotten the sugar. She ran and got it, a fluted glass Bloomfield dispenser. He took it and wrapped his hands around it, studying it. She noticed his napkin. He had been writing music. She had never noticed his hands before, had never been close enough. They weren't what she expected, not at all. He should have had beautiful hands, long fingers. His fingers were short and nails bitten.

"Like a Greek column," he said, holding the sugar aloft. "A little household icon. Do you lose many?"

"We have to keep pretty close tabs."

"Don't worry, I won't steal it."

She laughed. "I wasn't worried."

"Your heart, maybe, but not that. So, a quarter to four?"

"Sure," she said.

"Promise?"

She held up two fingers. "Word of honor," she said, regretting the words as soon as they were out of her mouth.

She blushed. She had heard rumors, the way he flirted with words and music. "Well, I've got to clear these tables . . ." She backed up, almost stumbling. She grabbed a tray and cleared number five. Miss 1995 had left her a plug nickel, vintage 2015.

"A plug nickel, can you believe it, Pete?" she said to the cook. Pete was going off duty.

He shook his head. "Some people, they think it really still is nineteen fifty. James got a Buffalo nickel from her last week—who knows?"

"Yeah, she's sweet on James."

The cook put on his dark glasses. "Well, I'm outa here. Gonna fight them rays."

"Wish I could join you."

"Condolences," he said, uncapping a Coke for her. She chugged it and then peeked outside. Her station was clear.

The jock had left her a dollar coin. At number six, next to the almost full cup of coffee and sugar dispenser there was a gleaming silver coin. A Kennedy.

Could it be an accident? Those things didn't grow on trees. She cocked her head. Maybe she shouldn't take it. She picked up the coffee cup and started back to the kitchen, then paused when she saw the balled napkin under the table. She picked it up and put it on the tray.

In the kitchen she unballed the napkin and smoothed it out. It was just a melody, a simple little scherzo in B flat minor.

She studied the notes, trying them on her inner ear. A chill went through her. She smoothed the napkin as best she could and pressed it in her book.

She clutched the half dollar in her hand and hummed the melody. Yes, that was it. As beautiful as the cold silver, as pure as ice. The scherzo was perfect—maybe it was her lucky day after all.

3:42 P.M.

The newspaper by his plate was folded to column four, showing a picture of Miss Shawneeville, 1995. She was a pretty thing, tears and all. Sort of plastic, though. There was an item below about the switching of the bells. The sacred "Blackwell's Tune" would be no more. A crying shame, that's what it was. It was bad enough that they had ruined those bells with their neglect; now they were going to compound the error by retiring both bells and bell ringer and replacing them with a bloody Teutonic tune and a mechanical bell ringer. Ever since the reunification, the Huns had been taking over. He shuddered, thinking of the maternal grandmother he had never met. A Dutch woman with a short brown bob, she had perished in the camp at Spandau. Such unspeakable horrors the Germans had loosed upon the world.

"A damn shame," he said to Pat.

"What, Max?"

"The bells. Balls, I hate Wagner."

Pat quirked an eyebrow.

"Goddamn 'Parsifal's Tune,' " Max went on. "Wagner was a nasty, arrogant, self-indulgent anti-Semite. Everyone knows that."

"Oh, settle down. Bells is bells."

"Bells is bells. Hah!" Max laughed bitterly. "That's what you know." He looked at the clock. "I've got to go," he said, not looking back, just grabbing his check and slapping money down at the checkout.

"Hey!" Pat called. Max ignored him, pushing through the swinging doors. Bells ain't just bells, he thought vehemently. It made a difference, damn it. Hell's bells! The old tune had grace and character. It had been alive. The new tune would be static.

He stopped. The ground seemed to come up before him suddenly. There was a metal telephone token in the slot of the pay phone. A picture of an elephant with tusks was embossed on the metal. He picked it up and dropped it in the slot.

"What number are you calling?" the canned voice asked.

An elephant never forgets. Or forgives. He gave them the number for the Shawnee College Library, then asked for the clavier room; he held his hand over his mouth as he spoke. "This is a friend speaking. I want you to listen carefully. There's a bomb wired to go off when you ring the bells. You must not ring the bells. I repeat, you must not ring the bells." His voice seemed to echo back, like a face reflected in a mirror—a strong voice, confident.

The masculine voice on the other end of the line was cordial, restrained. "I understand perfectly, sir. Can you give me your name?"

Max smiled. "The Shadow. That's all you need to know. Don't ring those bells, and no one gets killed."

When Max finished speaking, he simply replaced the receiver and went out, into a world washed new and clean. He was smiling when he crossed the street. Not even a shadow of the past haunted him as he walked. He whistled "Blackwell's Tune" all the way up the long walk beneath the canopy of elms.

White clouds floated against a blue backdrop, and through them raced the pale moon, shimmering in and out the blue like the bare buttock of a young gauze-swathed dancing girl. The birds sang as Max walked. Pigeons fluttered above his head, settling down to watch him from the apple-blossom-sprinkled lawn. Squirrels frolicked in the grass, and poetry flowed around him: "Oh a wonderful stream is the river of Time/as it runs through the realm of tears/with a faultless rhythm and a musical rhyme/and a boundless sweep and surge sublime/as it blends with the ocean of years."

He reached the top of the first plateau and paused. There was so much silence that there was no room for sound. He was in no hurry. He took a deep breath of sweet air and looked ahead.

"There's a magical isle up the river of Time, where the softest of airs are playing." Mahler Hall waited at the end of the Mall like a great goddess.

He climbed the steps and pulled open the great door and went inside. The music room was empty. He walked over to the open piano and stared down at the keys. Ivory, what a shame. Poor elephants, doomed to play other people's music, reduced in the end to "Chopsticks." He flexed his fingers and played.

4:01 P.M.

The man with the fox-colored eyes closed his frosted door to shut out the noise below. Some joker playing "Chopsticks." He wheeled back to his desk. "Heaven punishes those who despoil silence," he announced, as he began struggling with the little piece of music. It was a miniature scherzo, a diabolically simple little thing from the Purgatoria score. Its size, however, belied its importance. It was the core of the symphony; it was the key. If he could crack that one simple thing, the entire symphony would be his.

He put his hands to his ears and called up the inner muses, but the muses were quiet. The solution would not come. It was not his day. Everything had gone wrong today. Word of honor, indeed. Even the girl had lied.

He knew what the master had ordered for this passage: a dying away, like the melting of a cloud into the etheral blue, but the melody evaded him. Ball after ball of formerly flat and hopeful paper was resigned to the wire mesh can.

Amanda's internal alarm woke her. Her face felt flushed. She took her mirror from her purse and looked at herself. Freckles! She had been out in the sun too long. It must be a quarter to the hour already. She had better get going or she would be late. She hopped off the marble platform and hurried across the lawn to Mahler; she took the steps two at a time. As she grasped the heavy metal door ring, she looked back up at the library bell tower clock. How could that be? It was past four. The bells had not woken her. The sky seemed hungry for noise.

She entered the hall and walked toward the music room. The door was open, and from within came the sound of someone playing "Chopsticks." It couldn't be Bannon. She peeked in and saw the young man with reddish-gold hair.

He whirled around and his eyes met hers and held. "And

viol strings that outsing kings," she thought, her heart bounding up.

"Sorry," he said. "Did I put your ears in peril?"

She smiled. "You just need a little harmony."

"I feel like we've met," he said, coming toward her with hand outstretched.

She smiled. "I don't believe so."

"Name's Max Caine," he said. "You're a student here, aren't you?"

She nodded. "Amanda Zephyr."

He shook her hand. "Nice to make your acquaintance."

"Hey," she said, "do you know anything about the bells?"

"Bells?"

"They didn't ring. I was sort of counting on them."

Max smiled and shook his head. He looked at his watch. It was a minute past four. "Not missing much," he said. "Wagner."

She screwed up her face. "I never did like Wagner. Missed an important meeting with a professor, though. He'll probably be mad at me now. He's trying to teach me to play with pathos, like a German." Her brow furrowed. "I lost track of time. Too late now. Well, if I'm not disturbing you—I guess I should practice."

"Can I listen?"

She laughed. "I guess. If you want." She got out her case, took out her cello and bow, and rubbed the bow with rosin. Hers was a respectable French cello by an unknown maker; the wood was warm gold, a wavy-grained spruce more than a hundred years old, time enough for the oil-based varnish and linseed oil to oxidize, time enough to make the instrument impervious to solvent, untemperamental. She set the end pin of her cello, took her stool, and touched bow to the tamastik-covered string.

"Any requests? How about a Viennese waltz?"

"Play 'Blackwell's Tune,' can you?"

She laughed. "Easy as pie." She bowed her head and played the little piece with precision and clarity. When she was through she looked up. The man's eyes were wet.

"Strange," he said.

"What is?"

"Nothing," he said. "Play something else, anything."

She reached in her pocket and brought out a paper napkin and set it on the music stand. Time to sanctify the house. Let it happen. Let the bow wander, lead the way. Let the right hand open the expressive door; let the left hand swing like a well-oiled weather cock. She looked up when she was done.

"Are you okay?" she asked.

"I just felt a little dizzy there."

"Maybe you should get some fresh air."

"Maybe," he said. He walked outside and stood at the top of the stairs, watching the bell tower in the library across the piazza. He thought he saw a man standing behind the faience, looking down.

Suddenly she was beside him. He didn't speak, just started walking, looking straight ahead until they reached the pathway leading to the shrine. He looked at her, and she cocked her head and gave him the most dead-serious little smile. He reached out his hand and took her wrist and started off, but he didn't have to drag her, she followed like a thistle close to his leg. The great cat rose coolly above them. He didn't know what came over him then. He was seeing the saucy pinup, maybe, nothing more. He grabbed her and kissed her.

Bam. That was the sound her fist made when it pounded against his jaw. She burst into tears, and her face contorted with anger and mistrust. What the hell was wrong with him today? Was he trying to get himself fired? He reached up his hand to her and would have stopped her from running if she hadn't had the speed of a doe. He watched after her, longingly, knowing that he had really blown it this time.

L 2020

Eel's head jerked forward. She woke with a start. She had been playing Wormwood and had nodded off. She looked up at the holly screen. The dragon lay on his side, his scales already losing their glisten. A lukewarm hiss rattled from him every few seconds, but he presented no danger. He was dead. She had won.

What now?

She hit the REVIVE button.

PASSWORD?

She typed in the number 6543.

GOD MODE ON.

REVIVE.

She watched it emerge from its eggshell, watched it uncoil its scales. Dragons grew up quick. She would have to be careful. She watched the holly till the dragon had dried itself and let out its first steamy puff of air. She took a deep breath and waited to see what phenomenal world the Universal Mind would dream up next. What dark night of the soul lay down the next staircase? Suddenly her skin shivered.

She felt herself, back within her mind, bound by her skin-bound ego. It was a hallucination, of course, but she let herself shiver. Perhaps she didn't want to go down the staircase after all. Suddenly she felt tired of playing. Her stomach grumbled.

She saved the game, and went downtown for some soya

cakes and a hot cross bun. She made a Möbius toy from a
strip of computer holes and played with it while she watched
the Blue Lady eat a slice of blueberry pie. In the background
the Muzak machine played a syrupy version of Relham and
Ravinsky. What was the truth anyhow? Modern physics had
reached a crucial abyss. On the other side of the hole resided
alchemists and magicians. They were occupied with making
matter sing, busy turning lead to gold.

11:50 P.M.

It was almost midnight, and Max couldn't sleep. He got
up, dressed, and took a walk across campus. He came past
Mahler Hall and started down the walk, taking the shortcut
through the pines. As he stepped out of the pines onto the
sidewalk he saw someone who looked familiar. He stopped.
A shard of memory seemed to embed itself. The woman had
black hair cut shoulder length; she was struggling with a cello
case. The girl in Mahler Hall. All those years. Miss October.
He searched for a name.

Amanda.

"Amanda Zephyr," he said, suddenly, surprising himself.
His surprise was no less than hers. She stopped and turned,
but her face was a polite blank.

"Yes?"

He took off his cap. "You don't remember me. I met you
years ago, in Mahler Hall. You played a song for me on that
thing. I'm afraid I made rather a jerk of myself after."

She cocked her head and rested her case on the pavement.
He stepped toward her, into the glow of the street lamp.

"*You.*"

"Still hate me?"

She laughed and tucked a strand of soft hair behind her ear.
"You know what's funny? I was so mad then, but after—I
don't know. Over the long haul I guess I have to say it's one

of my fonder memories." She raised a hand and touched her cheek. "I was the jerk. I was sort of upset that day."

He found himself smiling like an idiot. The wind rippled up then, tousling the hairs around her temples, silver mixed with black. His heart was beating double time, and the ground beneath his feet seemed to be coming in waves.

She was smiling at him and laughing, a deep bell-like laugh. And then it was beginning, the fairy tale, the enchanted tale, beginning in all its ripe maturity. Once, upon a time. Introductions first.

"Maxwell Caine." He held out his hand, and she took it.

"Happy to make your acquaintance. Again."

Neither of them moved then. Hidden in the tight knot of their hands was a memory.

Once, upon a time, Max thought, looking into her deep violet eyes. "Do you like coffee?"

"Yes." She didn't take back her hand.

"I've got some freeze-dried stuff in my condo."

"The real thing?"

"Just a few ounces left. I ration myself."

"Sounds like heaven."

And it all began again. Up the path toward the grassy knoll and the panther shrine. Behind them Mahler Hall, its great iridescent eyes beaming down at them as they walked beneath the sapling canopy. The great cat seemed to be breathing as they approached, its stone flanks pulsing with a steady cat rhythm, its golden eyes watching them. What was love but space and time measured by the beating of a heart?

And then the bells began, the notes cascading like a waterfall, friendly spirits. Blackwell's Tune.

"Max?" she whispered. "Is it a dream?"

"Shh."

"But, I—"

"I know." He leaned down and pulled her to him, and smoothed out the seam in time with a kiss.

2040

Sunday, April 15, 3:33 A.M.

Eel's head was spinning, and there was buzzing in her left ear. She seemed to be drunk on some strong grape-based substance. Then her head stopped spinning, and the room began. That was worse. She opened her eyes to bright light, and took a breath of air. She had been with a man . . .

No, she pushed away that dream.

Aqua Velva. That's what Max wore. She had been sleeping, and Max had come. He had rescued her and told her a story.

That's nice. She closed her eyes tight.

"Hey, don't do that!"

Someone was talking to her and waving lights across her closed eyes. The voice wasn't angry, but it sounded worried. Do what?

"Miss Lacoste?" She smelled after-shave lotion. Aqua Velva. Not Max though. Not his voice.

She opened her eyes. She was standing at a phone, ready to punch in a number. She seemed to be wedged somehow, catatonic, unable to move. What was she doing there? What did that stranger want with her? Then she focused and saw his face. She knew that face. The man attached to it looked familiar, as well. He was holding a brown shoebox.

"I say," he said, "that was quite a jolt we took." He set down the box and started looking at his instruments. "A really big proton flare—rocked our socks off. You okay?"

222

She closed her eyes again and tried opening them slowly, but she still got an ill mem ref. Clay Adams was sitting in the big chair with his feet on the desk. He was smiling.

"I think so," she ventured, but she felt the hesitance in the vocal tones. She realized the buzzing in her ear was a dead signal. "Maybe I misdialed."

"Try again. I want to see his face when you give him the good news."

She rubbed her eyes and peered at the keypad. 6543. Why couldn't she dial? Was this the way Alzheimer's began? Had she popped the pull tab on her brain? An old ditty was going round and round in her head: "He thought he saw an albatross, that fluttered round the lamp; he looked again and found it was a penny postage stamp." This way to la la land.

He must have read her eyes. "You still don't remember? Maybe we better take you to Neuroclinic."

"No," she lied. "I'm fine."

He tented his fingers. "You sure?"

"I'm sure." Just say whatever came into her head. "Six-five-four-three, is that the code?"

He nodded. Maybe what she was supposed to say would come to her when she dialed. She must have taken a really massive jolt. She took a deep breath, and when his back was turned she lifted the shoebox. Inside were two voice tapes and an elephant coin token.

"What was that name again?"

"Caine, Maxwell. Hey, you sure you're okay?"

"I'm just having trouble focusing."

"You were about to phone our local hero and tell him he gets a bonus bouquet of credits. Six-five-four-three. That's the code."

A shadow of a memory flickered in her mind. Brother, was she mixed up. Maxwell Caine, wasn't that the name of the man they were trying to trip up? Wasn't that the killer? Something about looking for an ivory knife? Negating a perfect crime?

No, it wasn't.

Yes, it was.

Inside the brown shoebox had been a coin, worn smooth, and a picture of a man on celluloid, young and vigorous, Caine. A perfect story, number 665. And the next case? Number 666? Of course, the devil always wore a disguise.

"May I see the file?" she asked.

He handed it back to her and she opened it. Case 665 was a bomb scare at the Shawneeville library. There was no bomb of course, it was just a protest, an effective one. The Shadow, he called himself, and his interference led to a giant public outcry. A local radio station took up the crusade; money was raised to buy new bells so the town's sacred tune could continue being played. The investigating officer was one Maxwell Caine. According to Rookie Bob, so was the culprit. But there was no proof; besides, the statute of limitations had long passed.

The Shadow was a joke that worked, a trick, a trompe l'oeil. A joke at the expense of Death. A perfect crime. A large smile broadened her face. It made the man behind the desk smile, as well.

"You seem to be back, finally."

"Mostly." She took a deep breath, absorbing her present. She had won, albeit in an odd and roundabout fashion. Hold on, Eel, just give yourself a minute to catch up. Handle it. "The true test." There were two Maxes, weren't there? Max had crossed his heart and hoped to die if he didn't come back on the same track. And now he had gone and jumped the track, gone off to weave daisy chains. Not that she blamed him. Why settle for a conviction when you can have the girl and still foil the bad guy? The statute of limitations expires when there are none left who remember you and can testify to your passing. In a moment, the statute had expired. There *was* no worm in this section of the onion skin. Max was a local hero.

Things were coming into focus now. Memory was just so

much electricity, just electrochemical stimulation and charges. The glutamate transmitter carried the impulse across the synapse to the receptor, where the voltage cocked the trigger. It took the *arrival* of the impulse to pull it and fire the pulse into the primal neuron circuitry, recording a memory trace, locking in memory. If one arrived before one departed, one could unlock the memory and throw away the key. Someone had just inserted the key and taken out Max's card file and all the cross references. In a minute, that Max would be gone from her biography, along with all the physical traces. Oh, they might be there, but they would be like the socks and the frobnitzs, temporarily on loan, visible only in small quickly vanishing snatches of jamais vu. She knew. She had been there before.

She looked up at Clay Adams and smiled. He was green behind the ears, a rookie in the detection of crime. This was his first time down the wormhole, and he was still dizzy, eager to make excuses for a world gone topsy turvy. He had bought the new layer hook, line, and sinker—gone out fishing for a whopper and caught a minnow. She couldn't help but smile. One day, maybe a day not so far off, he would stumble onto a case where his own psyche crisscrossed and set off down River Destiny to catch himself a killer. Meanwhile let him slumber thinking his terra was firm. She smiled. She would like to be along when he caught himself a biggun.

"So, Lacoste, what are you going to do with your part of the prize?"

"Spend them as fast as I can. Maybe take a holiday before the next case."

He laughed. "Tomorrow's a holiday anyhow. Well," he said, "You going to call him now or not? Or do you want *me* to congratulate him on his nice little artistically plotted little crime?"

"You really think it's art? I thought pols detested art."

"Oh, not as good as the D.B. Cooper but definitely creative thinking. I did my best; I admit it when I'm licked. You both deserve the credits. So, you going to buy me breakfast now that you're rich?''

"Breakfast?" She felt dizzy suddenly. "Er, could you excuse me just a minute?" She got up and went over to the thick shade and lifted it. The sky was still pink. It was an old UFT joke, knock, knock.

"Yup," she said. "The sky's still pink."

"Were you in doubt?"

"Just for a minute. Maybe it was something I dreamed last night. I got mazed up. It's all antimatter now."

"You're still here." He said it as if it had significance. Maybe it did. She let the wisps of memory referents sift past. Fragments of names, flashes of time, riding in a car with the top down and the wind blowing her hair, eating a bag of donuts, a poor doomed girl with an unusual name. Caine, she thought, I hardly knew you.

Numbers—she had a hard disk in her brain for numbers. 6543. An easy number to remember, especially when one knew its significance. "I think I'll try now."

"Their unit indicates they are awake."

She punched Caine's number. An old man's thin face filled the holly.

"Are you Maxwell Caine?"

He smiled. "Speaking." She saw Adams look up from his task and shoot her a question with his eyes. She shook her head and mouthed the words: bad connection.

The tingling began at the back of her neck. It wasn't a bad connection. It was a perfect connection. Memory flooded in with his eyes and his voice. Ah, Max, we had fun, didn't we? You and me on the isle of long ago? His glasses were clear, and through them she saw his twinkling blue eyes. The memories competed in her mind for space. Sort them out: the knife never stabbed. The girl never died. The killer never killed.

Relham never won the prize. There was no Relham Hall, never had been. Just a mirage, all of it.

In the background she heard a woman's voice. "Max, who's calling so early?"

Eel smiled a Cheshire cat grin. "I'm sorry," she said, "I've got a bogus picture, sir. I'll ring you later."

She broke the connection. She smiled, clinging just a moment longer to the remnants of memory: elephants, Gummi Bears, a fragment of lovely music. It was all flowing past at astonishing speed. The last sweet refrain of the love song sang itself to sleep. And was no more. All of it utterly irrelevant. He hadn't even recognized her.

She turned back to Adams. He looked like a man who was hungry for breakfast.

3:44 A.M.

In the tall, white tower of the Happy Hunting Pueblos, an old man was rocking in his black Shawnee rocker. When the phone rang, he looked over at his wife; she was in the music pod with her earphones on. Her nightmare had woken them both; he looked at her protectively, glad she seemed to have forgotten. The phone rang again. He stopped rocking, got up, and activated the portascreen. On the screen a young woman's face shone. She was smiling at him, almost as if she knew him.

"Mr. Caine?"

"Speaking." He looked at his wife; she had taken off her earplug.

"Max, who's calling so early?"

He shrugged.

"I'm sorry, I've got a bogus picture, sir. I'll ring you later." The screen went black, and Max walked slowly back to his rocker.

"Who was it, Max?"

"Some young woman."

"Chasing young women now?" She laughed.

He smiled. Then for no reason at all he came over and leaned into the pod and gave her a kiss.

"What was that for?"

"For my wife."

"You're full of surprises, aren't you, Mr. Caine?"

"Yes, Mrs. Caine. Feeling better now?"

"Yes, much. Must have been something I ate. I haven't had a bad dream in years and years." She stretched her hand out and touched his.

"Now don't go getting any ideas, Mandy."

"What sort of ideas would I be getting, Max?"

He didn't answer, just took her hand and pulled her gently from the pod and embraced her. Old urges stirred.

"Wish you were young again?" she said.

"I wouldn't trade this moment for anything," he said. "Love me?"

"Always," she answered.

About the Author

Pamela West was born on August 29, 1945, in St. Louis, Missouri. By the end of second grade, she had attended six different schools; then her father joined the Army and the family settled down. She graduated from 6th grade at Oakview Elementary, Silver Spring, Maryland; from eighth grade at Fort Benning, Georgia; and from high school at Cairo American College in Egypt. She is a 1967 Barnard College graduate.

Her first novel, *Madeleine*, was published in 1983. *Yours Truly, Jack the Ripper* appeared in 1987. Both are historical mysteries, based on extensive research.

Pamela West lived for fourteen years in an idyllic central Pennsylvania college town where she helped raise her two children and edited dissertations for the university. A high school reunion in 1985 took her to Washington, D.C. As a result she is now married to her former high school sweetheart and resides in northern Virginia. During the spring and summer, she can be found rooting for her favorite professional soccer team, the Washington Stars.